Searching High and Low

by Mark D. Heires

Searching High and Low

Trilogy Christian Publishers A Wholly Owned Subsidiary of Trinity Broadcasting Network

2442 Michelle Drive Tustin, CA 92780

Cover design by: Grant Swank

For information about special discounts for bulk purchases, please contact Trilogy Christian Publishing.

Manufactured in the United States of America

10 9 8 7 6 5 4 3 2 1

Library of Congress Cataloging-in-Publication Data is available.

ISBN: 978-1-68556-963-1

E-ISBN: 978-1-68556-964-8

Dedication

I dedicate this story to my wife, Peg. Without her heart, help, and support, this novel would never have been written. I also thank my mom for the bit of DNA she spliced into my being, which infected me with her love of writing.

I also dedicate this story, with profound appreciation, to all the soldiers who courageously gave so much to the rest of us. Many enduring lasting scars that the realities of wartime service imbedded within the inner workings of their hearts and souls.

Finally, I dedicate this story to every family who has suffered the loss of a child in any of its forms. Remember that God chose the sacrifice of His Son to be His enduring example of the magnitude of His love for the world.

Guam, August 2, 1945
In the Dark of Night

A flash of light penetrates the eyelids of Lieutenant Eugene Walker. He counts three seconds, then, hearing an explosion to the north, breathes a sigh of relief. Flinching at the second flash, ducking as the shell rips through the air overhead, wincing at the explosion well to the south, he realizes that his heart is pounding so hard that it's shaking his chest. Trying unsuccessfully to think of a prayer, he plunges his hand into his pocket to touch his rosary while jumping out of his muddy foxhole as the third howitzer round flashes.

Though he is just nineteen, Lieutenant Walker is a gunnery expert. He knows that any forward artillery officer worth his salt brackets his intended target by intentionally firing the first two rounds short and long. After observing their impact locations, he can then more quickly rain destruction on his objective. So, it's the third round you have to worry about.

He also knows that inbound shells travel well over the speed of sound. You may see the flash from the shell that has your name on it, but you will never hear it. Most soldiers who have spent any time on the receiving end of bombardment know that you will never hear the one that kills you. And those that are unlucky enough to experience an unexpected, devastating explosion piercing utter quiet will never live long enough to feel peacefulness in dark silence again.

But, most importantly, he knows that panic is the deadliest foe. When pushed to their psychological limit, inexperienced soldiers may not be able to fight off the primal instinct to jump up and run. That's when the exploding shell's shrapnel will kill them for sure. It's this thought that drives him to act. He's their leader; he must save these kids.

He fills his lungs and bellows, "Stay down! He's trying to zero us!" Then he curses through clenched teeth as he lunges back into his foxhole just as the round explodes as bright as the sun, nearly shattering his eardrums and causing the mud under him to quiver like jelly. Fighting every fiber of his own survival instinct, he jumps up, runs, then lunges into the adjacent foxhole just as the next shell explodes much closer than the last.

Looking at the terrified faces of its sodden, mud-covered occupants, he forces a casual smile and says, "Don't worry, guys, they're just trying to keep us awake."

Just keep us awake, he thinks. That's a laugh. They're trying to blow us to bits.

In the next foxhole, he finds Sargent Davis in the fetal position. He is singing as usual. When Walker taps him on the shoulder, Davis turns his head and smiles before his eyes darken.

"If you run around like that, you're going to get yourself killed!"

"Relax, Sergeant. I made a deal with God."

On cue, they are stunned by a huge explosion that was way too close. When they pull their blackened faces out of the mud, Davis shakes his head, "Well, lieutenant, I just hope you got the deal in writing."

Though seeing his lips move, his ears are ringing too much to hear Davis. The acrid odor filling his nostrils causes his hair to stand on end. He is overcome with the feeling that something is about to happen that will change his life forever.

Part One—The Lost Coin—March 1961

Margaret, wearing one of her husband's ragged old coats, is shivering as she stares at a pile of stainless-steel parts now drying on an old bed sheet in the dilapidated shed that years ago was used as a chicken coop. She marvels that the unmistakable smell of dung from the ghosts of those chickens still hangs in the air. She has gotten accustomed to most aspects of farm life in the six years since she married, but getting used to the pungent odors emanating from a working farm operation has continued to illude her urban sensibilities.

From across the farmyard, she hears the high-pitched rumble of her husband's feed grinder wind down and stop. She pounds her fist on the table in frustration, causing the pile of parts to clang. She watches the rattling pieces in horror, hoping against hope that none fall onto the dirt below. If that happens, she will never finish in time to have Eugene's dinner ready at twelve. Her husband has been patient with her struggles to become a good farm wife, but late meals, that's another story.

She has just spent an hour washing and rinsing the cream separator. The hardest part of the job is carrying the huge galvanized wash basin of warm, soapy water from her kitchen. It had taken her back months to get used to the weight of it. But the hard work of a farm wife eventually hardened her body and mind to the near-constant abuse.

She shakes her head as she resolves to reassemble the parts in record time. The once unfathomable task is still intimidating. The multiple pieces are a menacing array of notches and grooves that all have to be placed into an exacting alignment, or they won't fit together at all. Every time she is successful, she recites a quick prayer of thanksgiving. Rushing as never before, frustrated by pieces binding in misalignment, she struggles on, finally seeming to have it together correctly. Then, she is aggravated to discover that an important piece seems to be missing, a big washer that holds the disks in the necessary alignment. This is also the moment that Dicky pops his head in the door.

"Where are your gloves, Mister?"

"'Ear," answers Dicky while holding up his arm to show a black mitten dangling from a piece of red yarn. The boy doesn't speak very well for his age. This fact irritates Eugene but doesn't concern Margaret because she is well-schooled in the patterns of child development from her years at Iowa Teacher's College.

"I'm almost done, dear. I just have to find where I put the washer. It looks like a silver coin with a hole in it."

Her mention of a coin causes the parable of the woman who lost a coin and then turned her house inside-out, looking for it to pop into her mind. Remembering Bible stories is one of the many lasting vestiges of being the daughter of a devout Christian minister.

The door whacks shut as Dicky goes outside. A moment later, he pops his head back in the door, holding the washer in his bluish fingers.

"Coin!"

"I threw the baby out with the bath water!" Margaret exclaims, realizing she had thrown the contents of the wash pail outside the door, including the all-important washer.

She hugs Dicky, saying, "You're a great little helper!"

He is delighted.

"Now, let's get to work on dinner before your father skins me alive."

#

Eugene is sitting on a milk can repurposed for use as a stool at a makeshift table consisting of a sheet of plywood resting on two ancient sawhorses. The ramshackle, which serves as his business desk, is strewn with bills which he is attempting to itemize on an empty feed sack using the stub of a pencil barely long enough to retain its John Deere logo. Before he got married, he had so successfully share-cropped the farm that he decided to buy it. That put him into debt, and things have only gone downhill ever since. Scratching away with his right hand while resting his head on his left, he is startled by a loud kick which causes the door of the feed grinding room to lurch open.

"Why are you writing it out yourself, Geno? Just get on the intercom and tell the secretary to do it," says the intruder.

"Geez, Dub, you scared the heck out of me!"

David W. Davis is Eugene's best friend. They served together in Guam near the end of WWII. Eugene was the platoon commander of a forward artillery group. Dub was a gunnery sergeant.

"A feed sack Geno, are things so bad you can't afford a sheet of paper? I can bring you a roll of toilet paper if that will help," Dub says, smiling.

Eugene looks at his friend with a dumb grin. "No thanks. Just bring over a couple of shotgun shells so I can blow my head off."

"Why do you need more than one? I don't think even you could miss from that range!"

"Okay, that's it!" shouts Eugene as he rushes towards Dub, tackling him to the ground. Eugene, a perfect physical specimen, towers over Dub, whose short, stocky build resembles an oil drum. After a few seconds of wrestling, Eugene has his opponent subdued in a headlock.

Being locked together in the dirt with his best friend is medicine for his spirit, but the dust stinging his throat jolts Eugene's mind back to Guam. Instead of fun-loving wrestling on the ground, he is back on that small, filthy island. An unexpected enemy mortar round had caught the squad out in the open, landing just a few feet from where Eugene was standing. The blast knocked him to the ground, unconscious.

Dub crawled to Eugene and shook him, "How bad are you hit?"

After Eugene opened his eyes, they looked for wounds. They were shocked to find none of the various shrapnel holes in his uniform had bleeding underneath.

Dub, with eyes like saucers, asked, "Do you believe in miracles?"

Eugene, still stunned, blinked his eyes open and shut, "I, I don't know."

"Well, Lieutenant, I think you should."

His consciousness now snaps back to the shed, still locked together on the floor with Dub. Terrifying flashbacks and nightmares of the carnage he witnessed on Guam, which haunt him all too frequently, have diminished in recent years. This one, with its happy ending, is much more tolerable than most.

After coughing from the dust, Eugene asks, "Can you come in for some dinner?"

"Thought you'd never ask. Margaret has been begging me to come over every time you leave!"

Eugene tightens the headlock as he says, "That's funny. She keeps begging me to ask you to stay away."

Both are dusting themselves off as they walk across the farmyard to the house.

"How bad is it, Geno?"

"I only have enough feed for two more weeks, and no one will lend me another dime."

"Man, that's rough."

"Promise you won't say anything to Margaret."

"You've got it, Geno. What are you going to do?"

"When the feed runs out, I'll be forced to sell the hogs and steers. With that money, I can pay off some of the bills, but even then, I'll still owe too much for anyone to float me another loan for planting next year. If I can't plant, I'm dead."

Dub, seeing the hurt in his best friend's eyes, whispers, "What can I do?"

"I have no idea. Remember when you found me this place? I really thought I was home for good."

#

Margaret is relieved when Dicky, who is watching out the window, tells her that Dub is coming in with Eugene to eat. The meal is late, but with Dub there, she knows all will be forgiven. Eugene's old army buddy's running mouth always relieves tension. She sometimes wonders if they would still be together without him to cheer things up. There's something very special about their brotherhood that allows Eugene to let down his guard, relax and have a good laugh. Margaret is secretly jealous of the closeness they share. When she tries to lighten his mood, it tends to have the opposite effect. Lately, the only time that Eugene seems to truly relax is when Dub is busting his chops about something. As he walks in the door, his easy smile warms the room.

"Man-oh-man!" exclaims Dub. "Why don't you leave this bum and marry me? Pot-roast, cornbread, potatoes, and gravy are too good for this guy."

"Oh, this stuff? The only reason I cooked was that I was hoping that you'd be joining us. For him, it's baloney, mustard, and Wonder Bread." They all have a much-needed laugh.

#

After eating, Dub's mind goes back to Eugene's troubles as the back door whacks shut. Not knowing what else to do, he falls back on his old standby, busting his chops.

"Let me know when you get tired of Margaret, Geno. I'll be happy to take her off your hands."

"That's a mailman for you, always chasing every wife on the route."

"A town milk route would be much safer. The farm husbands are usually close by and have a shotgun in the machine shed. I can't count on all of them to be a poor shot like you."

"Well, don't forget about the muzzle spread, old buddy. And why do you always act like you are a better shot than me?" asserts Eugene with a smirk.

"Because, if I had my M-one, I could pick off the crow on that wire over there," Dub says while nodding to the south.

Dub can tell by Eugene's expression that he is desperate to try to take his bravado down a peg or two. Everyone in their squad knew that Dub was probably the best marksman on the island. Dub watches Eugene holding out his right arm, comparing the size of the crow with his thumbnail.

"Nope. That crow is 350 yards away. That's fifty yards beyond the range of an M-one."

Dub studies the crow, then his buddy's face. He knows Eugene was trained to accurately judge distances and how to calculate trajectories in his head, a skill beyond most humans. When Eugene was inducted, the exam officer flagged his file for officer's training because his math skills scored off the charts.

"Since I don't have my rifle handy, I'll have to take your word for that," says Dub. "All I know is that you couldn't hit the broad side of a barn."

"See that barn? I could hit that with no problem. And seeing your back side is about that big..." They both laugh. "So, you better hope Margaret has a good pair of tweezers to pull buckshot out of your barn-sized behind."

After more laughing, he adds, "Now, you'll have to excuse me, Dub; I have manure that needs hauling."

"I think I've just been a victim of some."

Both turn their heads when they hear the screen door whack.

"Drive tractor?" Dicky asks, running towards them.

"Good luck with the other wives, Dub."

"Hang in there, old buddy," Dub says as he hops into the passenger seat of his car to finish his deliveries. As he drives away, his thoughts now his own, he feels a lump in his throat, knowing that Eugene is in big trouble.

#

Seeing Dicky's innocent face, his little world so insulated from his own problems, Eugene decides to indulge the boy. No matter how hard he works on the farm now, it probably won't make any difference.

"Okay, buster, I guess it's about time you start pulling your weight around here. Let's see if we can get the old girl started."

"Yay," says Dicky as he comes clumsily running.

The old Farmall F20 started out life bright red; now, twenty-five years older, she sports dull rust. Starting the old girl's four cylinders can be an unwanted adventure at times, and if you don't know what you're doing, it can be downright dangerous. Eugene hops into the saddle to set her brakes, put her in neutral, and set her to half-throttle and full choke with the ignition off. Then he mentally rechecks all of these before hopping back down. He pulls the crank out of the tool bin bolted onto her frame. He slides the crank into the opening just below the radiator with the handle pointing down.

"You want to give her a crank?" he asks Dicky, smiling.

Dicky tugs at it.

"Did you eat spinach today?" he asks.

Dicky shakes his head no.

"That explains it then. You'll need to eat more spinach." He moves Dicky well away and tells him not to move from the spot. He grabs the crank and pulls up hard, causing the engine to turn.

He turns the ignition switch from "off" to "on," and then he spits in his gloves, rubs them together, and says, "Here goes."

He reminds himself to only crank the thing one-half a turn because if he cranks it more than that, the handle could break his arm or even come around and break his jaw. He pulls the crank up hard. The engine pops, bangs, sputters, and dies.

"Oh, so you want to give me trouble, you rusty pile of iron."

He gingerly wrestles the crank back to the bottom position, warns the thing, and then pulls up hard. This time after bumps and grumbles, the engine is coaxed to life.

"Yay!" says Dicky.

"Well, let's hop up there!" Eugene nearly shouts over the noisy engine.

Once aboard, he maneuvers the small boy onto his lap. "You think you can handle her?"

Eugene puts it in gear and the machine, like an old workhorse, lurches forward.

"Take the wheel."

Dicky laughs as he tries to steer. The tractor is heading directly towards an oak tree.

"Turn that way," Eugene says, pointing. When the tractor doesn't turn, he helps the wheel around. "That's it, son. You'll be doing the plowing next spring."

Dicky happily bouncing up and down on his lap reminds him how much he loves this place and the huge role finding it had in numbing the demons that haunted his mind.

Searching for Peace

In September 1945, Eugene had come marching home from the war after VJ Day, with tens of thousands of others who had been deployed to the Pacific Theater. He traveled by military plane to the west coast, where he was soon discharged. He caught a passenger train that took him, with dozens of other discharged men in uniform, across a land that looked unbelievably peaceful. His parents met him at the whistle-stop on the north end of Epson, Iowa. It was great to be home at first. But, on the third Sunday morning, when he told his parents that he wasn't going to church again, things came to a head. His parents, devout Christians, fervently believe that it's sinful to stay home from church—they would never tolerate that.

After they angrily left for church, he packed his duffle, placed a note on the kitchen table, and left. In town, he called Dub. His army buddy picked him up an hour later.

On Guam, Eugene was drawn, like many other men, to Dub because he, like a cockroach, could survive and even thrive no matter what happened. His lively chatter raised everyone's morale, and his habit of blatantly never taking unnecessary chances somehow added to his folksy charm. When they were being shelled, he would borough himself deeply in a foxhole, curl up in a ball, and plug his ears with his fingers while humming "The Yanks are Coming."

Eugene liked how Dub had carried his unique knack for survival into the post-war world. For one thing, he knew everyone. With his connections, he was able to find work for both of them and often arranged a free place for them to temporarily bunk. But still, good, permanent jobs were almost impossible to find with so many returning soldiers looking for work at the same time.

Having tired of living as a vagabond, Eugene told Dub that he would like to give farming a try. In no time, Dub had asked around and found an available eighty-acre farm near Summit. After they looked it over, Eugene knew why it was available. The land was muddy and full of rough, round stones large enough to break any plow. The land was available because, in its present state, it was unplantable.

The previous owner had lost the farm during the Great Depression. The small farmhouse and farm buildings were long abandoned and overgrown. The acreage was currently owned by a successful farmer who had bought it for a song and then tried without success to find someone dumb enough to share crop it.

"This place is a mess, Geno," Dub said. "You need to walk away from this one."

Still, Eugene could see it had potential. His father had told him years ago that good farmland costs top dollar. If you want a deal, buy land that no one else wants because something is wrong with it. Underneath all the problems, you will find fertile Iowa top soil, the best in the world.

In the present case, the land, once cleared of the stones, which would be no small feat, could be planted, and if it proved to be too wet for crops, it could be dried up using buried drain tile. He knew it was a risk and that it might take years, but being young, single, and penniless, he figured that he didn't have much to lose.

Still, Dub had pushed him to walk away. But Eugene told him that when they drove over the last hill, and they saw this godforsaken mess at the end of the road, he knew right then that this was where he was going to put down his roots.

So, after some negotiating, a share crop agreement was worked out. The landowner would supply cash to put in a crop, and Eugene would do all the work, and together, they would equally share the profit. He would need to remove rock to make the land farmable. As for drainage tile, the owner would supply materials only after it proved necessary. Any improvements to the house and buildings were Eugene's responsibility. He knew that potential ownership, which he dearly desired, was years away. But he thought that maybe, just maybe, if he worked hard enough, it might come to pass.

Later, Eugene told Dub the real reason he wanted the place.

"Dub, Guam is still in my head. Back there, when we were getting pounded, I forced my mind to be somewhere else. I closed my eyes and thought of the most peaceful place I could imagine. I saw a broken-down farm on the end of a long dirt road, a road that nobody else would use except for me."

"And this is it?"

"Yes. If I can't find peace here, I never will."

#

Losing his itinerant work companion had gotten Dub into reluctantly thinking about a more permanent job for himself. As luck would have it, and of course, by knowing practically everyone, he was among the first to hear that the post office in the tiny town of Apex had an opening for a rural carrier. At first, he thought he would have no interest in working for another large government organization like the army. But he had to admit that he was tired of going from job to job, especially since many were either dirty or menial or both.

When he found out rural mail carriers don't need to where a uniform nor are they provided a government vehicle, the idea started to grow on him. He could just jump in his old car in whatever he happened to be wearing. The task required him sitting on the wrong side of the front seat, awkwardly steering with his extended left arm and pushing the gas pedal with his extended left foot so he could more easily access the galvanized mail boxes mounted on wooden posts every half-mile or so. The otherworldly way of driving appealed to his contrarian aspirations. While working for a large bureaucracy, he could just make up his own rules as he went along. It seemed an undignified occupation, but that suited him too. Roll out of bed, pick up boxes of mail in Apex, drive on quiet, country roads, window open, wind in his face, no one to bug him, and every day he would roll into his best friend's lonely place for a beer, give his hard-working buddy some grief, and when he tired of that, he would make his way home for another beer or two. What could be better than that?

#

The farm needed so much work when Eugene arrived that he scarcely knew where to begin. He would work outside until the sun went down and then come inside to try to make the rundown house more inhabitable. The outside work was brutal, rolling the endless supply of watermelon-sized stones onto a sled, then, after pulling the heavy skid to the edge of the field, rolling them off again. During the first weeks, the labor tormented his body, but it did wonders for his wellbeing. His frequent nightmares became more and more rare, and it wasn't long before the work had tanned him and chiseled his body.

One day, when Dub stopped by with the mail, seeing Eugene, his bronzed and shirtless body glistening in the sun, remarked, "You look like a Greek god, Geno. I think it's time we go out and try to scare up some women."

"I think your body can use some toning first, Buddy, and I have just the workout for you."

Eventually, enough rocks were removed to attempt plowing. After a concerted effort and several visits to the Summit welding shop after hidden rocks had done their worst, the fields were ready for sowing. After planting corn and bean, eleven variously sized outbuildings were cleaned and repaired, and he spent time every few days mowing down the weeds around the house and buildings. One evening, while eating a late supper of a ham sandwich and metallic-tasting water from the well, he regarded, with no small amount of pride, the improvement of his now almost respectable corner of the world. He would like to have seen paint on the buildings, especially the house and the barn, but peeling dirty-white paint would have to do for the time being.

The air was still warm, and the wind was now whisper-quiet, with only the occasional chatter of birds to punctuate the approach to the ending of a pleasant day. He noticed that the plainness of the farm buildings contrasted wonderfully with the grandeur of the gently rolling countryside. Looking across the road to the west, the ground sloped downward as an inconspicuous valley towards a small creek about a mile distant. The view beyond the creek easily stretched for fifteen miles as a patchwork of fields dotted with distant farmsteads, and above, he marveled at the grandeur of an ever-changing sky that stretched to the heavens. Since he had been there, he has found himself considering the magnificence of that sky; at times, a canvas of sapphire brushed with luminous cotton; at other times, flat gray with tears of falling rain; and occasionally an angry violence that would strike terror into his heart; but frequently, perhaps when he needed it most, it was a golden, glowing sunset which lasted for hours as soothing ointment for his most melancholy thoughts; and when the dark thoughts he was hiding from, those that burdened his soul, the fading sunset gave way to a view which has endured since the fourth day of creation. In the comfort of that deeply quiet darkness, constellations and the sweeping brushstroke of the Milky Way sprang forth with stars as numerous as the sands of the oceans and the descendants of Abraham from the unseen and unknowable azure blackness of infinity. Yes, this is the place—even more than the place—he first saw in his mind's eye on Guam; a place of hard work, a place for forgetting, a place for living, and a place to grow old in peace.

Then, was that a flash of light? His heart jumped as his mind raced to understand it. After a few seconds passed, he realized that it was nothing. But his sense of peace was shaken. Then he wondered for the first time—was this place alone going to be enough?

#

Ten years went by before he found an answer. He remembers the first time he saw her—his healing angel.

He had spent the morning pulling the broken drawbar off of his plow, then took it to the Summit welding shop for repair. He had just stepped outside to look for a shady spot to wait. That's when she came out of the grocery store right across the street, carrying two brown paper bags. The crisp cotton dress, which tried unsuccessfully to hide the figure of a model, revealed flawless skin on her shins and arms. Its collar, along with her long amber hair, neatly piled on top of her head, framed a youthful face that reminded him of his favorite actress, Audrey Hepburn.

He found that he couldn't stop looking at her. When the bag tore and cans started raining down onto the sidewalk, he was at her side almost before he knew he had moved. It wasn't until he was putting cans into her bag that he noticed how greasy his hands were. That didn't help his confidence.

"Can you take this?" she asked, indicating the partially torn bag she was clutching. "I'll run in for another bag."

Eugene clumsily took the torn bag from her as his mind raced to think of something non-moronic to say.

He tried, "Stupid thing's falling apart," then immediately felt like an idiot.

When she returned, they worked together to repack the scattered groceries.

"I can't thank you enough," she finally said.

"I'm so sorry about the grease," he said as he noticed the black smears all over the bags. "I was getting a draw bar welded across the street and had no idea I was this dirty."

She glanced down at the bag and then up to look him in the eye, not saying anything for a moment. Her pause sent fresh waves of terror through him, thinking that she was waiting for him to say something. She smiled, as if sensing his predicament.

Mercifully she asked, "What's your name?"

"Eugene," he answered. Breathing a bit easier, he said, "Let me carry those for you. I don't want your clothes to get dirty because of me."

"That's nice of you," she said, handing him the bags. "I'm parked at the church."

The short walk gave Eugene time to relax his brain and mouth. He found out she was the new schoolteacher and her best friend was the minister's wife. When they arrived at her car, the church's minister John McBride was just coming out of the door.

"Hey, Eugene," he said, waving. "I didn't know you knew Margaret?"

"Hi, John. We just met."

After a few more pleasantries, all went on their way.

Two weeks later, he got a call from John encouraging him to ask Margaret for a date.

"What makes you think she's interested in me?"

John confided that his wife had persuaded him to call.

"I'm not saying she's gone nuts over you or anything, but she is interested." After Eugene didn't say anything for a minute, he added, "The church is having a social next Saturday. You can either ask her to go with you, or you can just show up."

#

The day that Eugene had walked her to the church, Margaret had immediately gone to the parsonage to tell her best friend Madeline all about the interaction.

"Are farmers always that dirty?" Margaret asked. "Everything he touched turned black."

"Of course not. A cake of lye soap or two, a briskly scrubbing brush for forty-five minutes, and you'll find they're almost as clean as anyone else. But do be careful about the bottoms of their shoes."

"It sounds like it would be a lot less work to marry a minister," Margaret said.

"I don't know, Margaret. He's awfully good-looking."

"Really? I might need those forty-five minutes to be able to tell for sure."

"I'd take him dirt and all. He looks like a John Kennedy, only a muscular one."

"Madeline! You're married and to a minister, no less. What would you do if I told John what you just said?"

"Don't you dare!" Madeline exclaimed as they both tittered like schoolgirls.

Margaret tried to act indifferent when Eugene arrived at the social, but inside she felt like she was back in eighth grade. After they had been talking for a few minutes, Madeline stopped by.

"How do you think the scrubbing went, Margaret?" Madeline asked while looking Eugene up and down and then at Margaret with a wry smile.

"Scrubbing?" asked Eugene.

Margaret blushed.

"Oh, nothing," said Madeline. "I have to go."

They both talked non-stop for two hours. She learned that he had fought in Guam but didn't like to talk about it and that he was raised Christian but no longer attended church of any kind. She learned that his split with the church led to a big falling out with his parents, who lived near Epson, about forty miles to the east. When she asked him about that, she learned he didn't like to talk about religion.

Despite these inner demons, Margaret was attracted to him. In addition to his good looks, she found him to be a kind, smart and confident man.

#

As Eugene drove home, he felt like a different man. Just a few hours ago, he was barely able to overcome the fear that she would certainly dismiss him for making a fool of himself. In less than five minutes, her charm, warm smile, jabbing wit, and infectious laugh had banished the butterflies in his gut. She somehow unlocked his tongue so that their conversation flowed back and forth like rhythmic waves washing over a sandy beach. He knew she was pretty from the first, but today, as they talked, he found beauty almost everywhere he looked, in the way her hair swirled on top of her head with auburn wisps that danced on the breeze, in the lithe line of her neck flowing gracefully to her shoulders that danced so slightly when she laughed, in her delicate hands, graceful in subtle expression, exerting almost a language of their own, in the warmth of her smile that turned slightly crooked when she teased him, and in the depth of her brown eyes like coffee under glass, eyes that sparkled when she laughed, narrowed to wrinkle her nose when she feigned shock at something he said and locked into his as if finding his thoughts before he had a chance to express them. As the pleasant hours too quickly passed, he realized that he had never felt anything like this before.

Ever since the war, he had been a jumble of nerves. He was haunted by the sights and sounds of the terror and carnage that only other combat soldiers could possibly imagine or understand. Trapped in his mind were images too terrible to talk about, images that, when triggered, would transport him back to Guam. But with her, as he looked at her, as he talked to her, as he listened to her, he felt something he hadn't felt since before the war—he felt relaxed and whole. She was a medicine, a strong drug that healed.

All of this caused him to think of little else in the days and weeks ahead.

#

It took a bit of time and doing for Eugene to convince her to marry him. As a minister's daughter and school teacher, she was essentially a town person. Could she be happy living out where she was grossly outnumbered by hogs and cattle? Could she learn to grow vegetables in a garden and then preserve them in jars? Could she live in a place where the nearest neighbor was a half-mile away? These gave her a bit of pause, but the thing she really struggled with was could she be married to a man that didn't seem to believe in God?

She had talked to John at length about this. John conveyed how he had met Eugene when Dub had invited him out to Eugene's farm to hunt pheasants. Then he told her all about what he had learned about Eugene while he was there. The minister found out quickly that Eugene didn't want to talk about church. But John had an instinct that despite the war memories churning inside of him, this intelligent man's personal strength would, with time, overcome their grip. He had told Margaret that he firmly believed Eugene was on a long, slow road back to God.

It wasn't an easy decision for Margaret; she knew that if she said yes, she would be making a vow to God to stay with him for better or worse until death. She followed the reverend's advice, which was to pray about the decision every day for a week, a week when she was advised not to see Eugene.

After praying, she sat quietly in a pew at the back of the church. As the light of day was fading, and with the darkness and quiet of the church warm and inviting, she realized a fact that was inescapable; he needed her. Then she remembered the scripture with Jesus saying that there is no greater love than laying down your life for a friend. She thought perhaps Jesus was telling her that there was no greater love than for her to spend her life, as in her lifetime, on this man, a man who needed her more than he even knew. They were married a month later.

Seeing Red—March 5, 1961

It's Sunday morning, although, in the fog of just getting up, Eugene doesn't realize what day it is. If he did, he would know that things were about to get worse.

As he heads out the back door at five, he can hear the tin lids on the hog feeders banging shut, punctuated occasionally by the squeals of those pushing and shoving to get at them. He is grateful that at least the hogs know how to feed themselves. The cows and steers are not smart enough to lift a finger, no less a lid, with their snouts. If they were, his morning chores would be a lot easier.

He shivers in the crisp air as he looks up to see a clear sky full of stars. The hill to the northeast is silhouetted with the faintest hint of first light. Is that pink, he wonders? He makes a mental note to be on the lookout for bad weather. In the dimness, he sees three cows walking single file towards his humble milking shed. Inside he is glad that he left the place in good order after last night's session. He pitchforks hay into the stanchion as the hungry old bags slip their heads through the slats. "You're a motley crew," he says as he turns the knob on the dust and cobweb-covered Philco, which crackles forth music punctuated with static.

"Okay, Eunice, you're first," he says as he bangs the clean bucket on the cement floor. The tinny ring of the stream hitting the bottom elicits a guttural moo from her. "You're welcome," he responds.

Out of nowhere, the head of a black, brown, and white cat pops out from behind the stanchion, meowing insistently.

"Okay, Holly," he says as he shoots a stream of milk at her as the grateful cat comically flails her tongue about her face and whiskers. She was just another unnamed farm animal until Margaret named her Holly. He, like most farmers, is glad to have a cat around to keep grain-stealing field mice at bay.

"Do you remember the first time Margaret came to the milking shed, Holly?"

Holly's meow seems affirmative, although he knows she is actually just begging for more milk.

The exchange makes him recall his new bride's reaction to his animated conversations with his bevy of animal ladies.

He recalls how Margaret had expressed shock at hearing what she termed "her laconic husband's chatty behavior." He had explained that cows would give more milk if they have music and hear a friendly voice.

"So that's how you learned about dating," she had said with a laugh.

He now laughs, recalling that she was probably right.

After sending the cows on their way back out into the pasture and mucking the fresh manure they left behind, he is on to the cattle. He opens the water valve to the cattle tank as he fetches large pales of ground feed to drop over the fence into the feed trough, a long wooden platform edged with thick planks to prevent their clumsy snouts from spilling their feed into the mud. The steers greedily munch away with their enormous tongues and bottom row of teeth. It takes several trips to the feed room to supply today's allotment. With the last of the feed in place and the cattle tank full, it's time to check on the largest population at his address, the hogs.

Five steers eat a lot, but one hundred quickly growing hogs eat like there's no tomorrow. Eugene slides the huge lid off of one of the refrigerator-size, cylindrical feeder bins seeing that it is nearly empty. Each of the four bins can hold sixty bushels. All told, it is enough to feed the ornery mob for not much more than one day. Filling the four bins will take about two hours. Feeling hungry, Eugene decides to head back to the house to warm up and eat some breakfast.

In the kitchen, he sees Margaret fussing with her hair in the bathroom mirror. That's when he remembers with a cringe that it's Sunday.

Dicky hears the door and comes running. "Sunny school, sunny school!"

Dicky loves Sunday school above all else. He asks if it's Sunday school, mispronouncing the word Sunday almost every morning. It's the only time he gets to play with other kids.

"Are you hungry, Sport?" asks Eugene.

"Mamma, say pancakes!"

"Sit down, boys. The griddle's already hot," says Margaret.

The boys watch impatiently as she drops lard on the hot surface. A minute later, she is flipping over four buckwheat pancakes. The smell of them adds to the stomach-growling aroma of bacon already filling the air. She puts three cakes on Eugene's plate and a small one on Dicky's. She starts four more and then butters, syrups, and cuts Dicky's for him.

"This is the life, right Dicky?" asks Eugene.

"Man-o-man," he answers, causing both parents to laugh.

"We may have to start calling you 'little Dub,'" says Margaret.

All three are eating quietly for a few moments.

"Why don't you put on some nice clothes and come with us today?" asks Margaret.

Eugene's stomach churns a bit as he says, "I really need to get the chores done before the weather moves in."

Margaret, looking towards the window, asks, "What weather?"

"The sun was pretty red this morning, that means we're going to have weather."

After an uncomfortable pause, she adds, "It's not for me, you know. It's not even for you, although I think it should be." Then she lowers her voice, "It's for him."

"Him?"

"Not right now, but when he gets a little older, if his father doesn't go to church, he will want to imitate that."

"Not necessarily."

"It's only natural," Margaret says with a bit of pleading in her voice. Then she whispers, "Please."

Eugene looks into her eyes. Oh, how he loves those eyes and hates to disappoint them. With a thoughtful expression, he quietly says, "I'll think about it."

Margaret's face darkens, then, with eyes squinting, she punches out, "You do that, Eugene!"

Wiping his mouth with a ragged napkin, he gets up with a lurch, puts on his coat, and heads out the door.

Outside, his queasy stomach is joined by his throbbing head; these Sunday confrontations are only getting worse. Before Dicky was born, Margaret left him alone about going to church. In fact, he thinks she was glad that he had walked away from his Catholic traditions. Lately, she's really getting on his nerves.

Before the carnage on Guam, he held his faith closely. He attended church and regularly prayed, as the regiment's chaplain suggested. He prayed for courage and victory. He also prayed, like most servicemen in battle, that he and the men under him would survive.

The regiment had trained for amphibious landing and ground battle in the jungles of Maui and then shipped out to Guam. This late in the war, none of the trainees had any delusions about easy fighting. But also, like all those preceding them, five minutes of actual combat blanched the rigors of training to make it seem as if it was just done for morale. The terrifying savagery of battle, the immediacy of cruel death, the hopelessness of survival shake the soul to its core to find there if real belief in God can be found. At one terrible moment, a moment he can't let himself think about, he found utter emptiness.

He now asks himself if he can pretend to have faith, for Margaret, for Dicky. Part of him would like to comply. It certainly would make things easier. But he can't let go of one inescapable belief. At the darkest moment of his life, he had learned that you survive by letting go of delusions. For once, a man is forced to look into that place, that deep and dark place, the place that sanity avoids, the place very few people will ever see, a place that once you have seen it, there is no denying it, there is no forgetting it, and there is no covering it up; for better or for worse you have to live with the core belief found in that place for the rest of your life.

As he is filling the third hog feeder bin, he sees Margaret, in Sunday best, holding Dicky's hand as they walk to the car. As on every other Sunday, Dicky is chatting excitedly about going to Sunday school. He also notices how stunning she looks in her Sunday best. When they happen to look his way, Eugene smiles, and waves. Dicky waves back as Margaret gives him a stern look. As a man, he knows that his convictions are everything, but oh, how he hates to disappoint her. As he continues grinding corn for a huge batch of feed, he can't stop thinking about Margaret.

#

As Margaret and Dicky bound down the dirt and gravel roads towards church, Dicky is bouncing up and down on his seat.

He is singing a simple but original song about Sunday school.

Hearing the joy in Dicky's voice softens the annoyance she is feeling toward Eugene. She decides she'll talk to Madeline about it after church. It always helps to talk to her best friend.

"What's in surprise box?" Dicky asks while grinning.

"It's a surprise, Dicky. You don't want me to tell you and spoil the surprise, do you?

"Tell!"

"That just wouldn't be fair."

"Please tell," he says softly.

"Well," Margaret replies, "will you promise not to tell anyone?"

"Yes!"

"Even Michael?"

Dicky nods.

Smiling, Margaret whispers, "Chocolate chip cookies."

"Yay!"

Margaret feels much better as they pull into the nearly empty parking lot of Summit Christian Church near the center of town. Dicky's enthusiasm is a wonderful tonic. Inside, Dicky finds Michael; then both run to the teeter-totter, which is just outside of the classroom window. Margaret watches them for a minute before she busily finishes preparing for the class.

Madeline walks in the door wearing a white blouse and grey wool skirt. Her blond hair is in a neat bun. With spectacles, she looks like she should be in one of those Hollywood movies just before the handsome lead takes off her glasses, pulls the clip out of her hair to reveal a stunning beauty.

She smiles and says, "How are you, dear? Do you need any help getting ready?"

"Madeline, you look wonderful!"

"Thanks, dear. John sprung for a trip to the beauty shop yesterday."

They talk about beauty tips for a few moments, and then Madeline asks about her lesson.

"After they run around a while outside, you know, burning up all that extra energy, I'll bring them in to hear the story of David and Goliath. We'll talk about the characters for a while, and then I'll have them use crayons to depict something about the story they just heard. It's an easy lesson."

"They'll love it."

"I do want to talk to you after church, though," says Margaret.

"Is it about Eugene?" They have talked about this before.

"Yes, I always feel better after I talk to you."

"Of course, dear. I will be happy to talk to you. Now can I ask you something important?"

"Okay," replies Margaret with apprehension.

"What's the surprise?"

"Madeline, you're worse than the kids! It's chocolate chip cookies; help yourself."

After church, the two women sit down for coffee in the parsonage kitchen while the youngsters play in the backyard. Madeline listens sympathetically as Margaret expresses her frustration with Eugene continuing to avoid attending church as a family.

"It won't be long before Dicky asks why his daddy doesn't go to church."

"What does Eugene say when you ask him?"

"He says he'll think about it."

"Oh, well, at least he is not refusing out of hand. John has a lot of respect for your husband. He thinks you should trust God to bring him back to church in time."

"Yes, I know. He told me that, too. But what do you think?"

Madeline pours more coffee into her own cup and then holds the pot up, offering more to Margaret. After taking a sip, she says, "I think it's a man thing, and I think John is a smart man."

Margaret takes a sip as she seems to think about it.

"Madeline, how would you, John, and Michael like to come out for some supper next Wednesday?"

Madeline smiles while holding out her cup. "Here's to supper next Wednesday."

"Maybe a little Christian togetherness will help things along."

Margaret smiles as they clink cups, not knowing that the impromptu dinner they have just arranged will never happen.

#

Eugene had yet again lost his battle with sleeping. He quietly slips into the bedroom to find his work clothes and turn off the illuminated alarm clock, which now reads 4:58 a.m., before it can shatter the predawn peace.

Margaret was not as upset as he was expecting when she arrived home after church. She acted as if the blowup hadn't happened at all. Later, while eating dinner, she told him that she invited the McBride's to supper Wednesday night. When he said he was delighted, she smiled at him.

Despite not wanting anything to do with church, he genuinely likes the pastor and his family. John is laid back for a minister, having never pressured him to attend his church. Plus, Madeline and Michael are the best friends of Margaret and Dicky. It promises to be a delightful evening.

Ironically, he felt relatively peaceful when he had fallen asleep, but that's often how it works. He has a fighting chance of controlling his mind during the day, but his sleeping mind is free to torture him at will.

His dream had started with him grinding feed; then, suddenly, mortar rounds started exploding in the farmyard. He looked towards the house, seeing Margaret inside the backdoor screaming for Dicky, who, somehow unaware of the danger, was sitting in the yard calmly playing with a toy tractor, to come inside. As he ran towards Dicky, a shell landed in-between himself and the boy. When the dust cloud settled, Dicky was gone. He awoke with his heart pounding just after midnight.

Having found the boy peacefully sleeping in his room soothed his shattered nerves. But the likelihood of returning to that dream hardened his resolve to not allow himself to go back to sleep. Feeling so upset at the dream's vision, which was all too real, made him realize how much his affection for his son has changed over the last several months. When Dicky was just a baby, Eugene didn't feel much of a connection to him. All the doting and wide-eyed wonder other adults exuded mystified him. When someone would ask him something like, isn't it wonderful? He had to fumble around to come up with a reasonable-sounding affirmation. But over the last months, Dicky's enthusiasm, curiosity, mimicry, and unbridled imagination had wormed their way into his heart in a profound way. The nearly constant presence of death during the war, in many ways, numbed his fear of it. Last night's terrifying dream had suddenly renewed and strengthened its hold on him. His own death is one thing, but the death of his innocent son—no loss could possibly be worse than that.

Later, sitting in the easy chair with these incessant thoughts, he tries to force himself to think about anything else. He recalls the farm bills stacked on his plywood desk and the dooming calculations on the feed sack ledger and what they mean. If the cattle and hog prices unexpectedly go up significantly, he might have enough cash to make it to the harvest. If he has a bountiful crop and the prices are way better than last year, he might be able to pay off his long-standing debts. He realizes once again that the only thing that can save him is a miracle. *A miracle?* he says to himself. *That's a laugh. Only suckers hope for miracles.*

Now, with his long tussle with the night at an end, he thinks about Margaret's growing unhappiness with him. He doesn't like that the magic that she brought to his life seems to be fading. This uneasy thought is still rummaging around in his head as he quietly dresses. Now bundled in layers of work clothes, he slips out the backdoor being careful not to let it whack shut. He is greeted by a blustery wind out of the southeast. The sky above looks evenly dark-gray, but to the east, a rusty-red halo hangs over the hill. Walking to the milking shed, he notices the three cows are already at the door looking at him.

"So, you girls see it too." Eugene believes animals instinctively react to coming bad weather.

Inside he turns the radio dial to find a weather report as he forks hay into the stanchion. Cold gusts are pushing through gaps and cracks all over the shed.

"How would you like some snow?" he asks the cows.

Right on cue, Eunice moos.

The radio crackles out the warning for a winter storm in the evening hours. When Eunice moos again, Eugene asks, "So, what else can go wrong?"

#

"It's a little late to be grinding, isn't it?" Dub asks after kicking open the shed's door in the early afternoon.

"There's a storm coming, old buddy. I'm grinding extra."

"I heard. The car radio said it could be the worst storm of the season."

"Which direction is the wind right now?"

Dub looks out the door at the weathervane on top of the barn.

"Southeast," he says.

"Yep, she's coming right for us." Part of Eugene's artillery training was an overview of weather patterns. Judging wind speed and direction is an important aspect of accurately targeting artillery rounds. In addition, knowledge of impending weather is a significant facet of military tactics and battle outcomes. After all, bad weather and tropical diseases took out more soldiers than the enemy in the long war with the Japanese.

Like on Guam, large weather patterns in the States rotate counter-clockwise. Thus, the southeast wind indicates to Eugene that the system, though still a distance away, is aimed directly at him. When it shifts to the northeast, he can expect the heavy weather to hit.

"Good thing I still have the tire chains in the trunk," says Dub. "Your dirt road is murder when it storms."

"Well, try not to get stuck. I'm going to be busy enough around here without having to pull your sorry tail out of a mud hole."

"You may even have to put tire chains on the tractor the way it sounds."

"I know. That's on the growing list of things I need to get done before the storm hits."

After Dub leaves, Eugene realizes that he is not that worried about the storm. If anything, he's kind of excited about it. It's just a storm. Winter storms are part of the game, but something seems different this time. He just can't shake the feeling that something terrible is about to happen.

The wind direction, now accompanied by dark clouds to the west, only strengthens his belief that the eye of a big winter storm is looking forebodingly down on his lonely corner of the world.

At about two o'clock, Eugene sees Dicky come running into the farmyard. He's bundled in a tan winter parka, blue snow pants, black rubber boots with a red stocking cap, and knitted mittens.

"Drive tractor," he says into a blustery wind.

"You're in luck. I have to move some hay bales into the milk shed."

Eugene has been rushing all day to minimize the outdoor work he will have to do over the next few days. With Dicky in tow, he starts his old John Deere with its attached pay loader bucket and then maneuvers Dicky into his lap.

"Have you ever hauled alfalfa?"

He shakes his head no.

Eugene drives to the barn, dropping the raised bucket to the ground. They walk together inside through the side door. The barn, nearly full with bales stacked to the rafters, feels warm and cozy.

"It's warm," says Dicky.

Eugene lifts the boy up and sets him on a bale.

"You stay here for a minute. I have to put bales on the tractor."

Eugene carries bales out two at a time and stacks them on the tractor's bucket. When he can't balance anymore, he goes back inside to get Dicky. He's frustrated to find that the boy is nowhere in sight.

"Dicky!" Eugene calls out. "I told you to stay put."

"Up here," Dicky says while standing on top of a stack of bales about twenty feet in the air.

"You get down here right now! I mean it!"

Dicky clumsily races to the ground.

Eugene, flushing red, picks the boy up and pulls his face within inches of his own.

"Never play on hay bales like that. They're dangerous. Do you understand me!"

Eugene watches as Dicky's face scrunches up and his eyes fill with tears. Too scared to talk, he nods up and down. Eugene knows that Margaret doesn't like this kind of discipline. She prefers to calmly explain the issue, no matter how long it takes. Eugene believes in direct, forceful actions. Besides, he doesn't have time for her approach on a day like this.

After moving the bales, Eugene starts using the bucket to scoop manure out of the stock pens and move it to the growing pile on the north side of the barn. In spring, he will broadcast the odiferous pile onto his fields.

About halfway through the task, a car pulls into the yard. It's Tom Magnus, a livestock buyer from Mansonville. Eugene had previously asked the buyer to come out after he realized that he would probably need to sell his hogs to stay ahead of the bills.

As Tom approaches the tractor, Eugene cuts the engine. The return to quiet is a welcome respite from his harried race with the weather.

"I see you've got a hired man today," jokes Tom.

"He works cheap," replies Eugene.

Farmyard conversations usually adhere to an unwritten protocol, pleasantries followed by the weather, agribusiness news and trends, back to the families, then the extended families. But today, the banter will abruptly end on the subject of the impending weather.

"I'm cold," Dicky says as he starts squirming on Eugene's lap.

Eugene gets down from the tractor and places the boy on the ground.

"Run into the house."

Dicky trots off in the direction of the house as Eugene tries to move the conversation on to selling hogs and steers. The wind has shifted forebodingly to out of the east, and the temperature is dropping—he's running out of time. The two men walk to the hog pen to talk about current prices and expected trends.

The increasingly bitter wind moves the discussion to a quick conclusion.

Looking up at the sky, Eugene says, "You better think about getting home before this thing hits."

Shivering, Magnus agrees. He waves as Tom heads off in the direction of his car.

Eugene thinks about heading to the house to grab another layer to throw on against the cold wind but decides instead to race his chores along against the coming storm. Eventually, his shivering body and growling stomach move him to pack it in for supper.

The sound of wind fills the air as he shivers from being underdressed. He pushes through the back door, where he is greeted by a welcoming warmth and the smell of roast.

Margaret looks at him blankly for a moment, then she asks, "Where's Dicky?"

Those two words are a glass of ice water in his face. He is cold, and with all the extra work, he is exhausted and hungry.

Part Two—Where's Dicky

"What do you mean? I sent him inside two hours ago."

"He didn't come inside, Eugene."

"He was heading straight for the house."

"Dicky!" Margaret yells into the quiet of the house.

When there is no reply, Margaret opens the door to the attic, then calls out again while bounding up the stairs.

"I'll check the basement," Eugene says as his boots pound down the rickety steps.

Meeting back in the kitchen, Eugene puts on his heavy coat as he tells Margaret he will search outside. He tells her to check the closets and all the rest of his favorite hiding places. Dicky, like most young children, loves to play hide and seek.

"Check behind the chicken coop and the grove to the east," Margaret calls out as he is leaving.

#

Margaret knows all too well that losing track of Dicky around home is nothing new. As an only child, he has grown accustomed to entertaining himself within his curious and unbounded imagination. When he gets bored inside, Margaret will bundle him up and send him out to play. Lately, he has created an imaginary world behind the chicken coop. The methodical arrangement of sticks, rocks, grass, and straw makes up a townscape to which he has added some of his treasured collection of little stuff, which normally resides on top of his dresser. His inside treasures include an orderly assortment of tiny boxes, window envelopes, a whistle, a Buster Brown clicker, metal buttons, political buttons, and all manner of the tiny prizes concealed in cereal boxes.

Another of Dicky's recent haunts is the partially hollow trunk of an enormous cottonwood tree growing among others along the south side of their dirt road about a quarter-mile to the east. After a half-hour of searching a few weeks ago, Margaret found him sitting inside that hollow. When she asked why he was there, he said he was waiting for a bear. He loves bedtime stories about bears.

#

Eugene calls out to Dicky as he heads towards the chicken coop. He realizes at once that even his loudest voice is mostly drowned out by the buffeting wind. Next, he looks behind all of the outbuildings. He sets his mind on checking the trees to the east and decides it will be faster to take the pickup. After checking the trees, he circles back and then stops on the road in front of the house. He stands on the truck as he peers in all directions, looking for any sign of movement. He climbs down to stand by the driver's door, where he lays on the horn, looking for any sign of life. He sees Margaret's face in the front window gazing at him; she looks scared. The light is starting to fade, and the clouds to the southwest are ominously dark. He knows they are running out of time.

#

When Eugene comes back into the house, Margaret can see in his face that he is as worried as she is. He tells her it is time to call the neighbors for help. The antiquated phone system is actually a help in this situation. The black plastic monstrosity hangs on the kitchen wall with only a blank circle covering the location of the rotary dial on more civilized phones. On its side is a small crank which Margaret turns in several long bursts, causing two hidden dome-shaped bells to clatter on her phone and all of the others in the neighboring houses. For normal calls, each household has a unique pattern of short and long rings. A series of long rings indicate an emergency, much like the large bell on a volunteer fire station or the steam whistle near an underground mine.

As the neighbors pick up their receivers, Margaret tells them about Dicky, and it isn't long before pickup trucks start rolling into the farmyard. Margaret watching out of the kitchen window, sees Eugene quickly sending them in all directions. Through the now open window, she hears him sending the first two to search near the creek a half-mile to the northwest, which is a place that Dicky loves to fish for chubs. He sends other men to search again in the trees along the road to the east. He sends two men north to the high point in the field in order to scan in all directions. She prays they will find him before the daylight is gone.

#

One of the wives, Luella Brennan, their closest neighbor, had come with her husband. She is aware that this isn't the first-time Dicky had toddled off. On one occasion, while looking out her kitchen window, she saw Dicky playing with their dog. She had marveled at the unknowable path of exploration which must have led him all the way there.

"So, he's done it again, I see," Luella says as she meets Margaret in the kitchen.

"I hate to say it, but I think I'll let Eugene tan his bottom this time."

Luella can see Margaret's eyes fighting back tears.

"Don't worry, dear. They'll find him any minute."

"From your mouth to God's ears," replies Margaret softly.

Luella thinks to ask if she and Margaret may offer a prayer but stops herself thinking it would break the brave face that Margaret is clinging to.

Besides, she tells herself, *it's not quite time to start praying yet.*

"How much coffee do you have, dear? Those men are going to need some when they come to the house," Luella suggests mostly as a way to help keep Margaret busy.

While filling the electric percolator from the spigot in the kitchen, both women notice the snow blowing in the air.

"Good heavens, it's snowing!" Luella says.

Over the next hour, Louella can see that the long minutes ticking by are taking a toll on Margaret's nerves.

"It's time to call for more help," Margaret says emphatically.

After cranking the phone with the ring for the operator, Margaret waits.

#

June Donner is trying to finish a lengthy novel which she borrowed from the Temperance Public Library.

June's job as a phone exchange operator, which many might think of as robotic, actually encompasses the entire spectrum of human emotion and none more intimate than the rural customers, which some of her colleagues have termed "the cranks." It's an ironic nickname since the rural folks, who have to funnel all phone communication through the operators in Summit, treat their regular operators as neighbors and friends. Calls going out with good or bad news are almost always shared first with the operator. Though most of the calls are routine, at times, June enables vital communications in life and death situations. Most customers under pressure don't think to call the police or firemen directly; they just call the operator.

She is in the fourth hour of her shift at the Summit telephone exchange located just north of Main Street, and so far, it has been an easy shift. Her reading is interrupted by two long rings clanging forth from the two round bells at the top of the switchboard she is manning. She pulls the transmission cord connected to her headset and secures it into the socket adjacent to the flashing yellow light of rural party Line 28.

"Operator," she says.

"June, my little boy is lost, and I don't know what to do."

After extracting the facts from Margaret, she assures her that help will soon be on the way. After disconnecting the call, her first call to the Summit police station is not answered. Telling herself not to panic, she successfully reaches the town's fire station. A few moments later, she hears the siren to muster the town's volunteer firefighters. Then, June tries unsuccessfully to reach the Summit police chief at home.

While thinking about the worry she heard in Margaret's voice, she notices the school parking lot across the street is full. She remembers there's a meeting of the National Farmers Organization tonight. Disobeying a company rule, she leaves the building to let the local farmers know about the lost boy. Several of the men who know Eugene immediately hop into their pickup trucks and head out to his place northeast of town.

#

Over the next hour, darkness falls as the temperature continues to drop amid the increasing wind. The snow, which started as a few flakes and now falling in earnest, is cast back up into the air by gusting wind. The flakes swirl like a swarm of locusts, stinging Eugene's exposed skin and buffeting his eyes, squinting into the darkening night. The narrow and muddy road, deeply rutted by spinning tires, is becoming more impassible as each new car or truck arrives.

Eugene is cold and tired as he stands in the farmyard as dozens of men cluster around him, wondering what to do next. Looking in the direction of the road to the east, he sees an ominous red glow flashing in the snow-filled sky. Moments later, a county sheriff cruiser pulls into the yard, closely followed by the Summit firetruck. Eugene cringes when Deputy Buckman emerges from the car.

Eugene knows him from Camp Hyder, where Buckman was an M.P. who seemed to have enjoyed going out of his way to make him and all the other training soldiers miserable. When Eugene had returned to the area after the war, he learned from Dub that Buckman remained stationed at Camp Hyder for the entire duration of the war. Thinking of how his fellow infantrymen, many of whom were killed or badly wounded in action, were treated by this backbencher caused him to quietly fume whenever he thought about it. In the years immediately after the war, when they had occasionally met in cafes or bars, Eugene, especially when inebriated, found it impossible to bite his tongue. Dub always tried his best to smooth things over, especially if jail time loomed ahead. In all cases, these interactions only solidified the animosity between the two men.

It seems surreal as Eugene watches Deputy Buckman walking towards him midst the howling wind and blowing snow. They express strained pleasantries and then go together, along with neighbor Don Brennan and Benjamin "Bull" Johnson, the Summit Fire Chief, into the warm house now full of people.

Once inside, Buckman motions for them to sit at the kitchen table as he opens his notebook. Eugene bites his lip as he sits down as Margaret, oblivious to the tension in the air, brings coffee for them.

"Cream or sugar?" she asks.

"Black is fine," replies Buckman. "Let's get to it. When was the last time you saw..., I'm sorry, what's your little boy's name?"

"Dicky," replies Eugene. "He came outside at two o'clock. He was with me until about three when he got cold, so I sent him to the house."

"He went outside at one," says Margaret. "He got bored inside, so I bundled him up and sent him out."

"I looked at my watch. It was two," Eugene insists.

Buckman is writing in his notebook. *"Dicky was last seen at about three o'clock."* Looking at his watch, he says, "So, he has been missing just over five hours."

Margaret and Eugene look at each other; the impact of that statement hits them hard.

Looking at Margaret, Buckman asks, "Is there a chance that when he went out, he didn't go to Eugene right away?"

Eugene's patience is running out. "How does this matter? Did you notice the weather? We have to find him, and soon!"

Buckman's eyes narrow as he shifts his gaze to Eugene. "I know we need to find him and fast. The people out there are running around in circles, so we need to get this organized."

Margaret jumps in, in order to try to break the tension, "He likes to play outside by himself. He probably did that before he went to find Eugene."

Buckman writes quickly as Eugene continues to fume.

"Do you know where his play areas are, Eugene?" asks Buckman.

"Yes, he does," says Margaret. "We've already searched them."

"I'll have you show me these places after we search the house."

"I've already searched the house, too," says Margaret.

"I'll help you do it again," Buckman says. Then trying his best to sound sympathetic, he adds, "It's important we thoroughly search the most likely places first before moving on."

"Well, let's get going," snaps Eugene. "Talking isn't searching."

"Bull, use the firetruck's search lights to search the roads in every direction he may have possibly set out on foot," Buckman says to the fire chief. Then, turning back to Eugene, he asks, "Are there any places he likes to visit in the area?"

Eugene and Margaret look at each other. They hadn't thought of that.

"He ran off to the Brennan's place one day to play with their dog," says Margaret.

"I can show the firetruck the way," offers Don Brennan.

"Good. Any place else?" asks Buckman.

"Rabbits," says Margaret. "The Hamilton family raises rabbits. He loves to see those. They live a mile further south."

Buckman tells the fire chief to take Brennan and head out in those directions. He instructs them to be sure to use the flood lights to search the ditches on both sides of the road. He tells Eugene to use other volunteers to search inside buildings and anywhere outside he can think of.

Buckman looks at the clock. "It's eight-fifteen. If we haven't found him, plan to meet back here at nine-thirty. We'll need to prepare a statement and a description for the ten o'clock news reports. Do you have a picture of Dicky, Margaret?"

"I don't think so. We don't own a camera."

"What about relatives or church?"

"I think Madeline, the minister's wife, took one."

"See if you can get it for me."

#

Margaret is impressed by how thoroughly Buckman searches the house. When they were finished, there could be no doubt that he could possibly be anywhere inside. Then, he reminds Margaret to try to get a photograph of Dicky, so she calls Madeline right away.

A half-hour later, Madeline and John walk in the door.

"You poor thing," Madeline says while hugging Margaret.

"We would have been here sooner, but the roads are really getting bad. I was stuck in the mud until a tractor came along and pulled me out. Your neighbor, Tim Hamilton, is pulling cars out of the mud non-stop."

"God bless him," Margaret says.

Margaret's heart fills with wonder as she finds the house now so full of people that all chairs are full and folks, mostly women, lean against the walls. The kitchen table is filling with food. A stream of searchers, many of whom were not dressed for the ever-worsening weather, are flowing into the house to drink coffee and eat the cookies and cakes brought in by the neighbor women.

John and Madeline stand with Margaret as she is now looking out the new-room window onto the farmyard. Eugene had put this small addition on the north side of the house so they would have a more adequate living space. This room is warmed by a dark-brown, boxy fuel oil burner. The cozy space with carpet, knotty pine paneling, a sofa, and a television is, by far, the most comfortable room in the house. Today, the view out of this room's window is surreal. The always empty farmyard is full of parked cars and pickup trucks. A dozen or more men are wandering haphazardly in groups of threes and fours. Snow, driven by the wind, seems to be falling sideways, and occasionally gusts seem to punch at and flex the room's large window. The family burn barrel, which is usually next to the garden to the north of the house, has been moved into the farmyard. Flames and smoke, buffeted by the harsh wind, illuminate a group of men trying to warm themselves around it.

"There must be a hundred people searching," John says.

As they continue to look outside, standing shoulder-to-shoulder, she feels first Madeline and then John put an arm around her.

She drops her head on Madeline's shoulder as she says, "It's in God's hands, isn't it?"

"Of course," answers John. Then he recites an extemporaneous prayer petitioning God's protection for Dicky and praying for his quick return to his family.

#

Deputy Melvin Buckman has been on his car radio with Sheriff Sheldon Mackintosh for fifteen minutes, all the while trying desperately to keep his boss from finding out that he feels like he is in way over his head. Though the deputy has been in law enforcement for almost twenty years, if you count his time as an Army M.P., he has never led a case of this magnitude all by himself. He is also amped up because he knows that fate has dropped a real opportunity in his lap. This is the kind of case that could get his name in the newspapers. The sheriff hasn't said it out loud, but at his age, he must be thinking about retiring. If the stars line up just right, he might be able to throw his hat in the ring.

Armed with the sheriff's advice, he's starting to gain some confidence in handling the situation. But still, he's jumpy because he decided not to tell the sheriff about his history with the lost boy's father until absolutely necessary, and if that's not enough, he doesn't know how he's going to work closely with a guy that hates his guts.

At nine-thirty, Buckman finds Eugene to ask him to return to the house for a quick meeting.

When Eugene icily stares at him, he says, "I know this is a difficult situation, and I know that I'm the last person on earth that you would want to trust, but Eugene, I have a little boy too."

As the deputy struggles for something else to say, Eugene's eyes seem to burn white-hot. Finally, Eugene says, "We're wasting time. Let's go."

Inside, Eugene then Buckman take their wet coats off and hang them on the backs of empty chairs around the kitchen table. Margaret scoops them up to hang them by the oil burner to dry.

Buckman sits at the kitchen table and motions for Eugene to do the same. A hive of women buzzing around arranging food, cleaning dishes, and sweeping floors slow to a halt as the men sit down around the table covered with food. Margaret brings a tray with full cups of coffee from a huge urn that Madeline brought from the church.

"Help yourself to coffee and food," says Margaret.

Holding up his hands for quiet, Buckman says, "I need a description of the boy for the news."

Margaret and Eugene are staring blankly at him.

"You know, how old, how tall, what does he weigh."

"That's his height," Margaret says, pointing at the pencil marks on the door molding.

While Eugene hops up to fetch a yardstick from the closet, Margaret adds, "he turned four on November second."

"About three foot six," Eugene adds.

Buckman writes down the height, and after a bit of discussion, he writes down the collective guess that the boy weighs about forty pounds.

"What was he wearing?"

"He was wearing a hat, coat, snow pants, and yarn gloves,"

"Colors?"

"Let's see," Margaret says thoughtfully. "His cap is red; gloves are black." After a pause, she asks Eugene, "What color would you say his coat is?"

Eugene shrugs. "Dull green?"

"The snow pants are faded blue," she adds with uncertainty in her voice.

"Did you get the picture?"

"I have this one," Madeline chimes in, pulling it out of her purse.

The picture shows three children from a Sunday school class. Dicky is in the middle. The candid photograph caught Dicky with a distant expression on his face. Buckman sees that it's a flash image with good sharpness.

"They should be able to crop this and blow it up. Let me know if you find a better one."

Buckman looks up at the clock, which reads nine-forty-five. "I have to phone this information in to the sheriff. He will have it broadcast on the radio and TV for their ten o'clock newscasts.

Buckman chews on a sandwich as he talks to Sheriff Mackintosh over the phone. He notices Margaret setting a sandwich in front of Eugene, telling him he has to eat something. He tells her he is not hungry before taking a reluctant bite, then he devours it and takes another from a tall stack.

Hanging up, Buckman puts on his coat and asks Eugene if he is ready to resume searching outside. As the door slams shut, the deputy is shocked to see how bad the weather has gotten. The temperature has dropped twenty degrees; there are broken tree branches sticking out of the snow that is already four inches deep. When he turns to Eugene, he has to squint to keep the blowing snow out of his eyes, and he finds he has to yell against the howling wind. First, he asks Eugene to take him to the two places Margaret mentioned Dicky liked to play. He soon discovers that if there were any clues to see, they would have been buried by the storm.

Squinting through the night, he directs Eugene to take him into the barn. Inside, the unheated barn seems comparatively warm and quiet but dark.

Turning on his large flashlight, Buckman says, "I want to search inside the buildings. Hopefully, this weather will make him want to get inside."

But he is thinking, *God, help the boy if he is out in the weather alone.*

#

Inside, Margaret turns on the radio and television for the ten o'clock news reports. The radio news leads with the story about young Dicky. It gives his description and asks people to be on the lookout and to report to the sheriff or the operator with any information. The television report leads with the weather. After the first commercial break, they come back with the announcement about four-year-old Dicky Walker, lost near his home in the country northeast of Summit.

Not long after the news hit the airwaves, even more cars start rolling into the farm. At about ten-thirty, Dub burst through the back door. Margaret, who had been staring out the window, goes to meet him in the kitchen.

#

Hugging her, he says, "Oh, Margaret, I just saw it on the news. I had a heck of a time getting here."

"Mud?" asks Margaret.

"Mud, snow, and so many cars on the road that I had to drive at a crawl." He sees that her eyes are red and moist. "Where's Eugene?"

"He's outside with Deputy Buckman somewhere."

"Buckman?" The name hits him like a mortar round. How many times has he had to restrain Eugene, so he didn't kill the guy?

"Yes, Buckman. He's been here for over two hours."

"I'm sure Geno's not thrilled about that. I better go out there and help keep the peace," he says while heading out the door.

He is practically running as he thinks about how much Eugene hates that guy. When he finds Eugene and Buckman seeming to be calmly talking, he breathes a sigh of relief. He puts his hand on Eugene's shoulder and tells him how sorry he is that he is just now getting there, and then asks him how he is holding up.

"I can't think about myself right now," Eugene tells his friend.

Dub has never seen Eugene look this bad. He looks like he's been hit by a truck. Dub grabs a handful of his friend's coat sleeve at his shoulder to get his attention. When their eyes meet, Eugene thanks him for coming to help, then looking around at all of the people, he asks Dub if he can lead some of them to search the fields around the farmyard.

"But how?" asks Dub.

Buckman speaks up, "Form a line of ten searchers spaced about ten feet apart. Walk them across the open ground until you hit a fence. Then bring them back in the opposite direction."

"It's so dark. How will we see anything?"

"I know, but try it. If you see it's not working, bring them back. Ask other folks to drive along the roads and use their headlights to try to check ditches, culverts, under bridges, in and around any buildings, near clumps of trees, anywhere where a person might try to shelter from the weather."

"Okay, I'm on it," says Dub with conviction. But as he leaves, his heart is sinking for Eugene, Margaret, and Dicky.

#

As they finish searching all the buildings, Buckman can see the desperation and exhaustion in Eugene's eyes, so he suggests they head back into the house. The place is now full of people, many of whom had come to help search in light clothing. These huddle around the oil heater in the new room and the pot belly stove in the kitchen. Remembering the sheriff's advice, he tries to focus his attention on the overall situation. He thinks about what has been done and what remains to be done.

"Did somebody catch tonight's weather report?" he asks.

"Yes," says Minister John. "They said the storm is going to strengthen overnight and last at least through the day tomorrow."

With all eyes looking at him, Buckman considers the situation. He has completed a thorough examination of the house and all of the other buildings. The weather, along with the darkness, is making outside searches both ineffective and potentially dangerous, especially to the volunteers that he has noticed are mostly underdressed for the steadily worsening weather.

With the room now deathly silent except for a radio playing in the next room, he looks at Eugene standing with Margaret. He has to make a very tough decision; he just hopes to heaven he is right.

He softly says, "I'm afraid we have to call off the search for tonight."

Sensing a backlash, he flatly lays out his reasons for all to hear. The inescapable logic serves to deflate the flagging hope of everyone present.

"The weather may not be much better tomorrow, but at least we'll have light," Buckman says. "It looks like we're in pretty good shape for food here. When you come back tomorrow, be dressed in your warmest winter clothes."

All the eyes turn to Margaret as she says, "He's in God's hands tonight." After a pause, she adds, "I trust God."

Eyes welling with tears, people reluctantly start to leave.

"Please keep your eyes open on the way home," instructs Buckman. "Call in if you see anything at all."

#

Eugene is numb as he sits near the wood burner in the kitchen as the others file out, leaving Dub, John, Madeline, and Margaret standing together nearby. John recites a prayer as Eugene respectfully bows his head feeling completely lost and alone. After the pastor and his wife leave, Eugene notices

Dub move to sit next to him. *Good old Dub*, he thinks to himself.

Margaret sighs and starts to tidy up the kitchen. Eugene hears her telling him to get some sleep, but he insists that he will sleep better if he personally checks the two culverts near the house and the area of the creek where Dicky likes to fish. He knows it's going to be a long and difficult night. Perhaps this lonely pilgrimage will somehow help him find some peace before trying to sleep. Dub wants to come along, but Eugene insists that he wants to do it alone.

Reluctantly, Dub says, "I will search by the roads all the way home, and I will try to get back here as soon as I can."

After putting the last of the fresh batteries in his flashlight, Eugene walks out into the night alone. The blowing snow is beginning to erase the innumerable tire tracks and footprints that seem to be everywhere. Out in the darkness by the road alone reminds him of making the nightly rounds to check on his men on Guam. Satisfied the culverts are empty, he hops onto the rusty tractor for the half-mile ride through drifts and ditches to the creek.

He sits down on the large rock where he and Dicky had fished with poles fashioned from branches knotted with string. The huge, round rock that was no doubt left there by a glacier found itself directly in the path of the tiny waterway, a tributary of Pine Creek. The water bouncing off the rock created an eddy whose whirling action carved out a little pool that sometimes hides a few fish, typically not much bigger than minnows. Eugene remembers how delighted Dicky was whenever he caught one, no matter how small. As the wind mercilessly buffets his face, a face already wet with tears, he tilts his head up to talk to God, something he hadn't done since his first days on Guam.

There, during the long nights of bombardment on that horrible island, a place that could not be more different from this wintry world, he had made his peace with dying. After the war, though haunted by flashbacks of the horrible carnage, he took solace in knowing that he would never again be afraid to die. That realization had given him peace and confidence. Now sitting in this cold, isolated place, he is suddenly and unexpectedly being forced to face the horrifying prospect that his nightmares had shown him; that thing much worse than all the other deaths he had witnessed; the death of his innocent, little boy.

The clouds part, revealing a single star. As he struggles for something to say, only one word comes to mind. Looking to the heavens, he says, "Please." Then he cries.

Tuesday, March 7—Missing 15 Hours

Eugene is back out in the farmyard at 5:00 a.m.; his tormented mind wouldn't let him sleep anyway. He finds the conditions even worse than the night before; wind now out of the northeast with gusts driving snow into flesh like daggers and drifts piling high in its shadows; a cruel wind transforming the bitter temperature into a blowtorch of iciness; a howling wind as if a voice proclaiming danger in an ancient language easily understandable by every creature on earth. There, penetrating the wind, he hears metallic banging; the clanging hog feeders' lids, a nagging reminder of the many dozens of mouths that depend on him and him alone for their food. He realizes that even in the throes of this battle with death, somehow, routine chores will still have to be done.

A few early arriving neighbors help Eugene finish his chores as they discuss how best to begin searching. They are greatly concerned about the road; huge snow drifts have made it impassable for cars. No strangers to this type of weather, farmers knew to bundle up in layers of clothing and to drive tractors, not pickups, over the almost impassable roads.

#

Margaret, feeling numb, doesn't remember sleeping but realizes she must have dozed off, if only a bit, during the worst night of her life. She said many prayers for Dicky. But she also prayed for the strength to hold on to her faith no matter what was coming next. She had immediately put her full faith in the Lord and felt strongly that Dicky would be quickly found. But with the termination of the search and then agonizing about her son still out in those conditions, she knew that her faith was in for an excruciating test. The morning finds her confidence gone, but still, she clings to hope. Her humanness pushes her to make a bargain with God. But her knowledge of the Bible forces her to accept the will of the Lord, no matter how difficult. Her troubled mind is reminded of Abraham being asked to sacrifice his only son. The realization that he proved he was willing to do it forces her to see that her own faith, though she had thought it strong, is woefully not. Her heart pounding, feeling a bit faint, she now prays for the strength to just make it through the day.

#

Briggs County Sheriff Sheldon "Mack" Mackintosh has gotten up early too. His sixty-eight-year-old joints ache worse than usual this morning; his arthritis always bothers him more when it rains or snows. He is listening to weather updates on the small radio sitting on his kitchen counter while sipping coffee and gazing at the snow, at times blowing horizontally out of the window behind the sink. He calls young Deputy Buckman.

"This is shaping up to be as bad as the '59 blizzard. The highway patrol has already closed highways 150, 63, and 218 to the north of here. So far as I know, Highway 20 is still open. I'm going to call the radio station and tell them to broadcast that I am urging people to stay off the roads today."

"Thank heavens the schools are all closed," says Buckman. They discuss a plan for the emergencies confronting them. They are facing the worst snowstorm of the year, which will inundate the department with traffic calls; jack-knifed semis and stranded motorists will be the order of the day.

"I want you to take charge of the lost boy search again today. I need to stay at headquarters to run emergency response for the county," instructs the sheriff.

"Yes, Sir! I'll head out right away."

"If you need anything, radio back to me. I'll do my best to get whatever you need. And make sure you have chains on before you leave town. And

Melvin, a boy lost in a snowstorm, is a big deal. The news people will be all over it. For now, keep me informed and refer all news questions to me. And one more thing, I can't imagine what that family is going through, so let them know that we'll do everything we can, as soon as we can."

"On my way, Boss."

#

The deputy doesn't get very far when he sees that it is even worse than he feared. The air is full of huge flakes, and the stuff on the ground is blowing right back up into the air, making it almost impossible to see. When he turns north onto the farm roads, it becomes even harder to drive, and without any way to discern the road edge, he is in danger of plunging into a ditch. But, he knows this is his big chance to prove himself to the sheriff.

He turns on his emergency lights while feeling a little silly doing so. He is determined to try to make it to the farm this morning, no matter what. The gusts are so strong that they fight his steering, and they scour much of the road surface clear. But at intervals and especially where a structure impedes the wind's path, huge drifts form and grow. He stares intently, trying to discern anything out of the milk being swatted ineffectively by the thumping wiper. At intervals, deep drifts suddenly appear directly in front of him. When the drift isn't too big, he makes it through after a bit of a thud. The bigger drifts are a different story. He is jolted to a stop in a drift taller than his cruiser. He spins his tires forward and back until the snow-packed tire chains regain enough traction to allow the heavy cruiser to lurch out of the drift's icy grip.

He steps out into the elements to get a better look at the huge hill of snow. Seeing he has few other choices, he decides to give brute force a try. He backs up a quarter-mile and then accelerates to 60 mph while heading straight for the drift. The impact is stunning, sending snow flying in all directions. After he makes it through, he stops to check his car. Snow is packed into the grill, but he doesn't see any obvious damage. Outside in the weather, he tries to judge the condition of the road ahead. With many miles and countless drifts to go, he reluctantly decides he is not going to make it. He radios the sheriff that he is coming back to Temperance until they can clear him a path.

#

The deputy's report back to him is one more confirmation that this is going to be a very long day for all of them. The sheriff makes one more look out of the window and then immediately contacts the Briggs County Engineering Office and demands they dispatch at least one machine to open a path from Summit to the farm.

"I've got Summit Police Chief Gary Raymond telling me there are fifty volunteers in town who can't get out there. I've got a family with a toddler lost in this storm. I don't care how you do it, but I want that five miles open as soon as possible!"

#

By late morning a gangly road-grader has finally made its way to the farm from Summit. The final narrow dirt section, which was so muddy just yesterday, has frozen solid overnight, the one and only benefit of the brutal winter storm. Following behind it are several cars carrying volunteer searchers but the first car in line is deputy Buckman's cruiser with lights flashing.

Inside he finds Margaret standing at the kitchen sink, staring out into the farmyard.

"How did you ever make it here on those roads in a car?" asks Margaret.

"I followed the road-grader from Summit. And there were cars full of people who followed me. I tried to get here earlier, but I couldn't make it through the drifts. I'm really sorry I couldn't get here sooner."

"Eugene finished up the chores and has started searching with some of the neighbors."

"I'll go tell them to come into the house. I want his help to organize a search with the new volunteers. I'm sure the men would appreciate some coffee to help warm them up."

Buckman makes his way out into the storm, looking for Eugene and the men with him. His mind is reeling; he decides to radio the sheriff to talk things over.

"They've got one lane open from Summit. Right now, I have about forty people who can help search, and probably more are on the way. Over," radios Buckman.

"How bad is it there? Over." asks the sheriff.

"Visibility is awful, and I've never seen such big drifts. It's going to be tough searching. Over."

"Do the best you can, Melvin. Remember, always start in the center and work your way out. Over."

"Okay, Boss. We cleared the inside of the house last night. For now, I will re-search the farm buildings and then the immediate area with the men I have. As more arrive, I will expand the search outward from there. Can we get some dogs? Over."

"I'll try. I'm trying to contact the Civil Air Patrol search groups. They should be able to direct a larger area search if it comes to that. That's what they're trained for. Over," Mackintosh replies.

"Okay, Boss, if you need to contact me, you will have to call the house for now. I'll plan on radioing in every hour. Over."

"Good luck, Melvin. Out."

#

During the day, the road-grader makes the run back and forth on the dirt and gravel roads that lead to the black top just north of Summit. The drifting snow makes it an unending chore to keep just one lane open. Cars eventually fill the farmyard and are starting to block the narrow road. The small house is again filling with neighbor women bringing and preparing food. A radio is playing, delivering fresh news about the storm. At least once an hour, the statement about the lost boy, his description, and the request for searchers is read.

The stream of vehicles turns the frozen dirt road into a soupy mass of snow, mud, and water. Eventually, about a hundred and fifty people are searching in the area. Some are looking inside the buildings, the buildings that had already been searched numerous times. Others are braving the harsh elements, wading through waist-deep snow. Some form lines to systematically search the pastures and plowed fields. Ditches with deep snow are probed with long poles. The areas with trees are searched again and again. Nearby creeks are examined. Ironically, a seeing-eye dog from the Saint Vincent School for the Blind is brought in to try to pick up a scent. The horrendous weather conditions combined with the multitude of people who had been walking on every foot of land make it all but impossible for a dog to pick up a scent.

The now cleared road has also brought newspaper people to gather information for stories. They talk to officials as well as Eugene. Some even enter the house to speak to Margaret. Among the reporters is the editor of the Summit weekly newspaper. He scratches a storyline in his notepad that he will place in tomorrow's edition. *I was down there Wednesday, and it was a wintery quagmire. The snow was drifted to the rafters. All possible buildings and ditches were searched, but the storm's obscuring blanket had made it impossible to be sure of anything.*

#

Late afternoon, Dub enters the kitchen. When he finds Margaret's eyes, he suppresses the question he was planning to ask, already knowing the answer. Instead, he hugs her and then kisses her on the cheek.

"I wish I could have gotten here sooner. I've never seen the roads this bad."

After an awkward silence, he manages, "I brought your mail and the Messenger."

The Temperance newspaper's front page is dominated by the big winter storm. On the far-right side is a column with the small headline, *"Boy 4, Lost Near Summit."* Margaret looks lovingly at the picture of her son sandwiched in between the paragraphs of the story. The caption under the picture simply reads, *"Dicky Walker, 4."* The article gives his height and weight, what he was wearing, and when and where he was lost. It then asks everyone to be on the lookout for a boy matching the description and to call the tip line at the Briggs County Sheriff's Department with any pertinent information. The final paragraph outlines the Sheriff's plea for volunteers to carpool to minimize the number of vehicles at the location.

#

Though Buckman had thought that weather this terrible would have to improve during the day, if anything, it is getting worse. As the sun is setting, Buckman radios his report to Sheriff Mackintosh. After signing off, he heads into the house.

"Sorry folks, we have to call off the search again. The weather is just too bad to do any good overnight. But I do have some better news. Sheriff Mackintosh has Civil Air Patrol search teams from both Wellington and Willow Bend lined up for first thing tomorrow morning. These guys are professional searchers with all the top equipment, including an observation plane they can use if the weather permits."

Deputy Buckman, of course, does not tell them what the sheriff had surmised. Buckman remembers their conversation on the dark, snowy ride home.

"Melvin, keep this under your hat. If that four-year-old boy was outside when the storm hit and he didn't find shelter somewhere, well, not even an adult could have survived all that."

"So, you're saying he's probably dead."

"We can't say anything like that yet, at least not officially."

"I have to go talk to the family. What do I tell them?"

"Stay upbeat. If they press you, just tell them that we need to catch a break soon. My years have taught me to never give up on hope, no matter how slim, until it is no longer possible."

As the deputy's heart is sinking, he thinks about what he would do if it was his own little boy that was missing in a terrible winter storm.

Dawn Wednesday—Missing 40 hours

Margaret drags herself out of bed after hearing the backdoor clunk shut as Eugene leaves to tend to his early chores. She had been sleeplessly waiting for him to leave to spare herself from the possibility of having to talk about what is going on, especially first thing in the morning; what's left of her composure is much too fragile for that.

She sees that it has stopped snowing, but it doesn't really matter since the driving wind, which is rattling the glass in the kitchen window, continues to blast the dry snow right back up into the air. Squinting through tears with her face near its panes, she sees that the drifts around the buildings are almost reaching the eves and the rusty DeKalb thermometer nailed to the tree reads fifteen degrees.

"Dear God, where *is* he?" she says out loud.

The wind throbbing against the house during the night was a haunting reminder of what it must be like to be outside in these conditions. Margaret had prayed, perhaps for the hundredth time, that he was safe and warm inside somewhere, but where could that be? For the second straight night, Margaret was forced to cling to the hope of something unknowable, perhaps even impossible. She now prays for strength to hold on to that flimsy hope.

As the terrible reality of another bitter day confronts her psyche, she prays that this test of her faith will not last much longer.

#

The icy snow stinging Eugene's face is all too familiar. Squinting through the fog of falling snow, he sees Eunice looking in bewilderment at the huge drift blocking the door to the milking shed. He kicks into the drift to find the grain scoop he placed there for just such a predicament. With the door free, he allows the three girls to make their way inside so he can close the door behind them. Inside seems warm by comparison, if for no other reason than suddenly being out of the bitter wind.

After milking, he heads across the farmyard to grind feed. With everything that has been going on, he has already gotten far behind. The cattle and hogs are beyond hungry due to the slighted rations they have had to endure. The angry squealing hogs are easily heard above the noisy blasts of wind, as one, burrowing his snout into the icy soil and seeming to find a morsel, leads to a vigorous and noisy brawl.

#

Getting out of his warm car, the reporter, though now starting to shiver, hears a familiar sound over the howl of the wind. The sound leads him to the door of a drab, wooden structure.

After struggling to shut the rickety door, he shivers and says, "Man, it's nasty out there."

Eugene glances his way and then returns to scooping grain into the grinder chute.

"I'm Frank Frydenberg from the Des Moines Tribune," he states over the din of the grinder. "I was hoping I could ask you a few questions."

"I'm pretty busy here," says Eugene flatly.

"I can help with that. I ground feed for my dad almost every day when I was growing up."

"Where was that?"

"Near Ottumwa, seriously, I can scoop the grain and ask questions at the same time."

"I'd rather just do it myself," says Eugene. "But go ahead."

Frydenberg asks several questions while making notes. He asks about his livestock, the size of his farm, how long he has been there, and what he did in the war.

"You ask a lot of questions."

"Sorry about that. I really appreciate your talking to me with everything you have going on."

Frydenberg has learned that in order to get the answers he really wants, he has to develop a relationship, and in many cases, he has to be able to do that very quickly.

"Eugene, I know this is rough, but have you thought about with so much time that has passed if Dicky might not be alive?"

Eugene stops scooping then he shuts off the grinder.

Looking down, he answers, "He has to be inside somewhere... otherwise, he..." his voice trails off.

Frydenberg knows that the best way to get someone to say something difficult is to restrain the natural inclination to keep asking questions; he patiently waits for the awkward pause to drive him to continue.

After a moment, Eugene adds, "I really hope that someone took him." Another pause is followed by, "Otherwise..." his voice trails off again.

"By took him, do you mean kidnapped?"

Eugene looks at Frydenberg through bloodshot eyes and then nods.

Emerging from the grinding room, Frydenberg is surprised to see how many more vehicles and people have arrived. After instructing the photographer, who was trying to stay warm in the car, to get a picture of Eugene grinding feed, Frydenberg checks his notepad carefully before knocking on the kitchen door to talk to Margaret.

While waiting for Margaret to come to the door, two drab-green Civil Air Patrol trucks pull into the farmyard. He motioned for the photographer to get plenty of pictures. The scene with the uniformed Civil Air Patrol officers, their placarded vehicles, the Briggs County Sheriff cruiser, an Iowa Highway Patrol radio car, and dozens of volunteer searchers, including a group of Amish men who came in stark black horse-drawn carriages, causes his heart rate to increase. His mind races with the many story angles that have prize-winning potential.

He recalls with a smile how hard he had to lean on his editor to be able to follow this story based on an eleven-word teletype report and a reporter's time-worn hunch.

"Summit, Iowa (AP)—Boy 4, Dicky Walker, missing overnight in eastern Iowa blizzard."

#

Sheriff Mackintosh pulls into the farmyard behind the two Civil Air Patrol trucks. After introductions, Captain Hugh Stork of Willow Bend Civil Air Patrol unit asks Eugene where they can get out of the weather for a short planning meeting. Seeing that the house is already filling up, Eugene suggests that they gather in the grinding shed.

Captain Stork, along with Captain Bradley Winston of the Wellington Civil Air Patrol unit, outline the plans for the search. Captain Stork is in charge of searching inside buildings, and Captain Winston is to lead systematic outdoor searches. The objective for today is to thoroughly examine the four-square-mile area centered on the last place the boy was seen.

Laying a detailed area map on top of Eugene's makeshift desk, Winston pencils circles around the dozen or so farmsteads within the search area. Mackintosh and Buckman note the cache of weapons hanging on the wall behind the desk. Many appear to be war souvenirs, most notably a Samurai sword.

"Sheriff, I'd like you to speak with the owners of these farms to let them know we are coming and request they help guide the searches there."

Mackintosh points to Buckman, who nods affirmatively.

Captain Winston draws a pencil line around the paths of the wooded creeks within the search area.

"Do these roads have names?" he asks the sheriff.

"Nope, none of the unpaved roads in the county have names."

"Okay, I'll set up two teams. Team A will walk Pine Creek from north to south this road to that road, and Team B will search Buffalo Creek in the same direction bounded by these roads," he says, drawing lines indicating the search paths with arrowheads pointing to the unnamed roads.

"Searching in this weather is going to be brutal," says Captain Stork. "We were going to use a spotter plane, but with the current visibility, that would be pointless. So, we must rely upon ground searching, such as it is. If the visibility improves, we can have a plane out of Willow Bend in an hour."

Outside, the number of volunteer searchers has increased to over one hundred, most of whom are waiting inside vehicles or crowding around the downwind side of the farm buildings.

Captain Stork opens the door of his truck to grab its hand-help microphone. His instructions blast out of the truck's roof-mounted speaker. His directions divide the searchers into two groups of volunteers, with half forming on him and half forming on Captain Winston.

#

When Margaret opens the door for reporter Frydenberg, he takes note of the surprised expression on her pretty face.

"You're the first person to bother knocking in days."

"Sorry, my mom taught me to always knock. I'm Frank Frydenberg of the Des Moines Tribune."

"Well, come on in out of that nasty snow."

Frydenberg notices the kitchen table strewn with platters of sandwiches, cake, cookies, sugar, cream, and coffee mugs. On the counter is a steaming coffee urn with a red light glowing next to its spigot.

"It looks like you've been very busy this morning."

"All this is thanks to the neighbors. They've been bringing in food non-stop. Last night when I looked at the table piled with food, it reminded me of the story of Jesus feeding five thousand people."

Frydenberg smiles at Margaret as he burns that quote into his memory. He thinks to himself that this story has everything. Continuing in his friendly mode, he sits down with coffee, and he asks her about Dicky; what kind of boy he is, and the things he likes to do inside and out.

Margaret tells of his biggest love, Sunday school; it's about the only time he gets to play with other children. She tells about how full of imagination he is, using small objects to create miniature worlds out of everything he can find.

"He has a collection of all kinds of little stuff," says Margaret.

"That's fascinating. Would you mind showing me that?"

Margaret has Frydenberg follow her into his room. The small bedroom is simple yet tidy with yellowing wallpaper, bed neatly made with a cowboy-themed bedspread and a tractor calendar on the wall. His collection of little things is neatly arranged on top of both a cheap end table and a nonmatching dresser. All this evokes the mind of a curious young boy.

"Why a pile of envelopes?" asks Frydenberg.

"Maybe it's because you can see inside. He never lets me throw away an envelope with a window."

Margaret seems lost in thought. After a moment, Frydenberg points at an elegant broach asking, "Is this his?"

"Heaven's sakes, that's my great grandmother's broach! He's not supposed to snoop in our bedroom!" Margaret exclaims, snatching the broach off the dresser.

Frydenberg spends another half-hour in the kitchen talking to Margaret. He decides to hold off asking her any dark questions on this first visit. He has great background notes and has established a relationship, a very successful interview. Before leaving, he asks if she would mind if his photographer got a few shots in the house for his article. Margaret agrees.

Outside, Frydenberg is blasted with snow and wind as he sees several groups of men shoveling all the snowdrifts in the area down to the ground. He also sees a line of dozens of men passing hay bales along, like a bucket brigade, to the center of the farmyard, where they are being neatly stacked in a large, growing pyramid. A band of Amish men and boys are doing the stacking. Marveling at the stunning image, he quickly finds Jamie Ohlman, the pool photographer who accompanied him from Des Moines.

"Are you getting this, Jamie?"

"I just hope I brought enough film."

"What's up with the bales?"

"Captain Winston wanted the barn emptied to make sure the boy didn't get buried somehow."

"Keep snapping away, Jamie. Focus on the father, the guys in uniform, and be sure to get those Amish guys in your shots if you can."

"I'm on it."

"And keep looking for that perfect shot, the prizewinner. Save at least a half-dozen frames for inside the house. Get candid shots of the mother, the food on the table, and a couple in the kid's room. If the mother balks, apologize and back right off. Let me do any negotiating. I'm going to need her on my side if this thing keeps going."

#

When Dub pulls into the crowded farmyard, he notices a man wearing a trench coat and fedora hat coming out of the kitchen door. Inside he asks Margaret who that man is.

"A reporter," answers Margaret.

"Which paper?"

Margaret relates her exchange with Frank Frydenberg of the Des Moines Tribune.

"He's a long way from home," Dub says while pouring a coffee. "Here's today's Wellington Courier."

Margaret once again sees Dicky's picture included in the column on page one that forwards to another column on page five, which includes a photo of the farmyard full of cars and people with the house in the background. Margaret sits at the table while reading the article, which describes a family in trouble and how authorities, friends, neighbors, and even strangers are pitching in to help.

"It's a nice story," Margaret quietly remarks.

"Are you okay?" Dub asks her quietly.

"No. But I'm hanging on," she answers with sad eyes.

"I have to finish my deliveries," Dub says, then he stands up and kisses her on top of her head before going outside. "I'll be back when I'm done."

#

Eugene stares up and around the inside of the dusty, now empty barn. He has never seen it this way before; it seems immense. Stork and Buckman wave him over to examine the small pile of stuff that was hidden under all those bales.

"Does any of this stuff look familiar?" asks Stork.

There are several rags, a torn shirt, a mangled straw hat, old rat traps, a couple of gopher traps, three sinister-looking bale hooks, a flattened pair of very old work boots, and three unmatched shoes, one from a small child.

"That shoe wasn't Dicky's, was it?" asks Buckman.

"No," answers Eugene. "No one's worn a shoe that looks like that in years."

"I didn't think so."

Eugene squats down on his haunches running his fingers through the dust. He picks up a broken, rusty chain. Examining it closely, he realizes he is looking at what's left of a rosary. He drops it like it's hot and quickly stands; he looks pale.

"Anything wrong?" asks Buckman.

"No." After a pause, Eugene softly asks, "What's next?"

Stork explains that the next building to search is the hog house. He tells him that Doctor Charles Stenger, a Veterinarian from Temperance, will examine the hogs with a metal detector.

"If the hogs got him, there will probably be bits of zipper or metal buttons in their gut. It's a long shot, but we need to rule out the possibility."

#

Buckman lingers in the barn after the others have left. He's curious about Eugene's unusual reaction. After a moment of poking around, he finds himself looking at a small chain attached to a tiny cross. He sets this aside and continues to look for several minutes. It seems like nothing, but he takes the chain to his cruiser, puts it into an evidence bag, and logs it into his patrol book. It's just a hunch. There was something odd about Eugene's reaction to finding it.

Buckman then hurries to catch up with the others at the hog house. The process to examine each hog requires the assistance of a dozen men. The hogs are housed in a large clapboard shed that has small openings on two sides which allows them to wander out into a fenced lot to eat from the four large hog feeders.

First, the men herd them all inside and then allow one hog at a time out into a makeshift pen for individual examination. Over the next two hours, four hogs test positive for metal. These are marked with ear tags.

Doc Stenger tells Mackintosh he will oversee the slaughter of the four hogs but not to place much hope on finding anything significant because farm animals swallow metal all the time.

A bit later, Mackintosh motions for Buckman to come over to the sheriff's cruiser. Inside he points to the radio and tells him about an interesting lead that was phoned into the office in Temperance. The sheriff briefs him and then tells him to let the parents know what's going on.

Buckman finds Eugene and asks him to join him in the house for a cup of coffee. When he seems reluctant, the deputy reminds him that he hasn't eaten for hours. On the way to the house, he tells Eugene that they've gotten a tip that he wants to talk to the two of them about privately.

#

Eugene's mind is racing as he thinks about what kind of news would need to be shared with them privately. They find the kitchen nearly elbow-to-elbow. Buckman leans to Eugene's ear, asking him if there is a place they can talk alone inside. After a moment, Eugene suggests they can talk in the bedroom.

With the door shut, Buckman asks, "Do either of you know Mrs. Henry Todd?"

Eugene looks blankly at Margaret. She says, "That name sounds familiar, I think."

"She lives two miles straight east of here. She phoned in to tell us that around the time that Dicky went missing, a man in a blue car pulled into her yard, stopped for several minutes, and then left. That by itself doesn't mean that much, but the Temperance police had several reports over the last few weeks about a man in a blue car trying to get children to come with him."

Both parents tell the deputy that they don't remember seeing a blue car.

"Is it possible he wandered a half-mile or so down the road and then got picked up?" asks Buckman.

"I would say yes," answers Eugene. Margaret nods.

After thinking about it, Eugene suggests that they check with his friend Dub, who is the rural mail carrier for the area, to see if he noticed a blue car during his travels. Buckman thanks him for the suggestion and leaves them alone in the room.

Eugene looks down and quietly says, "I'm so sorry I didn't watch him go all the way to the house. This whole thing is my fault."

Margaret takes his chin, turning his face toward hers, and kisses him.

She looks into his eyes and kindly says, "We both let Dicky wander around by himself all the time. This is not your fault."

"But this weather… how can he…"

Margaret looks down and then whispers, "He's alive, Gene. I know it."

"How can you know that?"

"Because I'm his mother. A mother's heart knows many things. I think that blue car is the answer."

Buckman, the two Civil Air Patrol officers, and Eugene meet in the grinding room at six-thirty as planned. Stork summarizes the searches of the farm buildings, including those on the other farmsteads within the four-mile square. Winston reports on the wooded area searches. At one point, the group searching Buffalo Creek thought they saw a body under a patch of clear ice. It turned out to be a sunken log.

"But there's one big problem right now," says Winston. "Low spots, including ditches and ravines, are filled with deep snow. Even though the men outside made a textbook foot-by-foot search, even though they probed the snow with poles, we still can't rule out those areas until the deep snow piles have melted."

That sobering statement only adds to the feeling of futility in the back of Eugene's mind. All these people, all this effort, it's as if they're moving mountains with absolutely nothing to show for it.

#

Madeline, who had been worrying about the Walkers all day, hugs Margaret as she and her husband enter the house just before sunset. She is relieved to find her in better spirits because of the blue car development. It feels good to be with her best friend in her hour of need.

The authorities abandon formal search activities at eight p.m. Then, neighbors and friends, cold, tired and hungry from searching in the bitter conditions, make their way into the crowded house. Madeline offers food and coffee as they come inside. Her husband leads the group in prayer before they eat.

"We know that when the good shepherd loses a lamb, he will leave the others and then search until he finds it. We pray that with your help, Almighty Father, Dicky will be quickly found and returned to his parents."

As the searchers are eating, Margaret confides to Madeline that she doesn't know how much longer she can do this.

"I am trusting God with all my strength, but when I hear that wind and see how cold and exhausted the searchers are as they come in, then I think about Dicky, so small; I just don't know how he can do it."

Madeline doesn't know what to say. She hugs Margaret, and then the words, "Because God is with him," come from her lips without thought on her part.

Madeline, feeling Margaret's chest heaving in her arms, softly shushes into her ear.

#

After everyone has left, Eugene starts the old tractor; imagining Dicky is riding on his lap, he aims it through the night to the familiar rock by the creek. It takes him a minute to realize that something is different. For the first time since the storm hit, the wind has dropped off to almost nothing. Sitting on the rock, feeling comparatively warm in soothing silence, with twinkling lights on radio towers and farm lights in the distance, with the babbling play of the water over the stones, he feels almost peaceful. Perhaps, at last, there is a glimmer of hope, a hope-colored blue, the blue of a car.

Imagining Dicky sitting next to him on the rock, he says, "I miss you."

Thursday—Missing 64 Hours

Eugene is shaken awake by Margaret at five-thirty. He is greeted by the irritating sound of the radio, which is blasting in the house. After dressing, he makes his way into the kitchen, finding that Margaret has fresh coffee ready. As he pours a cup, the weather report comes on.

Mixed with a bit of static, the announcer reports, "Still another front will push through the area today, driving the wind back up to nearly thirty miles-per-hour. The blowing snow will continue until mid-afternoon when the temperature will rise above the freezing mark for a few hours before dropping back down into the teens overnight."

Eugene, having expected much better weather today, sighs with exasperation while putting on his winter work clothes.

"Rough night sleeping?"

"Longest night of my life," replies Margaret. "I don't know how much longer I can do this."

Eugene downs the rest of his coffee, then looks at her sympathetically.

"They have to find that blue car," Eugene offers.

"I prayed for just that all night," Margaret says softly through watery eyes.

Not knowing what else to say, he manages, "I need to get the chores done before the authorities get here."

#

Sheriff Mackintosh is up early, having gone to bed at eight. The long days this week are causing him to feel his age. Feeling unusually hungry, he decides to stop for breakfast at Reggie's Diner, located about halfway between Temperance and Summit on US Highway 20.

Sitting at the counter, he overhears a group of regulars, probably retired farmers, talking about the lost boy case.

"Just look at the guy, that Eugene Walker, standing there with his pitchfork. Doesn't he look like he would just as soon kill you as look at you?"

"That guy has a temper. I saw him shove a guy down in Clancy's and then dare the guy to get up. If it wasn't for Dub Davis, there would have been a big fight."

"You know what I see when I look at these pictures? I see hogs testing positive for metal and a guy grinding feed. I think he ground up the boy and fed him to the pigs."

"Come on," said one of the guys. "Don't you think that's stretching things?"

"Okay, well, let's see. There have been hundreds of people looking for that boy for days, and they haven't found a trace of him. How do you explain that?"

Back on the highway, the dark conversation rattles around in the sheriff's head. *This is just human nature*, he thinks. The more the boy's fate remains a mystery, the more people are going to talk about it. And the more people talk, the more people's imaginations are going to run away with them. But for him, this isn't just casual gossip. At some point, his job might force him to think the same way himself.

#

The wind and snow blast at Eugene's face for the third straight morning. The radio in the milking shed gives a static-filled update on the search for his son.

"Crackle...missing since Monday afternoon... crackle...last seen wearing... crackle...authorities are hopefully..."

Eugene asks Eunice if she has seen anything as a jet from her utter rings on the bottom of the galvanized pale. On cue, she moos. These sounds usually bring Holly, the cat, out of hiding. Eugene realizes that he hasn't seen Holly since the storm hit. This thought sluggishly roams around in his unconscious thoughts for a few minutes. As he dumps his pale into the tall silver milk can, he wonders if Holly might be with Dicky. He remembers seeing Dicky running after Holly many times.

Coming out of the shed, Eugene notices movement on the ground out away from the farmyard. As he walks in that direction, he notices the desiccated and mutilated remains of a wild flower; its stalk twisted and broken, leaves shattered, head decapitated, the tiny fibers holding it together untangling more slowly than the hour-hand of a rarely wound clock. Then, behind a clump of sugary snow is a shiny, jet-black crow picking pink flesh from a brown, white, and red, flattened mash of fur. Realizing that it's Holly, he picks up a fist-sized rock and throws it while screaming at the crow. The rock whizzing by causes the bird to flinch downwardly, look at Eugene, caw, hop twice and then fly to the top of the barn.

Eugene falls to his hands and knees, crying.

#

When Sheriff Mackintosh pulls into the farmyard at 7:00 a.m., Captain Stork of the Willow Bend Civil Air Patrol is waiting for him. Inside the sheriff's cruiser, Stork gets right to the point.

"That boy has been missing for over sixty hours, Sheriff. The most likely scenario is that he wandered off, darkness and the storm hit, and then he couldn't find his way back home. If he didn't find shelter somewhere within the first twelve hours, he's most likely dead."

After a pause, the sheriff responds, "That sounds about right, Captain."

"A little boy, under the best conditions, can only walk one mile-per-hour; more realistically, with the storm, he could do at best about half that speed. As far as endurance, a child typically has the stamina to walk one mile per year of age. But again, with the storm, I would figure the boy could have gotten two miles at the most."

Stork pauses to let that sink in.

"So, where does that leave us, Captain?"

"At the end of yesterday, we searched all shelters within two miles of where he was last seen. That means if he did, in fact, wander off, then he is most likely dead and buried under one of those huge snowdrifts out there."

Mackintosh rubs his chin as he is thinking.

"So, what about unlikely scenarios?" he finally asks.

After a short discussion, Mackintosh pulls an index card and writes:

1 He wandered off and got lost

2 He was kidnapped

3 He met foul play

#

At the morning planning meeting, Captain Stork gives time to Civil Air Patrol Lieutenant Francis Filmore. The lieutenant had begged for five minutes to pitch a highly unorthodox idea. He steps forward, dropping a copy of the Des Moines Tribune Sunday Magazine on Eugene's makeshift desk.

"I think we should call this guy," he says, pointing at the photograph of a man about sixty with white disheveled hair who could have passed for Albert Einstein.

The Sunday Magazine is inserted monthly into the paper's huge Sunday edition. The February magazine featured a long article chronicling a Danish purveyor of what was called extra sensory perception. Ebenezer Croissant was purported to have used his mystical power to find several lost persons, even at times from extraordinary distances.

"Who the heck is that?" asks Sheriff Mackintosh.

"He's a mystic in Denmark who has an incredible record of finding lost persons. If you read the article, you'll see what I mean."

"Well," said Mackintosh with a bit of a smirk, "He certainly looks the part." Then he turns to Stork, asking, "Where do you stand on this, Captain?"

"Ordinarily, I wouldn't give that guy the time of day, but we really need a break on this case. I almost hate to say it, but I think I'm inclined to give it a try."

Stork then turns to Eugene. "What do you think about it, Eugene?"

Eugene shrugs. "I think I'm willing to try about anything at this point. But my wife is religious. I better ask her how she feels about it first."

Surprisingly, Margaret says she sees this development as a sign of hope.

Later, she tells Eugene about how her father often preached about the power of the Holy Spirit and that, not knowing any different, she is hoping that this mystic is a man of God.

#

Sheriff Mackintosh calls the on-duty operator at the Summit Telephone Exchange, telling her that he authorizes the call. Then it takes her several minutes to connect with the overseas operator in New York City and several more to connect to the Denmark exchange. But then, incredibly, after only thirty minutes, Ebenezer Croissant is on the connection.

Unfortunately, they find Croissant's English skills are terrible. Finally, the sheriff recognizes the words, *"Deutsch sprechen."* A hurried search for a German speaker produces Wolfgang Staudenmaier, a retired farmer among the numerous volunteer searchers.

After a few minutes of indecipherable chatter, Staudenmaier put his hand over the mouthpiece, saying to everyone in the kitchen, "He says the boy is alive."

After several more minutes of German conversation, Staudenmaier relays that the boy is very cold and needs to be rescued soon. He also reports that they can find him three and a third miles to the southeast. He speaks a bit more German into the phone and then reports that there is a small shack located nearby.

"From there, go two hundred feet south. There you will find the boy near a clump of three trees." Staudenmaier recites to everyone in the room.

Margaret pulls her apron up to her face. "He's alive," she whispers. "That's what I've been praying for."

And that's exactly what I was afraid of, the sheriff thinks to himself, now realizing that he should never have allowed the call.

Captain Stork directs the search leaders to the grinding shed to study the map. Exactly three and a third miles southeast of the farm is a plowed field. About a mile further in that direction is a tributary of Pine Creek.

"That's the nearest area that has some trees," says Stork.

Stork asks Captain Winston to take a large group of volunteers to thoroughly comb through the area. As Winston is leaving, Stork pulls him aside to tell him to take Lieutenant Filmore along.

"This is his baby. If you leave him here, I'll probably tear his head off."

Then he asks Sheriff Mackintosh to stay behind for a minute.

He waits until the others have left, and then he asks, "What do you think, Mack?"

Mackintosh chuckles, "Go two hundred feet south? I think you should send a shovel with those guys to dig up buried treasure while they're at it."

"Did you notice the mother?"

"Poor woman. I don't blame her a bit. The worst part about this is that I don't know how we're going to be able to put this mystic back in the bottle where he belongs," Mackintosh says with an edgy voice.

"What do you think the press is going to do with this?" asks Stork.

"Well. Captain, have you ever seen a film with a pride of lions feasting on a zebra?"

#

Captain Winston feels like he has gotten a break. The search area identified is owned by Howard Greeley, who happens to have come to help search that morning. At Winston's request, Greeley hops into his search truck to guide him and the group of cars following to the subject location.

Winston struggles a bit to control the truck as he turns onto the rutted and snowy dirt road. The wind is even stronger now than when he arrived.

"Does this thing have four-wheel-drive?" the farmer asks as the vehicle seems to hop between the various ruts in the road.

"No, but there's chains on the rear tires."

On the way, Winston asks him if there are any buildings in the wooded area as described by Croissant.

"No," Greeley answers.

#

In early afternoon, Dub brings a large handful of mail and a few newspapers into the kitchen.

"My goodness," Margaret says, sorting through the stack of letters. She opens an envelope with a return address from Mrs. Sarah Severson, Dubuque, Iowa.

It reads:

"Dear Margaret,

I can't imagine what you must be going through. I have three young children myself. The oldest is a first grader named James Francis, who everyone calls Franky. Seeing your son's picture and thinking about you not knowing where he is fills my heart with pain. I want you to know that every night before we eat our supper, we say a prayer for you and your son. May God be with you during these difficult days."

Sincerely,
Sarah Severson

"What a lovely note," says Margaret softly. Then looking at the stack of letters, she adds, "Aren't people wonderful?"

"Yes, they are," replies Dub. "You need to see this newspaper too,"

Dub lays this morning's Des Moines Tribune on the kitchen table. A small headline on page-one states, *"Missing Boy Search Intensifies,"* byline Frank Frydenberg. Like yesterday, within the column on the front page is Dicky's face.

"I wish I had a better picture of him," Margaret says sadly. "He looks so distant."

The article forwards to page three, a full-page dedicated to the story with almost half of the space covered in photographs, including Margaret in front of the kitchen table full of food, Dicky's bedroom showing his collection of little things, the sheriff and Captain Stork talking with the Civil Air Patrol truck in the background, a group of Amish men stacking bales with their horse and black buggy in the background, a brigade of men, passing bales down the line with the barn in the background, Eugene grinding feed, a map on Eugene's desk with weapons hanging on the wall in the background, Doctor Stenger with Lieutenant Francis Filmore testing hogs with a metal detector, and a picture of Eugene holding a pitchfork.

The caption on the picture of Margaret states, "Mother grateful for the generosity of everyone." The caption on the picture of Dicky's bedroom states, "Dicky, a young collector," and the caption for the picture of Eugene states, "I hope he was kidnapped."

Among the storylines in the article is a conversation with Eugene where he is quoted as stating that he almost hopes Dicky was kidnapped at this point because that may be the only way that he can still be alive.

Overwhelmed, Margaret just shakes her head and says that all of this is just unbelievable.

"I'll have to thank Mr. Frydenberg if I see him again."

#

After Winston's search crew had thoroughly combed the assigned area, he asks Greeley if he knows of any other wooded areas nearby that have any kind of a shack.

Greeley slips his hands inside the bib of his overalls and says, "There's a large, wooded area three miles south of here. I think there used to be a hunting shack in there somewhere."

Winston realizes that searching this area, an area only vaguely described by Croissant, is going to take most of the afternoon.

#

Back from finishing his mail route, Dub pulls in and then starts looking for Eugene, finding him grinding feed.

"How you holding up, Geno?"

"Had better days. Did you hear about the mystic?"

"I heard that, but what's it about?"

"A guy with the Civil Air Patrol pulls out a magazine article about a mystic in Denmark who can find people with ESP."

"Really?"

"So, the sheriff calls Denmark from my kitchen."

"I hope he reversed the charges."

"Apparently, Briggs County's paying," Eugene says with a smirk. "So, they eventually get the guy on the line, and right away, he knows where he is."

"Well, that's a relief."

"He is shivering by some trees southeast of here. They sent fifty guys to look for him."

"Was he there?"

"They left three hours ago, so it's not looking good."

"How did Margaret take it?"

"She thought it was a hopeful sign."

"Poor thing," says Dub sadly. "I saw her for a few minutes earlier. I think she's holding on by a thread."

"I'm really scared, Dub. On Guam, I got to the point where I was completely at ease with the idea that I could die any minute. I thought I'd never have to fear death again. It never occurred to me that I would love someone else so much more than myself."

"Don't give up hope, Geno. I gave up on ever getting off Guam, I just wrote myself off as dead, but here I am."

"But what about Margaret, Dub. She's never had to face anything like this."

"Margaret has faith in God, Geno."

"I hope she never loses it. I think it would kill her if she did."

Dub seems lost in thought for a few moments. Then he looks at his best friend intently.

"Geno, even without faith in God, you'll both still have each other. No matter what happens, you'll both still need each other."

"If we lose Dicky and she loses her faith," his voice trails off. "It'll destroy her."

"You just can't let that happen. If she loses Dicky, then you'll have to do whatever it takes to make her hold onto her faith." After a pause, he adds firmly, "And that is for you just as much, if not more, than as it is for her."

#

As the light of day is fading, Winston's large group of searchers roll back into the farmyard. The weary men make their way to their vehicles to head home or into the farmhouse for a quick sandwich. Winston then gathers Stork, Mackintosh, Buckman, and Eugene into the grinding room.

Winston reports that they thoroughly searched the assigned area and two other similar areas nearby that Greeley pointed out. Then, pointing at the map, he shows the group the huge, wooded area further to the south where Greeley said there is a hunting shack.

"So, you're suggesting we keep following the mystic's advice?" asks Mackintosh.

The question is greeted by a prolonged silence. The sheriff stares at Winston, who then turns questioningly to Captain Stork.

Finally, Stork says, "Unless someone can suggest a better place."

Buckman, intently studying the map, says, "I think I know that shack. We used to call it the hermit shack because a crazy guy lives there."

"What's he like?" asks the sheriff.

"He's filthy, his clothes are like rags, and if you come anywhere near the place, he comes outside with a shotgun."

"Do you think he would hurt a child?"

"Quite possibly, yes."

"Well, that's your baby, Deputy. Take extra firearms and select a group of about five other guys who know how to use them. Bring them to me before you head out, so I can deputize them."

"Yes, Sir," responds Buckman.

"And for God's sake, don't let anybody get trigger happy. We need to talk to this guy, so if you have to shoot him, aim for his legs."

"Yes, Sir," Buckman says, thinking this is going to be the most fun he's had on the job since he joined the department.

Mackintosh then updates the group about the blue car lead. A seed salesman called the tip line earlier today to tell them that he was driving the blue car that pulled into Henry Todd's farmyard. He said he was making rounds with his customers and found himself on the wrong road. The sheriff tells them he spent an hour checking the guy out, and he has been ruled out as a suspect.

#

After the meeting breaks up, Mackintosh tells Buckman that he wants him to go with Eugene to update Margaret on the current situation.

"Why?" asks the deputy. "Eugene knows as much as I do."

"Because I want you to try to play down the mystic angle. I've got a bad feeling about it. We've gotten a few crackpot calls already, and I have a hunch that tomorrow there'll be a hundred more."

The house is crowded with people as usual, so Buckman meets with the parents in the awkward location of the bedroom once again. Margaret seems a bit disappointed with the news about the blue car and finding nothing at the location pointed out by Croissant. But then she perks right up upon hearing that they are searching in that area again tomorrow morning and seem to have found a shack in that general area.

"I don't think I'd get my hopes up, Mrs. Walker," tries Buckman. "If you think about it, all the directions that guy gave us are pretty much wrong."

Margaret looks at Eugene and then back at the deputy.

"God works in mysterious ways," she says softly, seeming hopeful nonetheless.

#

After the deputy leaves, Eugene feels Margaret holding onto his sleeve. She sits on the bed, pulling his sleeve down, causing him to sit beside her.

"What do you think about what Croissant is telling us?" she asks softly.

Eugene is conflicted about how to answer. Part of him wants to be honest about it. He thinks the guy is either a charlatan or a total crackpot. He's getting more frustrated by the hour because he is diverting the search effort from almost everything else, quite possibly in a totally wrong direction. But he can sense that she thinks about it differently. For her, this represents hope, perhaps the last tangible hope that either of them might find. What possible good would it do to crush her hope.

"I think they have to check it out," he says unevenly.

He sees Margaret's darkening expression.

"But how do you *feel* about it, Eugene?" she asks, emphasizing the word *feel* in a sarcastic way.

He knows, all too well, that she can see right through him.

He weighs his answer and then says, "I'm sorry, Margaret, but I'm having trouble believing the guy."

Margaret's face looks like stone now.

"Trouble believing! Of course, you do. Do you know what your problem is, Eugene? You don't believe in anything except yourself!"

"Sweetheart," Eugene says softly.

"Don't!" Margaret shoots out. "God is testing us, Eugene. You think about that! And if you know what's good for you, you'd better pray about it too!"

Margaret stands up abruptly and leaves the room.

Eugene can't help but hear Dub's words echoing in his mind, *Then you'll have to do whatever it takes to help her hold onto her faith.*

#

The sound of a ringing phone awakens Frank Frydenberg, who is dozing in his easy chair during the ten o'clock weather report. On the phone is a night-side reporter calling from the Tribune's newsroom.

"You told me to be watching the teletype for updates on the lost boy story."

"Did they find him?"

"No. It's better than that, much better."

"Yes!"

The reporter reads the teletype, *"Summit, Iowa—Renowned mystic, Ebenezer Croissant, called in Denmark to help authorities find young Dicky Walker lost Monday in rural eastern Iowa. Using ESP while speaking in German, the Dane reported that the boy was alive in a wooded area southeast of his homestead. Searching there to resume tomorrow."*

"Geez, I've got to get back up there."

Thirty minutes later, Frydenberg is knocking on his editor's front door. Ben Bray, chubby and looking disheveled in a worn, brown bathrobe, answers the door with, "What the heck is it now, Fry?"

"You didn't answer the phone."

"Yes, and there was a reason for that."

Frydenberg excitedly recounts the latest development in the hottest story they've seen all year.

"This story just exploded, and I'm eight hours behind."

Looking over the reporter's shoulder, he sees Frank's car parked on the street with its engine running, and someone is in the passenger seat.

"Is that Ohlman you've got in there?"

"We can be there in four hours. We've packed our bags. I want your okay to stay down there for a while."

"Good hunting, Fry," the editor says with a smile. "Bring me back a Pulitzer."

#

After everyone has left for the day, Eugene walks out of the backdoor and looks at his once peaceful farmyard; it looks like the 77th Infantry Battalion had camped here for a night and then moved out. As he passes through the rusted yard gate, he wishes for the dozenth time that he had stopped talking to the cattle buyer long enough to watch Dicky go through that gate because, if he had, then none of this would be happening. On the throbbing seat of the tractor as it rolls down the dirt road to the west, all the mind-numbing things that happened that day march through his mind.

When he reaches the solitude of the big rock by the creek, he closes his eyes and tries to imagine Dicky sitting next to him.

"What am I going to do about your mother?" he asks out loud.

Dicky has been missing three days. It seems so long, and so much has happened in that time that Eugene has lost all sense of what normal life should feel like. Thinking about Margaret, he decides that right now, he needs to take care of her with everything he can muster. He will pretend to have faith, if that's what she needs to believe.

"But can I do it?" he asks himself out loud.

How did that broken rosary get in the barn? he wonders to himself. Touching that broken rosary shook him to the depths of his soul, taking him back to the moment that changed him forever.

It was about halfway through the fighting to retake Guam, August 2, 1944. That gnawing feeling was something that he will never forget, a feeling so palpable that he could smell it. It was the acrid odor of cruel death.

His men were hunkered down, seeking sleep in bomb craters, a sleep they all desperately needed. Then the flash of artillery from Mount Barrigada sent his pulse racing. Not again. Time to risk his hide to try to calm down the men.

Shelling was hardest on soldiers who happened to have ended up in a foxhole alone. Private Tommy Warren was really rattled when Eugene suddenly jumped into his foxhole. Warren, whose brother was killed on D-day, enlisted soon after, lying about his age to get in. Tommy was in the fetal position, and it took Eugene several tries to get him to open his eyes. Eugene and Tommy, both Christians, attended field services whenever the chaplain was able to make one available. Now, seeing that Tommy was absolutely terrified, Eugene pulled his rosary out of his pocket.

"Here, Tommy, take this. This is the rosary given to me by the chaplain. He told me if I prayed that rosary every day that Mary and Baby Jesus would protect me."

Tommy took the rosary and looked at the small crucifix. "How come they say that you'll never hear the shell that kills you?"

Eugene could tell that his explanation only made him more terrified.

"Let's start a rosary right now," Eugene said.

Eugene stayed with him, reciting prayers for a time. Then, with Tommy feeling a little better, he left him to finish the rosary alone so he could go check on the other men. When he made it to the next foxhole, an immense flash and percussion stunned them all. After a minute, Eugene looked over the edge to see a big hole where Tommy had been.

He quickly crawled through the mud to find himself in an empty, smoldering crater. He could almost taste the acrid smell. Down in the mud, he noticed the little cross. He picked it up to find it was attached to a fragment of chain and a few black beads. As he pulled it, Tommy's dismembered hand emerged from the mud. He immediately dropped it in horror.

As he looked at the cross lying there, he thought about the promise he had just made to Tommy, the promise of his chaplain. Looking at the small crucifix, he pushed it down into the mud.

He tried to decipher the meaning of what had happened. When he got out of his foxhole in the morning, he knew the meaning. There are only two things that will help you survive; being a good soldier and lady luck, and he decided that lady luck wasn't someone you prayed to.

As his mind finds himself back on the rock by the creek, he notices that something is different. The snow is no longer blowing in the air, and it doesn't feel that cold. He reaches down to grab a handful of snow. Squeezing it, he realizes that it is above freezing, and then he notices that the wind direction has shifted from southeast to straight out of the west. The change in the weather lifts his spirits a bit. It's about time lady luck showed up.

Friday—Missing 86 Hours

Sheriff Mackintosh is drinking coffee while listening to the six-a.m. radio news in his kitchen. He is counting on his fingers the number of times the word mystic is said. The newscast is interrupted by the wall phone. Captain Stork wants to let him know that today's ground search would finally be supplemented with a spotter plane. He tells the sheriff to contact the state police to request a radio car to provide a communication link with the plane.

After setting that up, Mackintosh finishes dressing and heads out to support yet another day's searching. He makes a point of driving by Eddie's News Stand on Main Street. Along with weekly and monthly magazines, Eddy has a supply of newspapers big and small from as far away as Chicago, Omaha, and Des Moines.

The headlines on the stacks of papers on the sidewalk and wire racks confirm his worst suspicions; he sees the work mystic prominently displayed on all of them.

"Hey, Eddy, what's a mystic?"

"I don't know, Mack. I think it's like a magician."

"I'd say that's about right," the sheriff chuckles while flipping him a dime for the Des Moines Tribune folded under his arm.

#

A stream of milk is keeping time with the Polka music that is crackling through the cobweb-encrusted radio speaker.

"Eunice, what should I do about Margaret? I think her faith is going to unravel any minute."

Eunice continues eating as if she doesn't have a care in the world.

I guess it's up to me then, he says to himself.

Then, for the first time since all this started happening, his mind realizes something with complete clarity, something they tried to teach him in officer's training school, something he really learned in combat; an officer has to take charge, has to keep thinking, has to be the one that tells everyone else what to do; he has to be the one that everyone else will follow, even when he himself, doesn't have any real idea of where he should go.

In that moment, he decides that if Margaret is going to survive what he fears is coming, he is going to have to be the one to lead her to it. If she is losing her faith, the faith that defines her, that sustains her, then it is up to him to lead her back to it, even if that means betraying himself.

#

In the peace of the empty house, a house so rarely empty during the past four days, Margaret is on her knees praying. She has been studying her Bible concordance ever since Eugene went to his early chores. She has been looking up the Bible references for things lost. She had found there the story of young Jesus being lost during the Passover feast. After three days, He was found talking to the elders in the Jerusalem Temple. Thinking of how Dicky loved Sunday School and that it has been just over four days since he was lost, Margaret had called Madeline to ask her to again search the church for him.

A little later, Margaret read the parable of the good shepherd leaving his flock to look for the lost sheep. That is what Margaret is praying about this morning. After praying, Margaret pours a cup of coffee and rests for a moment in the family room. She notices something out of place out in the yard.

"Dear Jesus," she whispers when she sees a lamb, legs pulled under, sitting in the corner of the fenced yard. Finding Eugene, he tells her to call the Taylors and tell them that one of Norman's sheep has wondered off. The Taylor farm is just beyond the fishing creek to the northwest. Norman Taylor, the oldest son, has been raising sheep for just over a year.

Margaret prays again while waiting for Norman to come to gather the lamb. She knows it is a sign, and she is praying to know what it means. When her father preached about the lost sheep, he had said that the good shepherd is Jesus, and the lost sheep is anyone in need of salvation. *Dicky must be the lost sheep,* she tells herself. She prays all the harder that Jesus will find and save him.

#

Eugene watches as Captain Stork, standing in front of the map laying on Eugene's plywood desk, discusses his plan for the days search; the most complex day of searching yet; a search that will be aided for the first time by a spotter plane; and a search that will include a tactical assault on a shack. Stork tells the group he will stay with the State Police radio car to evaluate and respond to any new search opportunities discovered from the air.

Winston and Deputy Buckman, with the help of Greeley, will reconnoiter to ascertain the exact location of the hermit shack. Then Buckman, with a picked group of armed men, will approach and encircle the shack and then try to apprehend its occupant. After Buckman's operation is completed, the large, wooded area surrounding the shack will be searched by a significant portion of today's volunteers led by Captain Winston.

After the plans have been explained, Lieutenant Filmore, who the sheriff has started calling "Mr. Mystic" behind his back, speaks up,

"I think we should call Ebenezer again."

The sheriff exaggerates, looking at his watch, and then harshly says, "I thought Christmas was over a long time ago."

Stork, stifling a smile, says, "Give me your reasons."

"I think that we should let him know what we saw yesterday and see if he can add any insights. Look, I know this isn't standard procedure, but what have we got to lose?"

"Two hundred bucks for one thing," answers Mackintosh, referring to the cost of the overseas call.

After a thoughtful pause, Stork says, "Mack, we're almost at the end of the road. Let's give the guy one more shot."

The phrase, almost at the end of the road, hits Eugene in the gut. He then realizes that they can't just keep searching forever. With his pulse racing, his mind flashes back to Tommy, the private who was blown up while praying his rosary. They had to move out the next morning. They made a quick search for his remains, but the only thing they found was his hand and the fragment of the rosary.

Mackintosh seems to be fuming. After a moment, he agrees to make one more call, but this time from his office in Temperance.

Visionaries, Crackpots, and Professors

When the meeting breaks up, Mackintosh asks to speak to Captain Stork in private. Inside the sheriff's cruiser Mackintosh pulls out a stack of phone messages.

"This is yesterday's phone messages from mystics, visionaries, kooks, screwballs, and flakes. These crackpots are calling from all over the country. They probably pay membership dues. Here's a call from a Utah minister saying we would find him in a culvert. A woman from Ancillary called to give us the phone number of her favorite mystic; that was nice of her. Here's a guy from Utah that will come help us look for the boy using his forked witch hazel branch; that is, of course, if we wire him the train fare."

"I admit it's bad, Sheriff."

"Oh, this?" says Mackintosh, waving the messages. "This is bad enough, I guess. But did you notice that suddenly people from all over the country are following this story? But even that's not the bad part."

Stork, shaking his head, asks, "So, what's the bad part?"

"Yesterday, we had dozens of volunteers wanting to help search. Today half of the people showing up are not here to search. A lot are reporters, competing for access to the story, and the rest are gawkers and sightseers."

As if on cue, the two men notice a chubby, bald guy wearing a corduroy sports coat with leather patches on the elbows, sporting a plaid bowtie waving a book as he is speaking to a half-dozen note-taking reporters with Frank Frydenberg and Jamie Ohlman right in the front.

"Who's that?" asks Stork.

"Professor Quincy Tubman. He's the department head of the school of theology at Iowa Regional College in Willow Bend. He's brought along his graduate students."

"Why is he here?" asks Captain Stork.

"To get his picture in the paper," he says as Ohlman snaps away.

Getting out of the cruiser, they overhear Tubman lecturing about the dozens of examples he has studied that give strong evidence of the power of extra sensory perception.

#

After the planning meeting breaks up, Eugene goes into the house to tell Margaret and the folks there about the day's search. As he closes the door, an airplane roars overhead so closely that it shakes the house.

"That's the Civil Air Patrol spotter plane. The weather is finally clear enough to use it."

Eugene explains about the effort to find and question the hermit, the large search effort to the southeast, and that the sheriff is going to make another call to Croissant from his office in Temperance. Then Eugene steps into the uncomfortable part, the real reason he came back into the house.

"If you don't mind, I think it might be a good idea for all of us to say a prayer for God's help and success for today's search."

Margaret's face melts from surprise into a smile.

"I think that would be wonderful," she says.

As everyone bows their heads, Eugene recites a rambling petition for God's help with the dire situation. He finishes with an amen which is repeated by everyone. There is an awkward pause until Margaret, her eyes wet with tears, comes up to him and gives him an affectionate hug. Some of the folks pat him on the back. In spite of his inner lack of sincerity, he feels warm inside. In the back of his mind, he is hoping against hope that his insincere piety doesn't somehow backfire.

Professor Tubman is waiting when Eugene comes out of the house. With his students watching, he offers his assistance to the family.

"What kind of assistance?" Eugene asks a bit harshly.

"Well, I can advise you on matters of ESP," says the professor as if that should be obvious.

"Look," Eugene says as if he is contemplating punching the guy. "People are here to help search." Then he shouts, "If you're not here to search, leave!"

The heads of nearby reporters, including Frydenberg, swivel to take stock of the exchange. Tubman stifles his reply seeing the genuine rage on Eugene's face. Then with eyes wide, as if realizing the seriousness of the unspoken threat, he gathers his students to make a quick exit.

#

While recruiting a tactical posse for assaulting the shack, Buckman found two brothers who have frequently hunted there. They tell the deputy that they know where it is but think it might be empty. They usually steer clear of the shack in deference to its volatile inhabitant, but when they hunted there last fall, the shack seemed a lot more overgrown than usual.

Buckman takes his recruits into the grinding room to study the map. He notices a few of the men staring at the collection of weapons hanging on the wall. After a bit of prompting, the brothers show Buckman the approximate location of the shack on the map. He marks its location and then marks the point where they will park on the road. Asking about the shack's windows, he learns that there are none on its backside.

"Okay, you guys will quietly approach the shack from the back and stay undercover. Then, Johnny and I will approach from the front. When we're all in place, I'll call for him to come out. Johnny will be behind a tree, drawing a bead on the front door. If he comes out with a gun, I'll order him to drop it. Remember no shooting except under my orders. And if you have to shoot, remember to shoot for his legs. You guys out back are there to stop him if he tries to flee in that direction."

The deputy is really excited when the shack comes into view. The siding on the shack is rotted, and the whole thing is overgrown with dead vegetation. He uses hand signals to direct the group to the back of the shed.

At the fateful moment, he shouts for him to come out. This goes on for several minutes. Finally, after checking that Johnny has him covered, he continues to call out while slowly approaching the door with his eyes glued to the window. After pounding on the door, he opens it. He picks up a stick and throws it inside. Finally, with pistol and flashlight ready, he pokes his head inside and looks around. Empty, the place looks like no one has been there for months. Searching inside, the deputy finds a few personal papers with a name—Herman R. Hampton.

Buckman radios a report back to the sheriff. Mackintosh tells him he will initiate a manhunt for Hampton. Then he reports the developments to Captain Stork, who sends the group waiting to search the wooded area around the shack.

Then Mackintosh shakes his head as he says to Stork, "A hermit named Herman."

#

Madeline arrives at the house a little before noon. After she sets a warm casserole on the kitchen counter, Margaret takes her hand and leads her to the living room to sit together on the couch.

"I have something to tell you," Margaret says. Madeline notices that she seems excited. Madeline listens and then begins to smile as Margaret tells her that Eugene led a prayer that morning.

"That's wonderful," Madeline says.

"It's happening," Margaret whispers. "This whole thing is happening to bring Eugene back to God. It's an answer to the prayers I've been making every day for over a year. Now that he has faith again, God will return Dicky to us. Don't you see that it's just like Abraham and Isaac?"

Madeline knows that Margaret is referring to the Bible account of Abraham being asked by God to kill in sacrifice his only son as a test of his faith. Madeline searches her mind for what she should say. She takes Margaret's hands in hers; they feel warm and soft. She remembers what her husband had taught her to do when talking to someone lost in difficulty. He said to tell them that God is good and loving but that it's impossible for us to always know or even understand the will of God.

"It's wonderful that Eugene is seeking God, but sweetheart, only God knows what He is doing and why. We just have to keep praying and be prepared to accept God's will, no matter what."

After a few more minutes of quiet talking, Madeline convinces her to eat some casserole. After eating, Madeline tells Margaret that John wants to know how they would feel about having a prayer vigil for Dicky Sunday night at the church.

"Yes, of course, we would love to do that if Dicky is not found by then."

Madeline smiles, telling her she will tell John to plan on it. *Dear God, help my dear friend,* she prays in her head.

#

Lieutenant Kenneth Stallworth is the Civil Air Patrol officer assigned to fly with the private pilot contracted for the aerial search. He directed the plane to make several passes at tree-top level over the four-square-mile area around the farm. The high overcast combined with uniform white snow cover is not making things any easier. After covering the main search area twice at low altitude and then at higher altitude, he sends the pilot to fly over the wooded areas of interest to the southeast. Four miles further south of the shack location, they notice abandoned buildings adjacent to the east-west Chicago and Northwestern railroad tracks. That information is radioed back to Sheriff Mackintosh.

Consulting the map of that area, they discover the tiny village of Paris. Paris, built as a railway stop, has been abandoned for decades. With only about four hours of daylight left, the sheriff sends a group of volunteer searchers to investigate.

The Governor's Holding on Line Two

County Attorney Kenneth O'Dell is on the phone in his office in the county courthouse building overlooking Ansel Briggs City Park. He has been making a few calls to help Sheriff Mackintosh try to locate one, Herman R. Hampton. O'Dell knew the name right away. Hampton's brother Richard, a Willow Bend attorney, had called him back in August to seek his assistance in having his nomadic brother Herman committed. Herman, technically a resident of Briggs County, had been threatening their elderly father, and the threats had escalated to include almost every other member of the family as well. Hampton's subsequent commitment escaped the attention of other Briggs County authorities because he was taken into custody at his father's home in Lyon County.

O'Dell had just placed a call to the State Mental Health Institute to the south of Temperance to confirm that Herman Hampton was indeed still in confinement at the location. While waiting on the line, his secretary came in to tell him that the governor was on the other line.

"You're kidding," he says to her.

Then he says to the phone, "So, he's still a resident there? Okay, thank you, Nurse. I'm afraid I have another call I have to take." Then, after a pause, "Goodbye, and thanks again."

"Governor Norman Mallinckrodt called for me?"

#

Norman Mallinckrodt had just gotten out of a meeting with his staff. Among the topics discussed was improving his popularity. He was elected four months ago by the smallest margin in the state's history. The minority opposition members had taken to calling him "Landslide Mallinckrodt."

Don Slater, his chief political advisor, dropped a two-foot-tall pile of newspapers from all over the country on the conference room table. He spread the papers out so everyone could see the headlines he had circled in red wax pencil pertaining to the search for the lost boy in his state. Then he stated that they need to find a way to put the words *Governor Mallinckrodt* in all of these stories.

#

"He's holding right now on two."

Shaking his head, he pushes a button on his phone and says, "Kenneth O'Dell speaking."

"O'Dell, this is Governor Mallinckrodt. I want to talk to you about that little lost boy in Summit."

"He's lost *near* Summit, Sir. He was last seen in the farmyard Monday afternoon."

"That's the one. Are there any new developments today?"

"I talked to Sheriff Mackintosh at noon. Most of today's search activities are in the wooded areas southeast of his home."

"That's the biggest news story in the state you've got there. Heck, the story is being picked up by newspapers all over the country."

"The whole thing is a terrible ordeal for the family."

"Yes, of course, the family; it's bad for them, I'm sure. I'm calling O'Dell to see if there's anything I or my office can do. I'm sure you know that I can get the National Guard down there if you need more men. I'd be more than happy to do that."

"I'll pass your offer on to the sheriff. But volunteer searchers are one thing we have plenty of. About two hundred people show up at the farm almost every day."

"Tell me, O'Dell; you've been close to the action. What's your gut telling you happened to that little boy?"

"The thinking, and please don't share this with the press, is that there are three possibilities. Either he wandered off and got lost in the storm, probably dying of exposure, or he was kidnapped, or there was some sort of foul play at home. My gut tells me he is dead outside somewhere not far from home, buried in deep snow."

"Well, in that case, it's just a matter of time before they find his body."

"The problem is the snow. The area has been thoroughly searched, most places, dozens of times. They may need to suspend the search soon and wait for the snow to melt."

"Let me know right away if the search is suspended. In that case, I suggest that a massive search is planned for when the ground is clear. I'll supply National Guard boots and equipment. Heck, I'll get a flock of helicopters too. I will also see about getting the Red Cross to feed all those searchers."

"I'll certainly pass this on, Governor."

"You mentioned kidnapping. Are there any leads on that?"

O'Dell tells him about the blue car lead and the dead-end hermit angle. Finally, he explains that the family doesn't really have any significant money for a ransom.

"I'm sure you know that I used to practice law and that I was Attorney General for four years. I don't think I'd rule kidnapping out too fast. That's a nice-looking boy. Money's not the only reason criminals would take a child, especially one that looks like that. Tell the sheriff that I'm going to make a call to the FBI; they are now authorized to investigate kidnappings. I'll see if I can light a fire under them. This case has so much publicity right now. I think they'll go for it."

O'Dell tells his secretary that he is going to the search area for the rest of the afternoon. He has a lot of news for Sheriff Mackintosh. His first thought, when he was told that the governor was on the line, was that he was being let go. Mallinckrodt had made a campaign promise to consolidate county attorney positions by having several of Iowa's 99 counties share officers of the court.

Finding the sheriff, he first tells him the current whereabouts of the former occupant of the run-down shack.

"So, he's been locked up the whole time. That's great. Thanks, Kenny."

Then O'Dell spends several minutes explaining all of the governor's offers and ideas.

"What the heck do you think he is up to, Kenny?"

"Oh, this is all purely political. Like everyone else, he wants to see his name in the paper. But you really can't blame him, though. Nearly half the state voted for the other guy."

"Yeah, you're right. I've run unopposed so long I forgot what it's like to think about reelections."

"Do you really think the FBI will take the case?"

"One thing I've learned in all these years, Kenny. You'll never live long enough to have seen everything."

#

Late that afternoon, Mackintosh is told all of the searchers are returning to home base. The search from the air, the search in the area of the shack, and the search in the abandoned village of Paris have all gone for naught. A second call to Croissant in Denmark gave no new information. The guy just stuck to his original prognostication. He did ask at one point that the sheriff send him a detailed map of the area that he could study. On the phone, the sheriff agrees, but after hanging up, he concludes that by the time the map made it there, it would be too late. The sheriff shook his head in disbelief while telling all present that a prognosticator asking for a map is like a magician asking if the secret card you selected is red or black.

At the day's follow-up meeting, Captain Stork announces that the Civil Air Patrol is standing down until the heavy snow cover melts. No one, not even Eugene, objects. All of the searchers who have been there day after day realize that they have collectively searched the entire area completely, with most of the area having been searched dozens of times.

After starting his cruiser to head home, Sheriff Mackintosh opens the folded index card from his breast pocket. He draws a very light line through item number one—wandered off. Then he draws a light circle around item number two—kidnapped.

A few minutes later, he briefs Buckman about how to handle the private meeting with Eugene and Margaret.

"There's no way to know how the mother is going to take this news. If her husband is any indication, it may not be too bad."

"Are you sure you want me to do this, Sheriff? This type of news may be taken better if it comes from you."

"There's merit to what you're saying, Melvin, but you're the one that they've been talking to all along. Just my walking into the room at this point will be upsetting. They will not be thrown off by you doing so. Just hit the bad stuff on the top and quickly finish with what's going to happen next. Namely, we're all coming back with a huge search when the snow clears and that in the meantime, there'll be more resources to follow other leads, perhaps even with the help of the FBI."

#

Margaret is shaken when the meeting in the bedroom starts off bad and then gets worse. Every lead they have been following, including the blue car, the area the mystic described, and the hermit, are at a dead end. And she is even more upset hearing that they're halting additional searches.

"You can't just do nothing!" she screams.

Buckman nervously recites the sheriff's list of what will be happening in the coming days. Margaret lightens when she hears that the FBI might be getting involved.

She finally sighs and says, "We can't know what God is planning. We're having a prayer meeting Sunday night. I'm sure God will never turn away from so many faith-filled people."

After the deputy leaves them alone in the bedroom, Eugene asks about the prayer meeting. After explaining, she asks, "You are going, aren't you?"

He hugs her so that his face doesn't betray him, saying, "Of course. We need God's help now more than ever." His mind is surprised by how easy it was for him to mislead his true feelings; it was as if someone else had said the words.

Saturday—Missing Five Days

Expecting yesterday's mild weather, Eugene is disheartened by the brutal chill in the air. He curses as he looks up to the rusty weathervane on the peak of the barn. The wind has turned the squeaky arrow completely around to now indicate a light wind coming out of the northeast. He knows the wind will not stay light for long.

"God help us, Eunice. It looks like another storm is on the way."

Eunice seems to ignore him.

So, he screams, "What do you care!"

As he is milking her, he is venting a litany of his numerous frustrations. His life of peace has been shattered. His little boy is lost. Nobody is saying it out loud, but after five days, it is getting very difficult to imagine how he could possibly still be alive. His wife is holding onto faith that God will do something. He's started pretending to believe this, too. The authorities are waiting for the snow to melt. So, of course, there is another storm on the way.

The angry chatter upsets Eunice. She shifts her hoof, knocking over the pail of milk. Eugene picks up the pale and slams it into the wall causing the huge cows to pull back on the stanchions, causing the structure to creak as if it is going to break.

Coming to his senses, Eugene turns the radio dial so that music will calm everyone's nerves. He knows better than to waste energy on bemoaning his situation. But what can he do that will possibly help? Realizing that he has nothing to lose, he decides that he will pray to God to not let another storm hit the area. His affection for God is not really changing, but his sense of foreboding is becoming unbearable; a growing voice inside is telling him that he has to do something.

#

Frydenberg finds Eugene sullenly grinding feed when he enters the shed.

"You're up early," Eugene says while continuing to scoop corn into the grinder.

"I grew up on the farm too, so it's a habit I haven't been able to shake. Plus, it's the newsman's credo; to get the scoop, you have to get there first."

"Did you hear they've called off the search?"

"I'll bet you're angry about that."

"They searched four days by land and air. They just ran out of places to search."

"How's Margaret holding up?"

"Better than me. She's still holding out hope," his voice trails off.

Frydenberg pauses for a beat, trying to sense the perfect time to insert the obvious next question.

"Have you lost hope, Eugene?"

Eugene reaches for the switch, shutting off the noisy grinder. The crescendo of the droning motor and clattering steel winds down to an ear-ringing silence.

"Hope?" Eugene says flatly.

Frydenberg knows he has to wait for whatever is coming. As the seconds creep along, he chances a bewildered shrug, which seems to nudge Eugene to continue.

"After a massive search, not a single clue has emerged. It's as if he walked off the end of the earth. The plan now is to wait for the snow to melt. But, guess what, a second storm is on the way. All the kidnapper leads are dead ends. So, mister reporter, you ask me about my hope? It's growing thin."

After documenting everything Eugene said in his notebook, Frydenberg emerges from his car to try to interview Margaret.

"I see you still knock."

"My mom wouldn't have it any other way, Mrs. Walker."

"I think it's time you call me Margaret."

"Sure, Margaret, if you'll call me Fry." When she wrinkles her nose, he shrugs. "Everyone calls me that."

The reporter long ago learned that people tell their friends what they are really thinking, not people they address by their last name, and certainly not officials or reporters.

"I meant to thank you for writing such a lovely piece about Dicky."

"That's very kind of you to say so, Margaret. What you just said is why I became a reporter." But to himself, he adds, that, plus beating other reporters to a scoop, plus finding the angle they missed, plus, hope against hope, finally getting nominated for a Pulitzer Prize.

"Not at all, Mr. Frydenberg. I wrote a few articles for my college newspaper, so I know how hard it can be."

"It's Fry, Margaret. Which paper?"

"It's called The Panther Eye. I'm sure you never heard of it."

"Iowa Teacher's College in Willow Falls. It won a ton of awards back in the thirties."

"That's a long time ago, but I'm impressed you know about it," Margaret says as she smiles. Seeming to notice something, she stands up to look out the window as four cars pull into the farmyard.

"Look there," Margaret says, pointing. "They've called off the search, and the people keep coming, and look, they're bringing food."

"I've been a reporter for twenty years, and I've never seen anything like it."

"They just won't quit," Margaret says as she wipes new tears with her apron.

What a great quote, the reporter thinks to himself.

"It looks like you are going to be busy for a little while Margaret. I'll get out of your hair."

"Thanks again," she says, and then, after a momentary, awkward pause, she adds, "so much."

Taking a chance, he hugs her before leaving.

#

Instead of starting his rural mail deliveries, Dub drives directly to the farm. When there, he walks through the backdoor and drops the large mail bag hanging off of his shoulder onto the kitchen floor.

"Nobody in the Apex Post Office has ever seen anything like this. There must be five hundred letters for you."

"What!" says Margaret with eyes like saucers.

"I spent an hour sorting it. Here are the bills," he says, dropping the thin stack of bills wrapped with string onto the kitchen counter. "The rest are letters and postcards from people all over the country," he says as he opens the top, pulls out a handful, and drops them on the table.

Staring in disbelief, Margaret sees letters and postcards of all different sizes with return addresses from almost every state she can think of.

Margaret, with Madeline and a handful of neighbors looking on, says, "Aren't people wonderful?"

"Shall we see what they are saying?" asks Madeline.

Sitting at the table, they all start opening letters.

"Here's one from *Tacoma Washington*. It's from Saint Anthony's grade school, they say that they are all praying for you and Dicky. Isn't that lovely."

"Here's one from Fargo. A Mrs. Hiller says she has a four-year-old girl, and they pray together every night for Dicky."

"Oh, my," Margaret says, wiping tears with her apron.

"This one looks odd," says Madeline picking up a letter that is addressed with a black grease pencil. She opens it and quickly pushes it back into the envelope, looking upset.

"What is it, Madeline?" asks Margaret.

When she doesn't say anything, Margaret tries to take it from her. After a little tugging, Margaret reads the letter. It has only eight words printed in greasy black letters saying, *I know you fed him to the pigs.*

With everyone looking at her, Margaret dissolves into tears. Dub takes the note from her and tosses it into the potbelly stove slamming its door shut with a clang.

#

Kenneth O'Dell, wearing a black suit, hears his shoes clicking on the stone floors as he walks through the deserted hallways of the Briggs County Courthouse Building. He shuffles into the sheriff's office and slumps into the chair inside the door.

"I thought you lawyer types worked banker's hours," the sheriff says.

"Do you believe this? The governor sends his top aid to meet with us on a Saturday."

Mackintosh smiles, "The old boy is afraid the horse will ride out of the barn before he has a chance to get on."

"Horse?"

"Publicity, Kenny. Don Slater is a political horse from way back; he knows that the best kind of publicity is free. And if your guy is interested in national office, you want to have your guy mount up on a national story."

"You think Mallinckrodt is interested in national office?"

"Probably not, but if his name is floated around for national office, it makes his reelection a lot easier."

From down the hall, they hear the clacking of shoes getting ever closer.

"He must go to the same shoe store as you," the sheriff says with a smirk.

Don Slater fills the room with his imposing physical stature, booming voice, warm personality, and mind-numbing cologne. After introductions and adjourning to an ornate meeting room, Slater has Mackintosh bring him up to date on the twists and turns of the case.

"So, it's wait for the snow to melt, then a final, all-out search," restates Slater.

"My office is using the time to further investigate any kidnapping leads."

"Anything look promising?"

"Not really. The blue car, the hermit, and the mystic are all dead-ends."

"What else do you have?"

Mackintosh explains that they have a dozen or so tips to chase down, but none of these looks promising either.

"The governor got a commitment from the FBI to help with kidnapping investigations."

Slater pulls an index card out of his coat pocket.

Glancing at it, he says, "Special Agent J. Edmund Donovan and Agent Oren Joad will be here first thing Monday," before handing the card to Mackintosh.

"I wonder how long ago he took to calling himself J. Edmund," Mackintosh says with a smile. "If he's angling for Hoover's job, he should learn to be more subtle."

After discussing the FBI for a few moments, the conversation turns back to the big search.

"I want to sit in on the search planning. The governor is going to authorize the National Guard with soldiers, planes, and helicopters. He's going to get the Red Cross to support with food and any other supplies you can think of.

With your permission, I want to help direct all official publicity related to the search."

Mackintosh repeats the word publicity with a knowing look directed towards O'Dell. As the continued discussion is ramping down, Slater asks if they know where Frank Frydenberg is staying.

"Who?" asks O'Dell.

"He's staying at the Maquoketa Hotel, just down the street," answers the sheriff.

#

As Eugene comes into the house to warm up after grinding the feed, he finds Dub and Margaret sorting a huge pile of letters on the kitchen table.

"Are all those for us?" he asks.

"These, plus those over there," answers Dub nodding towards the overflowing mailbag leaning against the wall.

Staring in disbelief, Eugene asks what they are going to do with them. Dub tells him they're just sampling a few to get a sense of the overall sentiment.

"Well, over half are supportive. A few even have money in them," Dub says, pointing to three one-dollar bills on the edge of the table. "But some are mean, and a few are nasty, those we're throwing in the fire."

"How are we going to find any important mail in that bag?

"Don't worry, Geno. I already separated out all the bills for you," he said, pointing to the envelopes wrapped with string.

A little later, Eugene examines the overdue notices. After a little figuring, he realizes that he needs to sell all the hogs to deal with the numerous overdue bills.

#

Frank Frydenberg knows Don Slater from covering last year's gubernatorial race, so he is delighted when the governor's top political advisor knocks on his door.

"Great to see you again, Don."

"I'm starving. Do you know a good place to get dinner?"

"Not really. Let's ask at the front desk."

The Maquoketa Hotel, named after the river that flows through Temperance, Iowa, is easily mistaken for something else by first-time guests. From the street, one might think they are standing in front of a shabby boarding house, and even that's being a bit kind. The two would-be diners tap a bell to roust out the jack-of-all-trades clerk. After a bit of discussion about local eating establishments, the two men opt for the truck stop diner to the east of town.

At Reggie's, they find several truckers eating at its long counter. A large round table in the corner furthest from the door is occupied by a group of men wearing striped bib overalls and old, dirty caps with the logos of grain and feed companies. They find an empty table in the center of the establishment. A middle-aged waitress with the name Mavis stitched on her uniform brings them glasses of ice water. After ordering, Slater asks Frydenberg to fill him in on the day's developments.

"Shouldn't we talk about the nature of our relationship first?" asks the reporter.

"You want news. We want publicity; what's to talk about?"

"So, you let me know what the governor is going to do ahead of time, and I do what for you exactly?"

"Oh, not that much, Fry. You just make the governor look like a hero."

"What if I'm not very good at that?'

"Don't worry. I'll feed you the stuff I want you to run. If you don't agree with what I'm trying to sell, we can discuss it then. This thing could turn a half-dozen different ways from this point. We'll just have to make it up as we go along. Heck, it won't be that much different than the campaign."

Ground rules settled, Frydenberg recites a summary of the day's information from his notepad. Then, Slater recites from memory the actions that he's planning to make on behalf of the governor and what he had learned from his meeting with the sheriff and county attorney.

The conversation slows down when the food comes. Both men start to notice the loud conversation of the men at the corner table. They notice that the men are talking about the case, so they sit quietly to hear what they are saying.

"That Eugene Walker is a real hothead. When he got back from the war, he got into bar fights all the time. He even got in a fight with the deputy sheriff."

"That's what I've been telling you. I think he's as guilty as sin."

"But why kill a little boy like that?"

"He probably didn't mean to do it. He just lost his temper, and wham, the kid's dead. So, what does he do then? I'll tell you. He grinds the boy up with the feed, and the pigs take care of the rest."

#

Frydenberg calls his editor while looking out of the window of his corner room in the Maquoketa Hotel.

"What's going on there?" his editor asks.

Frydenberg relays the gist of the story he just read over the phone to the night-side guys on the news desk. Then he tells him about some of the potentially salacious angles that could emerge as the case plays out.

"This story is taking on a life of its own," he tells his editor.

"Your right, this story has more lives than a cat, and it can turn nine different ways, and with each turn, you can have every reader in the country on the edge of their seats. If the boy is found dead, what will the autopsy say? If the death looks suspicious, who did it: the parents, a neighbor, a serial killer, a nutcase?"

"But what if they don't find him?" asks the editor.

Then Frydenberg relays the dark rumor he heard in the diner. Then he asks his editor what he thinks they should do if they don't find him even after the big search.

"Well, first, call it an 'all-out search,' with a big headline. Then, if they don't find him, I guess we'll run a countdown series. One day since the all-out search, with a tip-line, then we keep counting the days. We can even run anniversary stories if he's never found. But I tell you this, Fry. The authorities are going to do something. And with the governor bringing in the FBI, that's almost as good as when they called the mystic."

"And there's another angle to the story," says the reporter. "The mother, a minister's daughter, is coming across as if carrying the faith of the Blessed Virgin. Don't you think people are beginning to wonder if she can remain steadfast in the face of any dark and salacious eventualities?"

#

Eugene comes into the house an hour or so after dark. For the first time since all this started, the house is empty except for Margaret. He finds her sitting on the sofa, looking at the various pictures from among the stacks of newspapers strewn around her. She looks like she's aged ten years.

Without saying a word, he removes his boots and moves to sit beside her. After a moment, he puts his arm around her shoulder. She melts into his side, laying her head against his chest. He takes a deep breath as if he is going to say something; then after a pause, he kisses the top of her head. He sees tears streaming down her face.

She whispers, “I’m scared, Gene.”

He draws both arms around her and says, “I’m scared, too.”

Sunday—The Plight of Job

Eugene is appalled to see the return of blizzard conditions rebuilding snow drifts since two o'clock in the morning. While milking, he feels the full burden of the situation and its hopelessness. The intensity of emotion burning his insides takes him back seventeen years to those haunting and unforgettable moments on the crater-pocked plain below Mt. Barrigada. In oppressive darkness, sweltering heat, morbid silence, and a quiet so cavernous, his thumping heart was easily heard. It was in the fleeting time between the distant flashes and their bone-rattling result; those three horrifying seconds, enough time to take one breath with enough time left over to wonder if it could be your last. Then comes a second flash, this one bright enough to blind, followed by an explosion shaking the ground so hard that he almost would not have been surprised if his teeth had fallen out.

A loud moo brings him back, making him realize he had stopped milking for several seconds. Heart still pounding, he sets his hands to work while thinking about what he can do for Margaret. He remembers how buying the farm had helped him cope with his rough reentry into normal life after the war. But even with the farm and Dub's steadfast friendship, he still struggled until he had met Margaret. More than anything else, it was Margaret that brought him back to actual peace and true happiness.

"I need Margaret," he says out loud. Then an answering voice in his head says, "She now needs you too."

As he is crossing the farmyard heading towards the house, a sedan carrying six men pulls into the drive. The visibility is terrible, and the snow is quickly piling higher. He makes his way to the car.

"Are you guys here to search?"

The men answer affirmatively. Eugene tells them that he appreciates their help but that searching has been called off and that, in any case, the weather is just too bad today. The men say that they might just search for a short time and see how it goes since they have already made the trip. Eugene tells them to be aware that the road might become impassable soon. He tells them that they will be gone most of the morning to attend church services. Then he thanks them again and heads into the house to change clothes.

#

With the weather so bad, Margaret is prepared for an argument about going to church. Seeing the volunteers arrive, she thinks he will use the excuse to not go with her. She is delighted when Eugene surprises her by coming in to get ready for church as he tells her what he told the guys in the car.

The road to town is still passable, but Margaret knows that it probably will not stay that way. Entering the church, Madeline hugs Margaret as Pastor John enthusiastically shakes Eugene's hand. That's when the pastor tells them that he is going to announce that they are having a special prayer vigil for Dicky at seven p.m.

Making their way inside, Margaret quietly makes sure that Eugene will be going to the evening prayer meeting; she is surprised and delighted to find out that he is.

#

A bit later, quietly sitting in the pew begins to wear on Eugene. He realizes that he would much rather be sitting in a dentist's chair.

Apparently, Pastor John has been giving a series of weekly sermons on the Bible character Job. The sermon begins with a recap of the first part of the story. Job, a man of very high social and moral standing, is being made to suffer setback after setback brought about by an argument between Satan and God. God is contending that he is a man of the highest character, and Satan argues that he will only remain so as long as his good fortune continues. When Job's life has been ruined, not knowing that he is being tested, he is left to wonder why God is allowing him to suffer. Expecting a boring sermon, Eugene is caught off guard by a discourse that seems to be speaking directly to him.

John then retells how after each loss, including his children, his wife, and his wealth, Job remains steadfast in his love and fear of God.

"Now that we are caught up on the story, I want to proclaim today's message, which is titled, Will God Hear Me," says the pastor in a soothing voice.

John then relates how Job, with nothing remaining to be taken away, is made to suffer a dreadful disease. Finally, after many hours of suffering, he heatedly asks God why He would do all this to him, a man who dedicated his life to serving Him.

"Then, God hearing him, gave His answer!" exclaims the pastor.

The pastor reads part of God's response, which to Eugene seems to not answer Job at all. He puts down his Bible and rhetorically asks them what God is saying. After a pause, he tells them that, at his first reading, he didn't understand either.

After a moment, he says, "What God is really saying is that His purposes, which are always good and true, cannot be understood in the context of an ordinary person's life."

Then he goes on to tell the congregation that since the fall of man, life on earth was ordained to be a struggle.

"It's meant to be hard; it is a place with disease; it is a place with losses; it is a place that can only be left by going through death."

After allowing that thought to settle, he says, "That's what Job heard and understood. He gave that answer to Job, and it's meant to be the same answer to us, always, even now. Ask God why He is allowing you to suffer? His answer is that it was done for His unknowable purpose. Is it an easy answer to hear? No. It's a hard answer that can only be accepted through faith."

The ending of the sermon hangs in the air. It has not been a lesson that fills a congregation with peace and joy.

Hearing the sermon gives Eugene a lot to think about. At the conclusion of the service, Eugene turns to Margaret, telling her that he feels that the sermon was speaking directly to him.

"That's what all good sermons are designed to do, Gene."

After a bit more talking, Eugene excuses himself to try to talk to Pastor John.

#

As Margaret is watching Eugene talking to John from a distance, an old woman tugs at her sleeve.

"I heard that you are the mother of the lost little boy," she says to Margaret.

"Yes, I'm afraid so."

"How long has he been missing?"

"Since Monday, almost a whole week."

"You poor thing. I know what you are going through. I lost my boy years ago."

Feeling touched, Margaret bends to give the woman a hug, whispering, "Whatever did you do?"

"I prayed every day at home and every Tuesday in this church. He was lost on a Tuesday."

"Didn't you ever want to give up?" asked Margaret.

"Many, many times. But whatever you do, don't ever stop praying. Do you want to know why? Because God will bring your boy back if you do. I know he will."

Margaret looks sympathetically at the old woman, saying, "God bless you, dear."

The old woman, looking a bit miffed, says, "I mean it. Promise me you will never stop praying. God will bring him back to you!"

Margaret smiles again, saying, "I promise."

Margaret, despite her current circumstances, feels profoundly sorry for the old woman. The distant look in her eyes, the unearthly way she talked, betrayed the numbed state of her mind. She knows that the poor, old woman, having gone through so much, being faithful in her prayers for so long, has, with her advanced age and loneliness, lost much of her sanity. She sadly wonders if God is showing her what her own future will look like.

Then, thinking about herself, how she has been secretly blaming Eugene's lack of faith for Dicky's continued loss and hearing of Job's losses, she suddenly is stunned by the likelihood that her little boy is almost certainly dead and that perhaps like Job, God has been testing her, too. She is staggered to realize that her long-held belief that her faith in God is rock-solid has always been a myth.

Margaret watches as Eugene continues to ask John several questions.

As the two men are talking, Margaret feels very distant as Madeline comes to talk to her.

"What is it, dear?"

"It's just that old woman," replies Margaret.

"Do you mean Mrs. Schmidt? What about her."

"The poor thing said she lost her son too."

"I'm afraid the years have not been kind to her. She's a sweet soul, but her dementia started to get really bad about a year ago. Now, most of the time, she's in another world."

"She did lose her son, though, right?"

"Her son was killed in a farm accident thirty years ago. The little boy was riding on a horse-drawn hay wagon with his father. They say the horse reared up, and the little boy fell under the wheels and was instantly killed."

"How terrible!"

"What did she say to you?"

Margaret explains that she told her to keep praying and that she knows that God will return Dicky to her.

"Why are you so upset?"

"Because I felt like I was seeing myself in thirty years."

She quietly cries as Madeline hugs her.

"She is right about one thing," Margaret hears in her ear, "we just have to keep praying."

#

Eugene is still talking to John when Madeline walks up to them to tell them that Margaret has accepted an invitation for them to join her and John for dinner at the parsonage. Eugene seems a bit reluctant until John tells him they will have more time to talk about Job.

Walking from the church to the parsonage is short but difficult. They're all squinting so much in the snow-filled wind that it is hard to see. John leads the way holding hands with Madeline, who is holding Margaret's hand, who is, in turn, holding Eugene's. Once inside, they are all surprised by how much snow is sticking to their coats and shoes.

The dinner table is quieter than normal because young Michael was invited to a neighbor's house for Sunday dinner. The dinner talk starts out relaxed, somehow avoiding talk about Dicky. Then several minutes go by with all eating in an uneasy silence.

Eugene is thinking about the situation.

"John, what do you know about miracles? I mean, do you think God still does them?"

John chews his food for a moment and then says, "I wouldn't be much of a minister if I said no, would I?"

"But have you actually seen any?" asks Eugene.

"Well, yes and no. I have prayed to God for many things that have then come to pass. But I can't know for sure if any of those were miracles." Then, with a quizzical expression, he asks Eugene if he has seen any miracles.

After a long pause, Eugene tells the story of the mortar round that should have killed him. When no one says anything, Eugene looks at John.

"Do you think that was a miracle, John?"

"That sounds like one to me," he answers.

"You never told me that, Gene," Margaret says softly.

Eugene glances at his wife, then looks away.

"Whenever I start thinking about those things, I can't stop."

After a moment of awkward silence, Eugene looks out the window at the worsening weather. He convinces Margaret to stay at the parsonage for the afternoon instead of making the unnecessary round trip to the farm and back for the evening service. Then, after a quick goodbye, he leaves.

#

Madeline can tell that Margaret is upset and needs to talk. The two women work together to clean up the dinner dishes, and then Madeline invites Margaret to sit at the kitchen table for a cup of coffee.

"What is it, dear?"

"I think Dicky is dead," she whispers with tears streaming down her cheeks.

"Oh, Margaret, it's too soon for that."

"I want to hold out hope. I need to, but last night I woke up and I tried to imagine him anywhere. I honestly couldn't think of a single place he could possibly be. If he's alive, he has to be somewhere, Madeline."

Madeline is at a loss for something to say. Finally, she asks, "Didn't you ever lose something, Margaret? I mean, really lose it? You looked everywhere and nothing. Then after you've given up, there it is, someplace stupid as if it appeared out of thin air."

Margaret had to admit that she had done that.

Margaret hugs her, saying, "You always know just what to say. You are my best friend. I will never make it through this without you."

#

When Eugene pulls into the farmyard, he notices some unfamiliar tire tracks quickly filling with snow. He thinks that more searchers must have come by to search and found no one there, just left.

After changing into his work clothes, he sets to work grinding feed and doing the late afternoon milking session. He is glad to have time by himself to think about the day. The story of Job has gotten into his head. Inside, he changes his clothes again and, finding Margaret's Bible, begins to read the long story. Later, looking at the clock, he realizes he needs to leave to make it to town for the evening prayer vigil.

Getting in the car, he notices that the wind has shifted to coming out of the northwest. While the snow is still blowing and accumulating, he feels fairly certain that the snowfall will die out overnight.

He's almost late when he pulls into the parking lot, which is only about one-third full. Inside, the church feels warm and bright. Madeline is getting ready to lead the church in song as he moves into the pew with Margaret.

"I was worried you might not make it."

"The snow is still pretty bad, but I think it is going to stop overnight." Then after a pause, he asks, "How was everything here in town?"

Margaret tells him that she is glad to have had some time to talk with Madeline about everything that is going on.

The prayer vigil starts with a few songs. Then John begins what he promises will be a very short message about the prodigal son. He emphasizes that after the prodigal son left, the father was sure he would never see him again. That is why he was so filled with joy upon his return. That's why he had insisted on a huge feast to celebrate God returning the lost son to him.

Then he opens his Bible and reads from the fourth chapter of Philippians.

He reads, *"Do not be anxious about anything, but in every situation, by prayer and petition, with thanksgiving, present your requests to God. And the peace of God, which transcends all understanding, will guard your hearts and your minds in Christ Jesus."*[1]

After a moment, John says, "Now, I want everyone here to say together all at the same time the petitions that are on your hearts." After a pause, he softly says, "Please begin."

The congregation begins a cacophony of words which being spoken together sounds like noise, but an unmistakable sentiment rings through to the rafters. The group prayer goes on for several minutes, eliciting tears from almost everyone there.

Driving home, Eugene quietly tells Margaret that it was a moving service. Margaret, with tears in her eyes, sadly smiles.

---

[1] Philippians 4:6–6 (NIV)

Monday—Missing One Week

Eugene wakes up, realizing he has slept through the night for the first time since Dicky went missing. It feels almost balmy as he heads out the door to start his chores. He reaches down for a handful of fresh snow, finding that it packs together in his grip; snow is on the verge of melting for the first time in a week. He tunes the milking shed Philco to find a weather report. A crackly voice says that it's heading for a high of forty degrees today. From that information, he knows two things, he knows that the road to his farm will become a quagmire, but he also knows that they are finally making progress towards having the big search.

He turns the radio back to the music station and chats with the cows until he has finished milking. His stomach is grumbling for some breakfast, but he decides to forge ahead with the feed grinding. Walking across the yard, he knows this could be the last day he grinds feed for the hogs. He wishes he could fatten them up some more, but he has run out of time to pay his long-overdue bills. Unless there is an unexpected delay, the livestock truck should arrive this afternoon.

After turning on the noisy grinder and starting to scoop corn into the chute, he notices that there is a bit of a mess beyond his makeshift desk. He stops the grinder, and after a quick inspection, he sees that someone has taken the war souvenirs that were hanging on the wall. He realizes at once that among those who stopped by the farm yesterday when no one was here were thieves. He is livid. Most of these didn't even belong to him. But thinking that someone was so low as to pretend to come here to help, only to take advantage of him, really makes his blood boil.

#

Nine a.m. finds Sheriff Mackintosh staring across his desk at two young men, both impeccably groomed down to the fingernails, both wearing identical crisp black suits and pencil-thin ties.

"Before you guys tell me anything else, I'd like you to tell me why the FBI is interested in a rural Iowa missing person case?"

"Officially, kidnapping," replies Special Agent J. Edmund Donovan.

"Well, I haven't spent much time in the big city, but I have spent thirty-five years in law enforcement. From my seat, kidnapping seems pretty unlikely."

Donovan pauses to adjust the knot driving his starched collar through two layers of skin. He sits back in his chair as he asks, "I think we could be working together for a while, Sheriff. How would you like me to address you? When we're not out in public, I mean?"

Mackintosh is not inclined to let his guard down just yet. But then he decides, what the heck.

"My friends call me Mack. You?"

"Mack, I like that. Everybody calls me Donovan."

"So, what about this case makes you think of kidnapping?"

"Kidnapping isn't very likely, Mack. But it is possible, and it's also the one and only reason the FBI can get involved in a case like this."

"That's pretty thin, Donovan."

The agent chuckles as he says, "Thin? It's practically invisible."

"Then why?"

"Because your governor was a Yale Law classmate of the president's National Security Advisor."

"You're kidding."

"That's par for the course in Washington. Look, Mack, you're stuck with us, so you might as well let us do you some good. We're officially here to look at kidnapping, so obviously, we're going to concentrate on that. But, as long as we're here, we can help you out with anything else that's nefarious. We'll leave the digging through snow drifts to you. But if a body turns up, we have the best forensics lab in the world."

"So, what do you guys want to do first?" asks the sheriff.

"We always start at the beginning. We'll want you and your deputy to take us through the case from day one."

The sheriff nods.

"Before I forget, Mack, watch out for Frydenberg. I think that reporter is in the governor's pocket."

#

Dub, having decided to swing by the farm before going to work, finds Eugene grinding feed.

"How you holding up, Geno?"

Eugene seems to be fuming. He switches off the grinder and points to the wall where their war souvenirs are supposed to be.

"Where are they?" asks Dub.

"Gone! Some mongrel took them while I was at church. Can you believe that?"

Dub can see how mad his friend is, but the irony of it is too much for him.

"So, the first time you go to church since you got back from the war, how long is that, fifteen years, and you get robbed?"

"Well, you got robbed, too, old buddy."

"I'm not really going to miss that Japanese sniper rifle. I hate to lose my old M1, though. Were you that attached to your samurai sword?"

His question seems to cause Eugene's anger to ebb a bit.

"It's not really the stuff," he says thoughtfully. "It's that people would take advantage of me in this terrible crisis. What kind of a person would do something like that?"

"Calm down, Geno. You have a lot more important things to worry about right now."

While shaking his head, Eugene says, "War Souvenirs, why does everybody go nuts over war souvenirs?"

"Right, how many guys did we see get injured or killed trying to pick up booby-trapped war souvenirs?"

"Too many, Dub," says Eugene softly.

While Eugene shakes his head, Dub remembers one of his buddies, who had survived the fighting, being hauled away on a stretcher with jagged metal sticking out of his gut. While he and the rest of the unit had stopped for rations, the guy, even after being warned against it, had gone into an enemy shack before the engineers had checked it for boobytraps. Ironically, that's why he had insisted on going in. He claimed the engineers were getting all the good souvenirs.

#

Ten a.m. finds the sheriff in a meeting room with the FBI agents, listening to Deputy Buckman taking them through his notes. He has just gotten to the part about the blue car phone tip. The deputy reports that Dekalb salesman Michael Morris phoned in to tell them that he was driving the blue car that upset Mrs. Henry Todd.

"So, that put an end to the blue car lead," states Buckman.

"Why?" asks Special Agent Donovan.

Buckman, looking up from his notes, says, "What do you mean?"

Donovan looks at the sheriff and tells him that the blue car tip in itself was a dead end, but the tip uncovered the other blue car that was prowling for children in the Temperance Park, the one just outside of the window of the conference room in which they are sitting.

"I didn't see where you found that guy," says Donovan flatly.

"I see you've read some of the newspapers," the sheriff says.

"Did you think we'd come here without turning this thing inside-out first?"

The sheriff, after thinking about Donovan's assertion, nods and agrees that they dropped the ball on that one. They had started looking for the local predator but dropped it when the salesman turned up.

Agent Joad is taking notes at the direction of Donovan as Buckman relates and now finishes his recap of the case. It's almost noon as he closes his casebook. Donovan dismisses Buckman and then asks the sheriff to join him for lunch.

#

Dub's rural mail route has brought him to the farm late in the morning. With yet another large mailbag over his shoulder, he enters the house. He is surprised to find Margaret alone in the house, sitting on the sofa, staring at a TV game show. When Dub walks into the room, she asks him to shut the television off. When he sits down next to her, he can see that she has been crying.

When he puts his arm around her shoulder, there's no reaction.

"I'm losing it, Dub," she says so softly he can barely hear her.

"You have to hang on," he says quietly.

"I know. Everyone thinks I'm a saint. I'm supposed to quietly suffer, accepting God's will. That's what my father always told me to do. Well, do you know what, Dub? That's very easy to say. Do you know what I really want to do?"

She abruptly stands and walks into the kitchen. When she sees yet another bag full of mail, she opens the potbelly stove and starts shoving handfuls of letters into the flames. Dub thinks he should stop her but decides to let her be. A square letter slips out of her grasp, falling like a leaf; it lands on top of her foot. They notice the very neat handwriting. It's postmarked from LaCroix, Wisconsin. She opens the letter, and they both can see impeccable handwriting with the salutation, *"Dear Margaret,"* and is signed by Sister Mary Alicia.

Margaret reads the letter aloud. It explains that she is a novice, having entered the order of The Sisters of Adoration, in strict training that doesn't allow her to speak, only to quietly pray. So, it is a welcome respite to be able to write one letter a week, and following her heart, she decides that this week she would write to her instead of her own family, hoping they will understand. She only knows about Margaret's troubles because of it being mentioned in chapel during the time of petitions. These daily petitions, which flow in from all over the world, are written and then prayed by the community together and then placed into a recitation packet for the vigilant sisters praying in the Chapel of Angels, the holy place where sisters of her order have been continuously praying day and night for nearly ninety years. She finishes by asking Margaret to remain strong in her faith, a faith so manifest in the newspaper stories, and that all of the sisters in her community will continue praying and waiting in hope for news of Dicky's safe return.

She sits at the table, looking distant. She hands the letter to Dub, saying very softly, "I almost threw this in the fire."

#

It's crowded as Mackintosh, with Donovan close behind, walks into Reggie's. They have to sit in the worst seats in the joint, the booth right next to the door. Every time the door opens, they are hit with a blast of cold air. They both order chili to try to stay warm.

"Why did you give this case to Deputy Buckman?"

"It wasn't carefully thought out or anything. We were shorthanded because of the storm, and he was the first person to get there the night it broke. So, I just gave him a chance to prove himself. I had no idea it was going to get this big."

"But he has a history with the father."

The sheriff had totally forgotten about these incidents. He realizes the years are catching up with him. He's fought against the idea of stepping down. This job that cost him his marriage has become too much a part of him. He realizes that he's going to have to try harder to stay on top of this thing. Plus, Donovan keeps impressing him. How does he know about the bad blood between his deputy and the boy's father?

"You guys do your homework. They had a couple of run-ins, but that was what, ten years ago? Hopefully, they've both managed to grow up since then."

"Do you think he's up to this job? It's a big case."

"Melvin? He hasn't done that bad so far."

"Too bad he didn't try to get bloodhounds out there before the area got totally contaminated."

"You ever play football, Donovan?"

"In high school."

"What position?"

"Linebacker."

"Don't look now, but you've switched to quarterback, the Monday morning variety."

"Fair enough, Mack. They teach us to push buttons and then see what lights turn on. It seems you have faith in your guy; that's the way it should be.

Your department's done better than most up to now."

"We did drop the ball on the other blue car."

"Don't worry about the blue car guy. We're really close to pulling him in, along with a half-dozen other perverts we have on file in the area."

"You keep impressing me, Donovan. But, tell me this, what do you really think happened?"

"They taught me to keep hunches out of it and, if I can't, to at least keep them to myself. Hunches have led too many cases in the wrong direction."

"So, what's next then?"

"We've gone over the case on paper; now it's time to see how the written accounts square with the scene and the players."

Mackintosh is just settling back into his office chair after lunch when he gets a call from Big Don Slater.

"Mack, the weather is going to break this week. So, I want to start making plans for the big search right away."

When the sheriff questions how he is so sure about the weather, Slater tells him he has it on good authority from the National Weather Prediction Center in College Park, Maryland.

"It's going to hit seventy on Thursday, so all that snow is going to be long gone on Friday. Do you think we can pull things together by then?"

"That's a lot of pulling in four days. But if you can get a commitment from the National Guard and the Red Cross, then I think I can get everything else set here."

The two men talk about the nature of the search for several minutes before tentatively agreeing to a planning meeting in the courthouse tomorrow afternoon. They agree that they will make a decision about going on Friday at that time.

"How's it going with the FBI, Sheriff?"

"They took up most of my morning. But I have to admit that Special Agent Donovan has hit the ground running."

"What does he think happened?"

"He won't speculate. He says that would compromise the investigation."

"Well, what do you think?"

"You don't want me to contaminate the investigation, do you?" the sheriff says with a chuckle.

"Sheriff, please give me a heads-up if you find out which way this thing is going to go," Slater says with a sharp edge to his voice.

#

Donovan had decided that he and Agent Joad arriving in the back of Deputy Buckman's cruiser was going to make a better statement than the two arriving in their own black Lincoln Town car. Seeing dried mud on the floor of the back seat makes him realize that the trip to the farm may not be too kind to his flawless, patten-leather shoes.

The twenty-five-minute drive to the farm takes them along miles of gravel roads. The rolling Iowa countryside is a patchwork of stubble-filled fields, some of which are occupied by grazing cows of various blacks, whites, and browns. Every half-mile, they pass a farmstead, each containing a handful of variously sized buildings.

"This place is really out in the sticks," says Donovan.

"Your first time in the Iowa countryside?" asks Buckman.

"Practically my first time in any countryside."

The last half-mile is muddy, with the deputy having to gun the engine while deftly spinning the steering wheel to prevent the cruiser from either getting stuck or sliding into a ditch. Donovan chuckles to himself, realizing that if not for Buckman driving, they wouldn't have been able to make an entrance at all.

Opening the car door, the agents are introduced to the odors associated with farm operations.

"Does it always smell this bad?" asks Agent Joad.

"Smell?" asks Buckman. "Oh, yeah, I guess we just don't notice it anymore."

"No kidding," says Joad with an incredulous look on his face.

After shooting Joad a stern look, Donovan says, "Why don't you give us a quick tour around outside, Deputy. And then we'll go in to meet the parents."

Donovan takes a stride to follow Buckman towards the grinding room. His foot slides off to the side, and he comes very close to falling down in the muddy ground. Looking at the mud on his shoes dangerously close to his socks, he shudders to think of how he would look if he had fallen.

Buckman, seeing the motion in the corner of his eye, turns in time to notice the near calamity.

"You have to watch where you step on the farm," Buckman says, grinning.

"That's the best advice I've ever gotten, Deputy."

"And you don't know the half of it."

Buckman takes the two agents on a quick walkthrough, following the timeline in his notes. Inside the grinding room, Buckman notices something is different. Then he realizes the weapons that were hanging on the wall are gone. He mentions this to Donovan, who asks Agent Joad to make a note to find out why they were moved. To himself, he considers that moving the weapons could have been intended to hide something.

Then checking his own notes, Donovan says, "I'd like to see the hogs."

As if on cue, a semi, with a *"Caldwell and Sons Trucking"* placard on its door, its diesel engine clattering loudly, pulls a multi-level livestock trailer into the farmyard.

A moment later, Eugene finds his way to the driver's door. Donovan motions for Buckman to join them. When the deputy returns, Donovan finds out that Eugene is selling all of the hogs. A moment later, Donovan is on the cruiser's radio talking to Sheriff Mackintosh. Donovan tells the sheriff to have the county attorney try to get a court order to hold the hogs temporarily pursuant to an FBI investigation.

"Why do you think he's selling the hogs right now, Mack?"

"I don't know. Maybe he needs the money."

"I want to bring the parents into your office tomorrow afternoon for questioning. There's getting to be a few loose ends. I think it warrants running both parents through the facts separately to see if the story is consistent."

"Do you think they might be involved?"

"Come on, Mack. This is standard procedure. You probably should have done this yourself last week. But now I'm glad you didn't."

After finishing the radio call, Donovan spends a few minutes making notes.

Then, finding Buckman, he says, "Let's go meet the parents."

Inside, after introductions, the group all takes seats around the large kitchen table. Margaret serves coffee, setting a tray with cream and sugar on the table; she wipes her hands on her apron and sits down next to Eugene.

"On behalf of everyone in the FBI, I want to offer our profound condolences for everything you've had to endure. When J. Edgar Hoover sent me here, he asked me to make a speedy investigation to help you two get a resolution just as soon as possible." Actually, his boss, not the FBI Director, had told him to take care of this quickly in order to get Governor Mallinckrodt out of the ear of National Security Advisor Bundy.

Eyes like saucers, Margaret asks, "J. Edgar Hoover knows about us?"

"Of course, this story has been covered in all of the Washington papers. He may even send you a note with all of those others," he says, nodding to the overflowing mailbag leaning against the wall. Realizing he is laying it on too thick, he quickly changes the subject.

"Let me tell you what we have going. We have a list of eleven suspects that are being sought as we speak by FBI agents and other law enforcement officials in the surrounding states. Top on our list is the owner of the blue car who was stalking children in Temperance and elsewhere a few months ago."

"I thought the driver of the blue car was a seed salesman," states Eugene.

"The Dekalb salesman was the man that Mrs. Todd reported. We know that. The man we are looking for now is a different person. We have reason to believe that he, while reportedly driving a blue car, was stalking young boys in the area, which put him on the top of our list. The others I mentioned are from our files of known offenders in the surrounding area. At this moment, we can't place them near here, but we are going to round them up and put some heat on them."

"How long will all this take?" asks Eugene.

"The Director told us to do it quickly. He's authorized enough manpower to, with a little luck, wrap this up in three days or less."

Margaret perks up a bit. "Do you think one of these men might have Dicky?"

Using his best sympathetic look, Donovan says, "Mrs. Walker, I can't make any promises." After a pause, he adds, "If he was kidnapped, and we don't know if he was, and if the perpetrator is on my list, and we don't know if it is, then, I think we have better than a decent chance to get your son back to you."

Margaret, hearing only, "get your son back to you," can only manage to say, "Oh, sweet Jesus," as she raises her apron to wipe the tears from her eyes.

Donovan closes his notepad and then says, "Thanks for the coffee, Margaret. It really hit the spot."

Then rising, he says, "I know it's so hard to be patient in a situation like this. I promise to make everything move just as quickly as humanly possible. Oh, one more thing, I'd really appreciate it if both of you could come to the

County Building tomorrow afternoon around one for an update. Hopefully, we'll have a lot of progress for you by then."

Donovan, now riding back to town while looking at the mud on his shoes, says, "Do you know a place to pick up some rubber overshoes and black shoe polish?"

"Sure," chuckles Buckman. "There's a Ben Franklin on the way into town."

A moment later, Buckman asks, "Did the Director of the FBI really say that?"

"He was thinking it," Donovan replies.

"That's what I thought," says Buckman with a smile.

"Is it unusual for a farmer to sell hogs in March?" asks Donovan.

"It's more about weight. Hogs are fattened to about two hundred and fifty pounds. Eugene's aren't nearly that big."

"So, why is he selling them now?" asks Donovan.

"Maybe he needs the money."

Donovan writes in his notebook and then shows what he has written to Agent Joad. It says, "Either he sold the hogs because he's short of money, or he is trying to hide something." The phrases, short of money and hide something, are both underlined.

#

Eugene is sitting in his grinding room reading the Bible. When he had talked to John at length about Job, the pastor suggested that he read about it for himself. Since then, he has spent a lot of his free time with Margaret's Bible. When he comes to Chapter 27, it shakes him to his boots. Job's best friend, who had turned against him, describes the plight of the unjust man. He reads, *"However many his children, their fate is the sword.*[2]"

---

[2] Job 27:4, NIV

He closes the book with a strong feeling that what he's just read is aimed at him because he had openly parted ways with God. Is this a prophecy? Is it a warning? Perhaps it's just his destiny. If he has to die into nothingness, he feels he can live with that; perhaps it is exactly what he deserves. But it's the reference to his son that is tearing at his gut. *I just can't live with that,* he says to himself. It's then that he closes his eyes and sincerely prays to God for the first time in years.

As he opens his eyes, he sees something clearly. When he came back from the war, he was just Eugene, one of many soldiers who had lost a part of himself overseas. But since then, Margaret and Dicky have become a part of him, much more than a part of him, and yes, even this lonely farm; the land now turned inside out, is a part of him too. He just can't let his defiance of God cause the loss of Margaret and Dicky; he just can't.

Eugene is surprised to see an Amish buggy pulling into the farmyard. He recognizes the driver, Elijah Yoder, who had come to help search last week. With him, holding the reins of the horse, is a young boy, not much older than Dicky. Eugene waves and approaches the buggy from the driver's side.

"Good to see you, Mr. Yoder."

"Please, call me Elijah. We're just taking the long way to town."

"Who's your driver?"

"This is my son, Gabriel."

"How long have you been driving, Gabriel?"

The boy looks away and seems at a loss for words.

"He's not much of a talker."

"Sounds just like my son, Dicky. I've been teaching him how to drive, too," says Eugene, smiling at the boy. Then he lifts the boy's hat off of his head with his left hand and rubs his hair with his right.

Then Eugene adds, "How many more like him do you have at home?"

"Just the one, here."

Eugene, doing his best not to choke up, says, "You keep a good eye on him then."

Walking away, he notices Margaret at the window is watching them.

#

Deputy Buckman, after finding out about the disappearance of the weapons, has just spent an hour going through the pile of newspapers related to the case that the sheriff has been obtaining from Eddy's Newsstand. The best picture of the apparently stolen weapons was in the Des Moines Tribune. He has taken the initiative to contact Frank Frydenberg to see if he can get a high-quality photograph.

A half-hour later, he receives a callback message from the reporter asking to meet him at Reggie's at four o'clock. Deputy Buckman is sitting at the counter when Frydenberg walks in.

"Hey, Fry," the bib overalls group calls out from their perennial corner table, "Come on over for a piece of pie!"

"Not today, guys. I've got a hot date here already."

As the reporter slides onto the stool next to Buckman, the deputy asks, "So, you've talked to those guys?"

"I'm a reporter, Deputy; I talk to everyone."

"I'm sure those guys gave you an ear-full."

"The voice of the man on the street is always an important part of the story."

On cue, a loud voice from the corner table yells out, "That's some hot date you have their Fry!"

Buckman chuckles as he says, "That's an important voice, right there."

"Local color," Frydenberg deadpans.

After ordering pie and coffee, the men start talking about the weapons photos. The deputy tells him, off the record, that the sheriff's office was not aware of the theft until they discovered it on a walk-through on Monday afternoon. Frydenberg expresses surprise that Eugene hadn't reported it, which seems to unwittingly open the deputy's mouth to his personal speculations about the case. Realizing that he is talking to a reporter, he reemphasizes that what he has just talked about is off the record.

"Of course. You're talking to a professional here. By the way, how's it going with the FBI?"

"Special Agent Donovan almost fell down in the mud when he stepped out of the car."

After a hearty laugh, Frydenberg says, "His first time on a farm, I guess."

"His first-time walking on dirt is more like it."

"Ohlman could have won an award with that picture," Frydenberg says. Then he adds, "Has Donovan been able to shed any light on the case?"

The deputy senses a changing direction, so he says, "I thought we were going to talk about me getting the photos."

The reporter hands a manilla envelope to the deputy. Buckman opens it and quickly examines a high-resolution enlargement of the weapons.

"That's a nice samurai sword," says the reporter. Then, after a quiet pause, he adds, "I think I'd be pretty angry if someone stole that from me."

Putting the image back in the envelope, the deputy says, "Well, maybe he's got bigger things to worry about right now."

#

As Eugene comes into the house for supper, Margaret asks him about the Amish man who stopped by. He tells her about the interaction.

"That little boy's name is Gabriel. His father was teaching him how to drive."

The conversation about the Amish family is like a tonic. They enjoy the most pleasant meal they've had since Dicky was lost.

"I have a very good feeling about the FBI investigation," Margaret says.

Eugene seems a bit lost for words. After a moment, his expression changes to a smile as he says, "I have a good feeling, too."

Margaret, looking at her husband closely, realizes that despite everything that has happened, he seems to be softening, becoming more approachable, especially to others. Seeing Eugene connect with the Amish man and his boy seems out of character in her experience. Feeling an unexpected glow deep inside, she kisses him more tenderly than she has in a very long time. Both are overcome with a floodgate of pent-up emotion; an irresistible force; a release of suppressed darkness, a bolt of lightning in a dark sky. Afterward, in each other's arms, there is a peaceful quiet that is so pleasant but fragile that neither is willing to speak, for surely it would shatter.

#

Frydenberg, back in his corner room in the Maquoketa Hotel, is transcribing notes from the jumble that he had covertly scribbled on his napkin at Reggie's. Now finished, he places a call to the home of his editor, Ben Bray, to petition his boss for resources.

The reporter tells his boss that this story is going to explode. He has crafted working relationships with both parents, Deputy Buckman and Big Don Slater, in the governor's office. He tells him that the biggest search in Iowa's history could go down as early as Friday.

"That search story is huge, but there are other things brewing that could be even bigger."

"You mean the FBI kidnapping story?"

"That's a story for sure, but it smells like there's another big one. The word on the street here is that the dad is a hothead, and some war souvenirs have turned up missing this week. I have a hunch that the authorities might take a hard run at the dad at some point."

Bray has several questions about his facts and hunches. When he is satisfied, they talk about the logistics of handling the story. The editor decides he will give Frydenberg a team of three junior reporters. One will be stationed in Temperance to phone in Frydenberg's notes, and two men in the newsroom will edit and co-write or ghostwrite stories as needed.

"What about another photographer?" asks Frydenberg.

"I'll send another one down for the Friday search. I'll let you work out how to deploy him with Ohlman. Heck, on second thought, I'll send two. Photos will tell the main story all by themselves."

Tuesday—Explosion

The normally subdued hallways of the Briggs County Building explode with the booming and unmistakable voice of Sheriff Mackintosh from behind the closed door of his inner office. Deputy Buckman, feeling his heart pounding, would rather be anywhere else.

"What did I tell you, Melvin! Don't talk to the press!"

"It was off the record," Buckman replies with a bit of defiance in his voice.

"Oh, so it was off the record," the sheriff says sarcastically. "Why didn't you say so?" Then he pauses, fuming.

"Let me tell you what off the record means," he starts more evenly. "It means he will print everything you said as," now inhaling before shouting even more loudly than before, "says an anonymous source familiar with the investigation!"

The sheriff stands up suddenly, which terrifies the deputy, who almost wouldn't have been surprised if Mackintosh had pulled out his gun and shot him at this point. The sheriff is now pacing back and forth, eventually standing in front of the window to look outside, trying to calm himself, remembering his doctor's warning about his blood pressure.

After what seems like twenty minutes to Buckman, whose own heart is racing, the sheriff begins speaking in his usual reasonable-sounding voice. He explains to the deputy that Frydenberg is a seasoned reporter who will stop at nothing to get himself a good byline.

"Stop at nothing means he will lie, cheat, steal, and try to cut a good deal with the devil while selling his soul. Do you get that?"

"Yes, Sir," Buckman replies meekly.

"Melvin, this case is big and getting more complicated by the day. The governor, the FBI, and the old guys in Reggie's will all be coming for me with pitchforks. But that's not what I'm really worried about."

After a pause, the deputy asks, "What really worries you?"

"I'm really worried about what these forces are prepared to do to that poor family."

#

Agent Danny Jackson, wearing faded dungarees, an inside-out black sweatshirt, and expensive black shoes, casually looks at the license plate of a blue 1954 Chevy Bellaire parked in front of Nate's Tavern on fifth Avenue in Dodge City, Iowa. He pulls a black ball cap out of his back pocket, putting it on his head. This is a signal to his partner and the representatives of the Dodge City Police department and Williams County Sheriff's Department, who are watching from hidden locations near the front and back doors.

Jackson takes careful stock of the five people within his eyesight as he walks in the front door.

"Hey, who owns the blue car out front? I'm afraid I might have put a small dent in it when I pulled in."

"The Chevy?" asks a man at the bar as he sets down his beer and turns to look at him. The man perfectly matches the description from both the FBI file and those given by the concerned citizens of Temperance. Agent Jackson takes note that he is drinking with his right hand.

"It's a very small dent. If you don't mind coming outside to take a look, I'll be happy to give you cash to cover the damages."

Feeling that it must be his lucky day, Harold Thomas Pell accompanies Jackson out of the front door. As he bends over to look for a dent in the driver's door, the agent pulls the man's right arm up to the middle of his back.

"Hey!" yells Pell.

"I'm Agent Daniel Jackson with the Federal Bureau of Investigation. I'm afraid you'll have to leave the rest of that beer inside and come with me."

#

News of the sheriff's dust-up with Buckman traveled fast. It didn't take long for Frydenberg to pass it on to Big Don Slater. It took the savvy political advisor only a few seconds to devise a way to put the information to good use.

Slater had called Reggie, whom he has been tipping very generously, to ask him when Deputy Buckman arrives for lunch each day.

As Slater walks in the door, Reggie nods towards the deputy eating his lunch at a table near the side wall. In short order, Big Don joins him at the table and starts innocent-sounding conversation. Knowing that the deputy is probably feeling like his career is on the rocks, the politician eases into the topic of greener pastures for a young law enforcement officer whose name has gotten a lot of recent notoriety.

"Governor Mallinckrodt asked me about you just yesterday. He saw your picture in the paper and seems to feel like you're doing a great job on a difficult case."

"You're kidding."

"I hope you don't mind if I call you Melvin. The governor knows better than almost anyone else what it's like to have to do a tough job in a difficult situation under the gaze of constant publicity. He couldn't stop singing your praises." Sensing his words are chipping away some of Buckman's natural skepticism, he rolls on. "He wants you to come to work for him when this thing is over. How does being on the governor's security detail sound, at the rank of, say, a sergeant in the Iowa Highway Patrol? Those guys have great pay and benefits, as I'm sure you know."

After a moment, the deputy manages, "Are you really serious?"

"Dead serious, Melvin. You'll have to keep all this under your hat for now, but I'd like to be able to tell the boss you'll give this your strong consideration.

Do you think you can do that?"

Not believing his good luck, Buckman glances around to see who might be listening and says, "Sure."

"Okay, the governor really appreciates it. But, seriously, Melvin, you can't even tell your wife yet. Is that understood?"

"Yes, Sir."

"One more thing, Melvin. The governor wants to be just as helpful as possible in this unfolding case. He'd appreciate it if you could just let me know if and when anything surprising unfolds so he can be prepared to respond as quickly as possible. Most people don't understand how hard it is, even for a governor, to get the heavy wheels of state to move without advanced notice."

"No problem."

Big Don feels good about how quickly he was able to tap into another source of information. The placard on his desk in Des Moines reads, *"Information is Power."* He laughs to himself, thinking about the unwritten antecedent to his credo—ignorance is weakness. In the present circumstance, Deputy Buckman's ignorance, not knowing that it would be nearly impossible for even the governor to bypass the standard training and the rigorous protocols to personally appoint anyone, no less an outsider, to an officer position in the Iowa Highway Patrol.

#

Knowing she has to go to the county building in Temperance today, Margaret reluctantly decides she should spend time making herself presentable. After putting on her Sunday dress, she fusses with her hair and makeup for several minutes before she is finally satisfied with her grooming. She opens her little jewelry box to find her favorite pendant, a graduation present from her father, a gold cross adorned with diamonds, four small ones at the ends, with the largest at its center.

After a little digging, she finds the cross hiding under a small velvet bag. Seeing the bag brings on a sense of uneasiness. Feeling ashamed because it flies in the face of her father's sense of theology, she opens the bag to take out the lucky coin given to her by her maternal grandfather. Her heart skips a beat at finding the bag empty. She runs her fingers through the box for a moment before rushing to dump out its contents on the kitchen table; the coin isn't there.

Feeling numb, she recalls her grandfather giving her the gold coin on her tenth birthday, telling her that an old person giving a coin to a child is an old German tradition. The coin was given to his father by his own grandfather on the occasion of his boarding the steamship City of Stuttgart bound for New York in 1860. She clearly recalls his gravelly voice.

"Hide the coin so no one will steal it from you. If you find yourself in a dire situation, spend the coin to save yourself. But if you manage to keep it, pass it on as a family heirloom. It will be a harbinger of good luck. But you daresn't lose it, for if you do, then it will be a curse."

The coincidence of losing the lucky coin at this time is unnerving enough, but making it worse was her own father's warning her against the sin of placing faith in an object of luck. He had taken the coin away from her when she was ten, telling her that possessing a lucky coin is like slapping God's face. It was only when she was an adult that he believed that he could trust her to possess the coin as a family heirloom, not as an omen of good fortune.

Now afraid and ashamed at the same time, she straddles the emotional fence of being cursed by her ancestors or being cursed by God.

The almost sanitary nature of the Briggs County Building, in contrast with the earthy reality of farm life, only adds to Margaret's uneasiness as she and Eugene blunder around trying to find out where they are supposed to go. Sheriff Mackintosh apologizes for not having someone meet them at the front entrance of the large building.

After friendly salutations and an offer of refreshments, the sheriff turns the meeting over to Special Agent Donovan. He eases into the proceedings with some well-planned light chat thanking them for yesterday's fine hospitality at the farm, contrasting it with a phony story of the bad manners he routinely encounters in the big city. Also, he comments lightly about the improving nature of the weather, telling them that the sheriff's department is pushing for a big search in the coming days.

"Now, let me tell you about our investigations. The driver of the blue car that was accosting children in this city was apprehended in Dodge City this morning. He's undergoing questioning as we speak. The FBI agent on the case is highly trained in all the latest interrogation techniques. I can tell you that the early reports are that the subject is seeing the benefit of being cooperative."

"Oh, thank God," says Margaret. "Does he have Dicky?"

"Prying information from a belligerent requires a bit of patience. It's a bit like snake charming. You have to play the right music to get the snake lulled into just the right frame of mind to get it to give up the information we all so badly need to have."

Seeing Margaret's frown, he adds, "Margaret, that's one of the hardest things I face in my job, telling nice folks like you, who have endured so much, to have patience. I've also learned that it's just not fair to make promises, but I am really hopeful for an answer as soon as this afternoon and certainly no later than tomorrow."

Wiping tears, Margaret nods her head quickly up and down.

Donovan then turns to the status of the other eleven individuals of interest. Eight have been found and interrogated. Seven have been quickly ruled out as suspects for various reasons. The eighth, Tyler Landry, an unemployed insurance salesman, was apprehended in his home in Blue Earth, Minnesota. He, too, is being interrogated. So far, he doesn't have an alibi for the time in question.

"So, in summary, we have three still at large and the two under intense interrogation, and I'm optimistic that those still at large will be quickly rounded up."

The sheriff now takes over the meeting, updating Eugene and Margaret about the improving weather, which will lead to the all-out search in the coming days, a search for which Governor Mallinckrodt is pledging very substantial resources, including those of the Iowa National Guard. After the nature of the big search, which is explained in broad strokes, the sheriff turns the meeting over to Donovan to wrap up. After summarizing what has been discussed, Donovan tells Eugene and Margaret that he wants to see them privately for a moment.

"There is one more thing that you can do to help the investigation," starts Donovan. He goes on to explain that he would like them to go through the details of the afternoon that Dicky went missing one more time. He tells them that going through this exercise in just the right way has proven to be useful in getting eyewitnesses to recall forgotten details that may have become lost in a dense fog of worry as the events unfold.

"Can you help us with that?" he asks.

When both agree, he directs Margaret to stay where she is to talk to Agent Joad and asks Eugene to come with him. Both look at each other, expecting they would once again do it together, but neither objects.

#

Ever since learning yesterday that he was going to be interviewing Margaret Walker, Agent Oren Joad has been preparing himself for the task. Up to now, Special Agent Donovan relegated his duties to taking notes and writing daily case summaries. So, he is grateful for a chance to prove his mettle to the powers that be. However, Donovan, as Agent in charge, has practically scripted his interview questions.

Reviewing and probing the all-important hours between noon and six p.m. on March 6 is the primary objective of the interview. However, it's equally important to press inconsistencies as they might occur while reading Margaret's reactions. All investigations attempt to discover the chronology of facts and superimpose those on other witness testimony while reading the behavior of the interviewee, looking for subtle markers that a response may be less than candid; FBI jargon for lying. The FBI devotes a great deal of emphasis and training in this regard. For Margaret's first interview, Donovan instructed him to use a kid-gloves approach.

During the first meeting at the farmhouse, Joad noticed that she was an attractive woman. Today, made-up as she is, he finds her to be stunning. So much so that he decides to drop telling her how nice she looks as an icebreaker.

Instead of using his planned opening line about how she looks, he adlibs, complementing the gold cross hanging from her necklace. She smiles and tells him it was a gift from her father.

Off to a good start, he pours a glass of water and smiles as he hands it to her, then he pours one for himself and takes a sip. He wants to make her as comfortable as possible. She thanks him.

He gives her the standard preparation asking her to relax and not think of him in an official capacity, rather just answer quickly and honestly, not worrying about crafting her words. He explains that he hopes that they can learn some of the details that, in the fog of the moment and in the telling and retelling, have gotten lost. Finally, he tells her it would be best if she calls him by his nickname Skip, and he will call her Margaret, if that's alright.

Joad leads the interview through the afternoon of last Monday, starting with the noon meal and leading up to the last time she saw Dicky leave the house.

"What time was that?"

"It was one o'clock."

"Exactly one?"

"Yes. He asked me to go out earlier, but I told him to wait until one."

"Why the wait?"

She pauses for a moment and then says, "I wanted to finish browning the roast for supper before bundling him up. I thought I might burn it if I let him get me distracted. He's very good at that, by the way."

"I'm sure he is," Joad says, smiling. "Was it his idea to go outside or yours?"

"It was his."

"Did he give a reason?"

"Do you have young kids, Skip?"

"No, I'm afraid I'm a bachelor."

"A kid his age has a short attention span. He plays inside until he gets bored, then he wants to go outside. It wasn't unusual for him to go in and out several times a day."

"But on this day, do you remember if he gave a reason?"

Margaret thinks for a moment. The Amish boy driving the buggy reminds her.

"Why yes, he said he wanted to go out to drive the tractor."

"Drive the tractor?" Joad says with a surprised look on his face.

"He meant sit on his father's lap while he thinks he is driving."

"And Eugene lets him do that?"

"Sometimes, if he's not too busy."

Satisfied, Joad moves the timeline along. Margaret tells him that after Dicky left, she was doing laundry. She had set up her ironing board in the living room so she could watch TV. He asks her which shows she watched during the day, knowing that they could potentially be used as time markers.

"Did you see Tom Magnus, the livestock buyer, in the yard that afternoon?"

Margaret says she remembers looking out of her window and seeing his car. When he asks, she recalls that it was a dirty, black four-door. When she can't remember what time it was, he asks if she remembers what was on TV at the time. She recalls that it was the game show, A Queen for a Day. He asks if she remembers noticing when the cattle buyer left. She did not.

The interview continues through to the time that they discovered Dicky was missing.

"Do you recall the time?"

"Yes, it was five o'clock. Eugene said he looked at his watch."

"Please try to remember if you looked at a clock. There's a red one on the wall of the kitchen."

"Don't you believe Eugene?"

"Of course, Margaret. But for any investigation, it's best to have two collaborating accounts if possible. Please try to remember."

"I'm sorry, I don't remember looking at the clock."

"What about the TV or the radio? Was there anything on those that you remember?"

"The radio wasn't on. Eugene turns it on when he comes in to supper for the market reports. Now I remember. I remember looking at the clock and thinking he was missing the market report. It was five-fifteen when I looked, and he came in just a little after that."

Joad makes a note of this discrepancy and circles it.

"So, let's see. Dicky was outside for just over four hours. Is that unusual?"

"I would say yes, for this time of year. When it's warmer, he'll often stay out that long, but in colder weather, he doesn't stay out much over an hour or two."

"Did you think about checking on him?"

That question causes Margaret's face to sadden.

"I wish to God that I had."

"Of course," Joad says sympathetically.

Now comes the tricky part, Joad thinks to himself. He tries to recite the next question as he had practiced it.

"Is your husband the one who enforces discipline on your son?"

"We both do."

"How would you describe his manner of imposing discipline?"

The question causes Margaret's eyes to widen.

After a pause, she grasps the cross on her necklace in her fist, then she flatly says, "His approach is fine, like any other father."

Joad notes how she is holding the cross in her fist. It's a classic signal that she is holding something back as if she is hiding her lie from God. He stores that information for later.

"Fine," he says with a smile. "Thanks so much for your help. I know it's a tedious way to spend an afternoon. I do feel like we got some helpful information."

#

The first of Donovan's questions for Eugene are essentially the same as those Agent Joad is asking Margaret, factual questions about the timeline designed to probe for inconsistencies or subtly veiled purposes. His interviewing tone up to this point is intentionally robotic. He did this, so he can now shift to a more casual demeanor to try to get Eugene to answer casually and candidly, a subtle mechanism to slide truth out of reluctant lips.

Setting down his notepad and pencil to make it seem like he is going off the record, Donovan, in a casual, offhand way, says, "Geez, Eugene, it must be tough to have to sell your hogs now, with everything else that's going on. I mean, what a time to run out of money."

Donovan wrote out this statement in several different ways. He was striving to have it sound like a sympathetic thought that just popped into his head. He wants Eugene to be off guard so he will quickly answer the question that he hadn't actually asked, the question hiding between the lines. That question is; Eugene, are you broke? The reason it's an important question is that money is among the top four motives for murder. The reason he doesn't want to ask it directly is that if Eugene gets a hint that he is a suspect, he will guard and second guess the answer to every question they may need to ask.

"What makes you think I'm running out of money?" Eugene says matter-of-factly.

"Oh, well, sorry. I was just told that your hogs are a little on the thin side for selling, that's all."

"When they're that size, we call them feeder hogs. Guys like me fatten them halfway and sell them off to the next guy who feeds them to market weight."

"This is interesting. So why not feed them the rest of the way yourself?"

"Actually, I planned to do that, but with everything that's going on, it's a real pain to have to feed them every day."

Donovan pours himself a glass of water and then pours a second glass for Eugene. This gives him a moment to think. If this guy is lying, he's really fast on his feet. But why not? He's a decorated combat officer, an occupation where those who hesitate or make bad decisions probably don't survive, and then there's the fact that he tested at genius level in the Army's screening examination. Deciding that pushing the issue any farther will alert a smart guy like Eugene that it's important for some reason, and besides, it's easy enough to independently look into his finances on his own. He decides to move on to his second "casual" question; time for a bit more acting.

Donovan stands, stretches as if he is taking a break before getting back to business.

He tries to act as if he is just now remembering something as he says, "By the way, I heard someone took your war souvenirs."

"Actually, most of those belong to Dub."

"Buckman said you didn't report the theft."

Then Donovan sits, reaches into a folder, and then slides a blowup picture of the weapons across the table to Eugene.

"So, which of these belong to you?"

Eugene identifies the samurai sword in the picture.

"Wow, I heard those can be really valuable depending on how old they are. It must be a great story how you acquired it."

"Actually, it was given to me."

"No kidding, by whom?"

"General Broderick."

"General Broderick?"

"He was our commanding general when we took back Guam."

"That must be really special to you then. Aren't you upset that it's gone, and even more so if it was stolen?"

Donovan had debated with himself about using the word *if*. The use of *if* is subtle but significant because it implies there could be another reason for it to be missing, possibly a dark reason. Donovan is now trying to appear casual while watching Eugene's reaction very closely.

Eugene doesn't say anything for a moment; he seems to be thinking. Then he tells Donovan that he was really upset at first. Not because he lost the sword but because someone pretending to be helping him was actually a thief. Then he says that he didn't have much attachment to the sword because it's from a time and place he would rather forget.

"Why did the general give it to you?"

"He had just awarded me a Bronze Star. Our unit had just won a tough and important battle for him, and I guess he was feeling generous."

"Why did you win the Bronze Star, Eugene?"

"I couldn't really tell you. He said it was for conspicuous bravery in battle. Bravery? I was more scared than anyone else. Like I said, I think he was just in a good mood."

Donovan picks up his glass of water; then, he walks to look out the window. He realizes that Eugene had not betrayed any of the typical mannerisms that would indicate he is holding something back. But, the content of his answers seems vague and evasive. He had read the official record of his actions in battle that warranted the medal. The military jargon, typical of these documents, ambiguously recounts what happened. He decides he wants to talk to someone who was there. Then he decides that is yet another reason to interview one Sargent David Dub Davis.

The rest of the interview about the afternoon's activities, including Eugene describing his conversation with Tom Magnus, the livestock buyer, agreed substantially with his earlier assertion about his motives for selling the hogs. He makes a mental note to have Joad interview Magnus to see if his version matches Eugene's.

He can see that the discussion about the last time Eugene saw his son is painful.

"I am haunted by that moment," Eugene says softly. "He said he was cold, so I sent him to the house. I try to force myself to remember seeing him going to the house," his voice trails off. "Why can't I remember that? It's all mixed up with me talking to Magnus and hurrying to finish the chores ahead of the storm."

Donovan senses he is hearing something important as if something subtle lies beneath his words. He tries to keep his objectivity while assessing what is said. Again, in this discourse, he seems completely sincere. Could this guy be that good of an actor?

Big Plans

Big Don Slater is the last person to arrive at the search planning meeting that he had so mercilessly pushed Sheriff Mackintosh to organize for this afternoon. He can easily see that Sheriff Mackintosh is beyond angry as he has been waiting for fifteen minutes with his secretary, Gladys Henry, Deputy Buckman, County Attorney O'Dell, Captains Stork and Winston of the Civil Air Patrol, Randal Radcliff, Director of the Eastern Iowa Red Cross and Brigadier General Michael Dishman. Dishman is in the second year of his four-year appointment as Adjutant General of the Iowa National Guard, serving at the pleasure of Governor Mallinckrodt. The sheriff's face turns scarlet when Frank Frydenberg follows Slater into the room.

"Can I see you in the hallway for a moment?" he says to Slater as he abruptly stands and strides towards the door. He waits at the door as Slater moves into the hallway. When Frydenberg attempts to follow, the sheriff shuts the door in the reporter's face.

"What is he doing here?" the sheriff says through his clenched teeth.

Big Don, not a stranger to smoothing ruffled feathers, calmly explains that getting the right kind of publicity will be essential to acquiring volunteer searchers on short notice. Mackintosh, calming down a bit, tells him that a local paper such as the Temperance Conservative would have been able to do the job.

"We're going to need wide coverage to get enough volunteers, Mack. We could have filled the room with reporters from all the local rags, but if you think about it, you'll realize that it's more efficient this way."

"Enough. We have to get the meeting underway."

Civil Air Patrol Captain Stork, acting as commander of all civilian volunteers, reports on the breadth of the search. He shows the group the planned fifteen square miles of the search area on a large map laid out on the conference room table. He proposes marshaling the searchers in the village of Summit, which should have sufficient parking to stage the massive search.

"But I'm afraid that pushing the search to Saturday is absolutely necessary. In order to handle this number of searchers, we will have to be able to use the parking lots of schools and churches, and we will want to have the public-school buses available. That's a lot of people, so we absolutely need those buses."

After an update on Saturday's weather and a bit of resistance, most of which comes from Slater, whose biggest concern is how a Saturday-born story will play in the news cycle, the need to move the search to Saturday is conceded.

The sheriff then gives the floor to Slater, who ceremonially greets everyone on behalf of the governor. He then has General Dishman list the resources that are being made available under the governor's declaration of "a situation of limited use in a non-emergency situation." The general is calling three hundred reserves from the 133rd Infantry Regiment into active duty, along with all the military vehicles as designated by its tactical commander and two MH-6 "Little Bird" helicopters.

The general then turns to Captain Stork, asking, "Do you think you can muster 700 volunteers, Captain, five days from now?"

"I understand that volunteers are still coming to the farm every day with no solicitation whatsoever. I suggest to publicly ask for a thousand, and I think we'll get seven hundred without breaking a sweat."

The sheriff then turns to Randal Ratcliff, asking, "Have you had a chance to develop a plan for the Red Cross to feed that many searchers?"

Ratcliff explains that he got a heads-up from Captain Stork and is planning to set up a large tent in a suitable location in Summit for coffee, water, juice, and doughnuts in the morning and then a cold lunch with sandwiches and various side dishes during the middle part of the day served by one hundred Red Cross volunteers.

"It will run more smoothly if volunteers at lunchtime are staggered, but we will get the job done in any case," reports Ratcliff exuding confidence.

"Very good," exclaims Mackintosh. "I'm appointing County Attorney Kenneth O'Dell as the tactical leader of Saturday's search. Refer all logistical questions to him."

The sheriff had informed O'Dell of the decision to put him in charge that morning. He had explained that the governor's office had insisted on the move. Big Don had, in fact, asked the sheriff to put O'Dell in charge at the direction of the governor. The sheriff realized that the governor could put a lot more pressure on the county attorney than himself, but feeling his age and knowing there is no upside to getting into a tussle with Mallinckrodt; he was happy to leave the headaches to O'Dell. Big Don, a master chess player, was thinking a few moves ahead; if the big search produced nothing, there would be more pressure on criminal aspects of the situation. With O'Dell tied up in planning the search, the governor's office would have more time to plan how to take advantage of the more complex criminal/political situation as the county's chief prosecutor plays catchup with the legal aspects of emerging criminal facts. At the end of the day, Slater is angling to get the governor as much newspaper ink as possible. National coverage, putting the name Mallinckrodt on the national radar screens is the prize.

Rocky's Army Surplus

Rick Rakowski is scrubbing the ever-present dirt off of the rundown storefront of his Army surplus store near the bridge to the Rock Island Arsenal in Moline, Illinois as a stocky man driving a dirty black car pulls up out front.

"Welcome to Rocky's," Rakowski says as the man is pulling an M1 rifle out of his trunk.

"Are you Rocky?"

"Guilty, as charged," he says as he drops his scrub brush into the bucket. "What have you got there?"

"Some war souvenirs."

"You a vet?"

"Yes, I am," the man says after a moment of hesitation.

"I'm Rocky, I was in the war too, but it was the first one. Nice to meet you." When the man shakes his hand without offering his name, Rocky starts to get a little suspicious.

Rocky, a WWI veteran, suffers from ever-worsening memory. At times he is sharp, and at other times, he struggles to keep up with the shop he has run for the last forty years.

Inside, Rocky looks over the items the guy brought in. The most desirable piece is a dusty samurai sword with brown leather straps neatly wrapped around its handle.

"Man, you've got a nice sword here. Where did you get it?"

The man's answers are vague. He doesn't seem to want to say where he got it. When he asks why he is selling the stuff, he just says it was gathering dust. Rocky sizes the guy up as someone who may have stolen the items. He has seen this before; vets bring back souvenirs from overseas and then toss them aside. Later, other people, if they somehow find out the guy has them, will steal them.

The guy didn't drive a very hard bargain, so Rocky was able to get them for a great price. As the guy is leaving, Rocky goes out to get his scrubbing items just in time to get a good look at the guy's license plate number. It's a yellow Iowa plate. He grabs a stub of a pencil and writes the plate number down on a scrap of paper, and sets it on his sales counter near the cash register. Whenever he buys items that he suspects are stolen, he puts them in the window and doesn't sell them for a few months in case the owner or the police come looking for them. Rocky hates to see a fellow veteran get the shaft.

#

Donovan meets with Agent Joad to review and compare their interviews with the parents while the details are still fresh in their minds. They start by comparing the answers to questions related to the timeline events of the afternoon when the boy went missing. Joad points out how he was able to get Margaret to remember some time clues from which he was able to improve the accuracy of the event timeline for the afternoon of March 6.

But the most significant finding Joad discovered was that Margaret was not candid about her answer about how Eugene disciplined the boy. After the two men list all the reasons they can think of for why she would behave this way, Donovan summarizes that they will want to probe this issue in future interrogations.

Donovan takes Joad through his interview with Eugene. After going through the timeline questions, he takes Joad through the probing of his finances, stolen souvenirs, and his troubled memory of the last time he saw his son.

"Do you think he was lying, Boss?"

"This guy is very intelligent. I feel like he's two steps ahead of me. It's best if I reserve judgment on his candidness for now. But I intend to check out everything he is telling me."

After Donovan summarizes the key facts from the dual interviews, he assigns Joad a list of investigation areas, including checking Eugene's finances, trying to find the souvenirs, and trying to talk to men in his unit about the merits of his Bronze Star.

"I can talk to Dub Davis about that last one," says Joad.

"No. I've decided to hold off on talking to Sargent Davis for the time being. He's too tightly connected with Eugene. I don't want Davis showing his intelligent best friend the breadcrumbs that I'm dropping. I might have enough trouble staying ahead of him as it is."

#

Donovan finds a callback slip from Dr. Truman Powers.

"This is Donovan. What do you have for me, Doctor Powers?"

The FBI's Chief of Forensic Science patiently walks him through the relevant aspects of "Sus Digestivorum." Patiently listening to the scientist, Donovan realizes that he is talking about how quickly pigs digest anything that's put into their mouths.

"So, there's no hope of finding evidence inside the hogs we have quarantined?"

"That's correct. Organic matter entering the gut of a hog is dispatched in eighteen hours or less."

"What about traces in fecal matter on the ground?"

"There would be teeth and perhaps up to one-inch fragments of large bone."

"What if said matter is ground with grain before feeding?"

"In that case, I think it would be like looking for the eye of a needle in a very disgusting haystack."

"So, practically a perfect crime," Donovan flatly says.

"Forensically speaking, yes." After a pause, Powers asks, "How is the grain fed to the hogs?"

After thinking, Donovan answers, "The feed is dumped into metal bins in the hog lot."

"So, the ground feed is dumped into the top of the bin." After a pause, Dr. Powers continues, "In that case, the high-density fragments, like teeth, metal, and maybe bone, might have settled to the bottom away from where the hogs could reach with their snouts. If you're lucky, there might be meaningful evidence still sitting in the bottom of those bins."

#

Donovan, finding the sheriff alone in his office, says, "I think it's time to let you know how I see this thing shaping up."

"Does that mean you're past the hunch stage?"

"A hunch is a theory with little evidence to support it. I want to tell you about a small pile of evidence that seems to be pointing in a disturbing direction."

"Do tell."

"Have you ever seen those connect-the-dot puzzles?"

"Sure."

"Okay, here's a few dots. There's a rumor that Eugene ground up the boy and fed him to the hogs. Then he sells the hogs. Then the sword that was in the grinding room vanishes. Then he doesn't report the theft."

Donovan goes on to explain that when he first heard the wild rumor about Eugene feeding the boy to the pigs, he thought it was just a product of bored, retired guys flapping their gums. However, when you connect the rumor with three other dots, an ugly picture starts to emerge.

After a pause, he adds, "None of this proves anything, it's just one of a couple of theories, but I want you to know that I will be very quietly looking in that direction."

The two men discuss this and other aspects of the case for an hour. As the discussion is winding down, Mackintosh says, "This all still seems a bit thin for a professional investigator. Why are you pushing this so hard?"

Donovan pushes his chair back from the table. After looking down at his notes, he looks the sheriff dead in the eyes. "I took a big chance angling for this case. I'm the youngest Special Agent in the history of the FBI. If I fall on my face now, it will be me personally embarrassing the FBI Director in front of the National Security Advisor to the President. The only way out of this for me now is with a big win."

Mackintosh can see that he is dead serious. "You're taking one heck of a chance. If you swing and miss, you'll be the guy who tried unsuccessfully to bury a war hero."

Donovan blinks in spite of himself as he says, "I haven't missed yet."

"Do you know the last stanza to 'Take Me Out to the Ballgame'?"

A slow smile comes over Donovan's face. "I like working with you, Mack. I'll need you to keep me honest. Is that a deal?"

Mack nods.

When Donovan gets up to leave, he has one more important thing to tell the sheriff.

"Eugene Walker is very intelligent, Mack. The top forensics guy at the FBI told me that if he ground up the boy and fed him to dozens of pigs, it's about as close as you can get to a perfect crime. I really need you to keep this suspicion as quiet as you can for now. If he is guilty and he gets a whiff of this, he may be able to block our every move."

#

Melvin Buckman has just finished eating supper with his wife and his two young boys when the phone on the wall behind him rings. His wife's hands are in the dishwater, so he picks it up.

Big Don Slater's voice sounds friendly as he asks the deputy if he has anything new to report.

"It's a little loud in here. Hang on a minute while I go take the call on the other extension." The deputy, whose hobby is souping up car engines, had a phone extension installed in the garage. He doesn't trust his wife to know he's talking to the governor's top aid, a fact that is no doubt too juicy for her to not tell at least one person in town, and in Temperance, one person would prove to be enough. After, he lifts the garage phone off of its cradle; he asks Slater to wait a moment more while he goes into the kitchen to hang up the receiver there.

It's really cold in the garage this evening; he finds himself shivering even with his coat on. So instead of being cautious, he forges ahead to try to speed up the ordeal.

"The FBI seems to think that the war souvenirs that were allegedly stolen might implicate Eugene Walker in the death of the boy. I'm not sure how and it's by no means certain, but apparently, it's a focus of investigation at this point."

Big Don's pulse quickens. He wants to shout, wow, but he plays it cool by saying, "That's interesting, Melvin."

Then he asks the deputy if anything else has caught his attention. The call doesn't last much longer as both men are in a hurry to wrap things up. Slater ends the call by asking the deputy to keep digging to see where this might go.

#

After hanging up, Slater calls Frydenberg to tell him about the FBI possibly being interested in the missing weapons. He intentionally leaves out how this could implicate Eugene, wanting to gauge the reporter's instincts on the case so far. After a pause, Slater asks him to imagine what might happen next if the all-out search produces nothing.

"Well, they might start looking at Eugene."

"Perhaps they already have," Slater says before filling in the reporter on the rest of what Buckman had said.

#

After hanging up with Big Don, Frydenberg calls his editor in Des Moines.

"Who in the name of everything holy is calling me at this hour?" Ben Bray says sharply into the phone.

"It's Fry. I want you to save me a column next to the big search planning story."

"What for and for how long? They put it to bed five minutes ago."

"I'll dictate the story to the news desk in twenty minutes. I just got a tip that the FBI is very interested in the stolen war souvenirs. I don't have it cold, but I have enough to wink at possible foul play by the dad."

"Wow! That's a huge implication. Who do you have it from?"

"I got it indirectly from the deputy."

"Indirectly? Who did you get it from directly, Fry?"

"Don Slater and I go way back. He's been milking the deputy."

"Big Don milking! Maybe I should put it in the agricultural section."

"This is a scoop, Boss. Nobody else has this."

"You sure you do?"

"Absolutely!"

After a pause, Bray says, "Okay, and I hope I don't regret it. I'll tell them to hold column space for ten minutes. If they haven't got your call by then, it'll have to wait."

After hanging up, Frydenberg writes down a sketch of what he wants to say, then dials the number. The call is answered five minutes after hanging up with Bray.

"Headline, stolen weapons mystery," he adlibs. Typically, it's bad form to bury the lead of the story by putting the key information at the end. In this case, in a short side-bar story, he reverses the pattern.

He finishes with, "The weapons not being reported as stolen, is thought suspicious, says an anonymous source close to the investigation."

As the copywriter is reading back the story, Frydenberg, though worried the managing editor might press him about the validity of the quote relayed by Big Don Slater, feels proud of his skill at unearthing this salacious tidbit and getting it on the record.

Wednesday—Things are Getting Ugly

Sheriff Mackintosh woke up with a headache. After taking two aspirin pills and starting a pot of coffee in his Westinghouse percolator, he opens his front door to pick up the Des Moines Tribune he is now paying Eddy to deliver each day. Unfolding the paper reveals a large banner headline, *"Lost Boy All-Out Search Saturday."* He chuckles to himself as he remembers he gave that one to O'Dell. He plops the paper on his kitchen table. He pours a cup of coffee, stirring in sugar and milk, tossing the spoon into the sink, then as he is lifting the cup to his lips; he is startled by the wall phone ringing just two feet from his left ear.

"Ouch!" he exclaims as hot coffee splashes onto his chest.

"Morning, Mack, did you see the Tribune?" asks Donovan.

"Just the headline."

"Check the last line of the small story on the right side."

"What the—" the sheriff's voice trails off.

"It's early. What time are you going to be in the office?"

"Give me a half-hour."

In the sheriff's office, Donovan reads the small article out loud and then says, "Who else did you tell about the weapons, Mack?"

"Just deputy Buckman," the sheriff says with irritation. "I'll have that guy in here in ten minutes."

"Hold on, Mack. So, your office has a leak; that's par for the course in Washington. When you have a leak, you can do two things, either plug the leak or use the leak."

"Use the leak?"

"Sure, a carefully timed leak of misinformation can be very useful."

"What misinformation?"

"I have no idea, now. Maybe an opportunity will present itself later, and maybe not. But there is another thing you can do to a leaker; that's a lot more fun."

"What's that?"

"Hang him in the wind, like torn underwear," Donovan says with a smile.

#

With the help of the IRS, Agent Joad is able to find the banker who is financing Eugene's meager farming operation. It seems that he was holding his own for several years by using a standard share crop arrangement with the land owner. In this arrangement, the land owner allows Eugene to use the land, including all buildings, for a fifty percent share of the profits from the harvest. The arrangement requires Eugene to report all his expenses to the bank so that a fair and honest profit can be calculated. Thus, Joad is able to see exactly how much Eugene profited year by year.

After the first seven years, Eugene was able to put up a down payment to buy the rundown 80-acre farm. As the owner, he needs to supply his own cash but doesn't have to share the profit. Unfortunately, poor farm market conditions degraded his working cash supply over the next two years. He was forced to start borrowing against his land. Then more bad luck: just as market conditions improved, he suffered significant hale damage two years in a row.

"Boss, the poor guy cashed in the life insurance policies on his wife and himself to buy livestock. He was hoping to be able to make enough money off the hogs to pay off his past-due mortgage loan. He's about two months from defaulting the mortgage, which would leave him dead broke."

"So, he's about as broke as a guy can get?"

After thinking for a moment, Donovan says, "You mentioned life insurance on himself and his wife. Do you know if he has a policy on the boy?"

Joad's eyes widen. "I'll find out."

#

Donovan taps on the sheriff's door and then slumps into a chair. He explains to the sheriff that he's been talking to the lab guys about the digestive properties of hogs. When the sheriff hears that everything consumed by a pig is voided in less than twenty-four hours, the sheriff asks about releasing the hogs they have quarantined.

"I'd like to hold them for a while longer."

"Why?" asks the sheriff.

"He's broke, and I want to keep that pressure on him for a little while longer. He seemed to be hiding that fact from me for some reason. Let's wait a few more days to see if his tongue loosens up about that."

"That's pretty rough, isn't it?"

"I'm afraid that comes with the badge, Mack. By the way, the lab guys want us to check the hog feeders for forensic evidence."

"Forensic evidence?"

"You know, teeth, bone, things like that. They feel that if the boy was ground up in feed, some of the heavy pieces might have fallen straight down the center, and if we're lucky, a few might still be in there."

"Interesting, I would never have thought of that."

"Here's the kicker. We'll need to get Walker's permission or get a search warrant if we want the evidence to be admissible, and if we find something there, we absolutely need it to be admissible. That could be our very last chance to produce direct evidence to prove that the boy is dead. I'm sure you know that prosecuting a loss of life crime without a body will be like getting those pigs to fly.

"So, let's ask him."

"I really don't want to tip him off yet."

Donovan and the sheriff quietly consider the dilemma for a few minutes.

Then, the sheriff says, "Ask for permission to search through the hog lot, not specifically the feeders. Tell him we need to rule out that he fell in and was eaten."

"The lab guys said that finding evidence in the feces is impossible," Donovan says.

"Sure, but the hog feeders you want to search are in the hog lot too, right?"

A smile grows across Donovan's face. "You're starting to grow on me, Mack."

#

Margaret sees Dub pull into the farmyard and park by the open yard gate near the back door. He carries in two bags of mail, one much bigger than the other.

"I'm sorry I'm a little late. I spent hours sorting your mail for you."

He explains that he wrapped all the normal mail into a small bundle, and then he had taken the liberty to open and sort all of the mail related to Dicky into two bags. When she asks which of the bags contains good mail, he shrugs as he points to the smaller one.

Margaret grimaces and shakes her head, saying, "Things are getting ugly."

She reads through a handful of notes from the good bag. One is a postcard from Sister Mary Alicia. She has drawn pink flowers in the margins.

"That's so sweet," she whispers.

She peaks into the top of the larger bag. On top of the pile is a postcard with, *"God knows what you've done. He will punish you for eternity."* She kicks the bag angrily with tears in her eyes.

"Kick it again," says Dub as he kicks the bag with all of his might. She kicks it softly, then melts into his arms, sobbing.

"Oh, Margaret," he whispers in her ear.

She looks up at him with eyes full of tears. "How can God let this happen to us?" she asks with an edge to her voice.

"There's no answer for that."

She lets go after a moment. She walks over to the big bag of mail and kicks it harder than she has ever kicked anything in her life.

#

Donovan receives a phone report from Danny Jackson, who is the agent in charge of the team rounding up the kidnapping suspects. Jackson tells him that all of the suspects have been interviewed or accounted for and that they all have been ruled out.

"That's a job well done, Danny."

"Thanks, Donovan. That means a lot coming from you. How's the case shaping up on your end?"

"Grinding it out as usual. This thing can still go a couple of different ways but Skip, and I are moving the ball down the field every day. You know, Danny, one day at a time."

After a little more chatting about the case, Donovan asks agent Jackson for a professional favor.

"Danny, can you see yourself clear to move Tyler Landry, the guy from Minnesota, back to possible?"

"I don't think that'll ruffle too many feathers. Why?"

"It might not be necessary, but I'm afraid if we totally rule out a kidnapping across state lines that someone will insist on pulling my plug."

"You might be right about that."

"Thanks, Danny. I really want to see this one through."

#

Agent Joad and Donovan are staying at the Maquoketa Hotel in Temperance. The quaint hotel is located within easy walking distance of the Briggs County Courthouse Building. The evening switchboard operator is an attractive young woman named Sally Brown. Joad, a bachelor, has taken to chatting with the young woman when she is not occupied placing calls.

"What time do you get off duty, Sally?"

"I get off at ten."

"I'd be happy to join you for a nightcap at Good Time Charlie's if you're interested."

Later, sitting in a corner booth, Joad gets Sally to imbibe two whiskey sour cocktails that he has persuaded the bartender to make a little stronger than normal.

"How do you like switchboard work? It seems interesting."

Sally giggles. She seems to be giggling more and more with each sip.

"Normally, it's the most boring job in the world. But lately, with reporters and Big Don Slater making so many calls, it keeps me on my toes."

"Who makes the most calls?"

"That's easy. Fry is on the phone the most. Sometimes he reads his stories to the writers in Des Moines that appear in the paper. I think maybe I should be a reporter someday," Sally says while giggling.

"That probably would be a fun job. How do you know he's reading his stories over the phone? You don't listen in, do you, Sally?"

Smiling, she leans in, putting her face close to his, "You're not going to arrest me, are you, Skip?" Then she winks the longest fake eyelashes he has ever seen.

"I didn't bring my cuffs with me," he says as he playfully pinches her nose.

"No. He tells me about it when he places the call, so I know it will take a long time. He's nice. I think he likes me, actually."

"Do you place calls for Don Slater, too?"

"Of course, I think he likes me too, but he's too old for me."

"Does he place many calls?"

"He calls Fry a lot," she says, giggling. "You would think he would just knock on his door."

"That's funny," says Joad while trying to pretend he is laughing. "Does he call anyone else?"

"Mostly, Des Moines calls."

"Any others?"

"Just one, 24242," says Sally. "Isn't that a silly number?" giggling as she sing-songs the number.

#

"So, who's 24242?" asks Donovan later, after listening to Joad report on his intelligence-gathering outing with young Miss Brown.

"That's the home of Deputy Melvin Buckman."

Smiling, Donovan asks, "Are you going to ask her out again?"

"I don't know, Boss, she's pretty, but I think the giggling would get on my nerves."

#

"So, you're telling me that you know deputy Buckman has been leaking case information to Frydenberg," the sheriff says to Donovan.

"Not exactly. I know that Big Don has been in several phone conversations with your deputy."

"Do I want to know how you got that information?"

"Don't worry, Mack. No phones were tapped, and no wires were used, just a little old-fashioned detective work."

"So, how's the information getting to Frydenberg?"

Donovan explains that Big Don and Frydenberg worked closely during the governor's election, so he believes that any juicy information known by one would be known by the other.

"But why would Buckman be willing to feed him information in the first place?"

"The same way all politicians get things they want, by promising something."

"But what can Big Don give Buckman?"

"He doesn't have to give him anything. A politician promises, giving is someone else's job."

"So, what do I do with a leaking deputy?"

"Put him on ice for now."

"On ice?"

"Yes, Sir. How about you give the boy a promotion. Appoint him to be O'Dell's assistant for the big search. Make sure O'Dell knows that he should delegate the kitchen sink to the boy. We want him so busy jumping through hoops that he doesn't have time to feed Slater anything except search-related information."

#

"There's an active life insurance policy on Richard R. Walker," Joad tells his boss.

"Dicky? In what amount?"

"Ten thousand dollars."

Donovan rubs his chin. "Skip, you've been studying his financial situation for a while now. How much would ten thousand dollars help his troubles?"

"It's not going to make him rich, but it easily covers all of his immediate debt and sets him up pretty well through to the end of the year."

"Well, there's no denying that this is a motive for murder; the prospect of losing the farm, gone with one swing of a sword."

Joad looks at him incredulously. "Do you really think he could have done that, Boss?"

"Actually, no, but we can't let our feelings rule it out. We have to follow the facts, and you can't deny the facts are heading in that direction."

"But we've been with this guy for a while now. Does he fit the profile for something like this?"

"That's not for me to say. That's a job for the psych boys. I think it's time to bring Ziggy in on the case."

#

Joad and Donovan are having a working lunch of burgers, fried potatoes, and pie in the courthouse conference room. Joad eats quietly, watching Donovan read the day's activity report written by himself.

When Donovan sets down the report, Joad says, "I have an idea I want to run by you, Boss."

"Nice job on the report, by the way. What's your idea?"

"I would like to set a little trap for Buckman that can prove he's the leaker."

"How would you go about it?"

"We make sure the deputy is waiting in the sheriff's outer office. Then, since the sheriff left his door open, Buckman hears the sheriff say he is going to talk to the Chester County Sheriff about an important witness. When that tidbit appears in the paper, we'll know for sure Buckman leaked it. We get Sheriff Johnson to play along. If anyone starts asking questions later, the witness in question is involved with an unrelated case."

Joad is watching Donovan's face as he seems lost in thought for a few minutes, then he tells his partner he has been thinking along the same lines.

"But instead of a mousetrap, Skip, how about a beartrap." After a pause, Donovan says, "You have a rundown of the stolen weapons, nothing particularly valuable, right?

"Just ordinary war souvenirs, Boss."

"Let's leak a story that the samurai sword is valuable antiquity, no details, keep it vague. If we get lucky, Fry is so busy he might run it without checking."

"How does that help us?"

Donovan explains that eventually, when the sword turns out to be nothing special, Fry will have some egg on his face. He also explains that getting out a story like that might help the sword resurface; for example, if it was actually stolen, or if someone who needs money has hidden it, the thing might suddenly show up somewhere.

"Somebody like Eugene? That's brilliant, Boss. How do I leak it?"

"Why don't you happen to run into Buckman at Reggie's. He should be there in about half an hour."

#

Lying in bed, Eugene has dozens of thoughts swirling in his mind like a tempest. Not the least of which is how shaken Margaret has become. Her love for him has been his only shield against the demons that have been haunting him for years. On top of all that, he feels personally responsible for Dicky becoming lost. How could he let anything become more important to him than making sure he safely made it back into the house? But worst of all is the dark feeling that his son is dead, a feeling that is becoming more indisputable with each passing day.

His mind is trapped in all of these thoughts spiraling out of control, repeating over and over and over. Exhaustion from too many sleepless hours over a period of days launches him into a terrifying realm, the place of demons that resides between his dark experiences of the past and the distressing reality of the present.

His disturbed mind places himself shivering in a muddy bomb crater, not shaking from cold but rather from terror. He sees a distant flash, the flash of an enemy round being launched from a cave on the distant mountain. He counts three seconds, and then a huge blast bounces him off of the ground. In that instant, with him two feet off of the ground, he sees his men huddled and screaming to him from their foxholes. He knows what he has to do. He times the blasts to dash to the next foxhole to tell them that they are safe. An unexpected blast knocks him to the ground. Terrified as the next shell is landing, he slides into a muddy hole. There he sees a dismembered hand holding a rosary, a hand that is still moving. Then, he realizes that it isn't an adult hand; it's the hand of a child. The hand opens so he can see it is holding a Buster Brown clicker. Then he can see Dicky lying face down in the mud.

He is screaming "Dicky!" over and over again as Margaret is shaking him violently, screaming herself for him to wake up. At last, fully awake, they sob together uncontrollably.

Eventually, Margaret goes back to bed. Eugene gets up. He finds a half-empty bottle of whiskey, a long-forgotten friend buried behind a scrub pail in the cabinet underneath the kitchen sink. Sitting at the kitchen table, the dusty old friend keeps him company as he waits for the morning, still hours away. Risking a return to sleep is out of the question.

Thursday—Dirt in the Snow

Joad, still groggy from getting up so early, is drinking black coffee from a paper cup as he waits in the idling Lincoln for the news truck to drop a bundle of Des Moines Tribune papers on the sidewalk in front of Eddy's newsstand. He has nodded off when the screech of the large truck's brakes shatters his peaceful slumber.

Shivering from the cold air, he unfolds the paper back inside the car. He scans the front page's columns dedicated to the lost boy story. He sees, *"In a surprising twist, an anonymous source revealed that the allegedly stolen samurai sword is an antiquity worth a large sum of money."*

#

When a stocky man, a regular customer, sits down at Reggie's counter, a cup of hot coffee is immediately set down in front of him, and the cook starts an order of bacon and eggs without his saying a word. While stirring a spoonful of sugar into his cup, the trucker sitting next to him folds the morning paper and sets it on the counter between them.

"Mind if I look at your paper?"

"Go ahead. I found it on the counter when I came in."

The paper has a large article about the planned search for the boy now missing for nine days. But when he notices the side article discussing war souvenirs stolen from the boy's farm, he sets down his cup cockeyed on its saucer, causing coffee to spill with some of the hot liquid making its way to his lap.

After a commotion of wiping and cursing, he scans the article to the bottom. When he sees the part about the sword being valuable, his pulse quickens.

"Geez!" he exclaims out loud before he gets up and leaves, forgetting about the bacon and eggs.

Three hours later, he pulls into a parking space in front of Rocky's Army Surplus in Moline. He stretches as he gets out of the car before slowly walking up to the storefront. He smiles as he sees the sword in the front window. A bell clangs above his head as he pushes open the aging wooden door. The place seems darker and dustier than it did the last time he was here as he walks up to the old, battered counter cluttered with junk. After a minute, he punches down the button on top of the round bell near the sign that reads, ring bell for service.

Not seeing or hearing any movement, he looks out the window to notice the deserted street. He moves closer to the window as he is thinking about just grabbing the sword and quietly leaving. As he is reaching for it, he hears footsteps creaking on the wooden floor, growing closer to him each second.

"I was beginning to think that nobody was here," he says as Rocky comes into view.

"I was in the back cleaning my rifle," he says with a smile. "At least that's what I tell people, so they will think twice before trying to steal from me."

"I was just looking at the sword in the window," the customer says nervously.

"A guy brought that in a few days ago. Hey, now that I look at you, wasn't it you who brought it in?"

"Yes, I'm sorry to say. When I got home, I started missing the stupid thing. You probably think I'm nuts."

Rocky starts talking about other customers who came back to buy things they sold him.

"I guess nostalgia is a funny thing," he finally concludes. Rocky is in a talkative mood. It takes a while for the customer to steer him back to buying the sword. He offers to pay a bit more than what Rocky gave him for his trouble. When another car pulls up out front, the stocky customer suddenly seems to remember that he's in a big hurry.

"What about the other stuff you brought in?"

"I don't really need that stuff. It's just the sword."

When the driver of the other car heads in a different direction, the customer breathes a bit easier. Rocky writes up the transaction on a slip of paper.

"Name?"

"Joe Anderson."

Rocky takes his cash and plunges the transaction slip onto an ancient receipt spindle adjacent to his antique cash register.

The Show

Big Don Slater is standing next to Gladys Henry's desk for at least the tenth time in the last twenty-four hours. On this visit, he is seeking confirmation that the sound system, podium, and portable seating will be ready at least one hour before tomorrow's eleven a.m. press conference; an event he had staged on the front steps of the stately Briggs County Courthouse Building to maximize the visual effect of the governor's visit.

"For the fifth time, yes," replies Gladys.

She then hands him the latest draft of the twenty-page press release outlining the logistical details of the all-out search.

"Is this the final draft?" he asks while thumbing through the document.

"Apparently, that's totally up to you," she replies with a sarcastic voice she has honed with over twenty-five years of secretarial work. "If you want fifty copies of this by eleven tomorrow, it had better be."

Slater sits down in a chair as he carefully scans the document.

"Geez!" he exclaims. "'Mallinckrodt' is spelled wrong on page six."

Mrs. Henry chuckles as she slides a corrected copy of page six across her desk.

"You got me!" Slater admits, now chuckling himself. "I like you, Gladys. How would you like a photo of yourself with the governor?"

The governor's limousine is scheduled to arrive a little before ten with a state police cruiser along to help avoid travel delays. Besides, it never hurts to arrive with some swagger. The extra hour will allow time for a conference room run-through of the carefully orchestrated event. The governor's remarks, which were written by Slater and polished by the communication's office in Des Moines, can be tweaked at that time if needed. Big Don is starting to relax about the big show he has worked so hard to prepare. The stated purpose is to make an appeal for hundreds of volunteers. Slater's real purpose is to grab a large handful of free publicity showing the governor looking as noble as possible.

#

"Hey, it must be Thursday," Rocky says when he sees his brother come into the store with a bag and a thermos.

His younger brother, Thomas, makes the drive across the Mississippi River from Davenport every Thursday for lunch. Thomas enjoys his brother's company but also likes to check in on him to see how he is managing with the store and his health. Just two years ago, Rocky was in much better shape. Unfortunately, Rocky has slowed down considerably, but Thomas is most concerned about his memory which seems to be getting worse almost every week.

After his usual friendly greeting, Thomas is looking at the items in the front window.

"Where's the samurai sword you had in the window?"

After learning that he sold it that morning, Thomas shows Rocky the article in the Des Moines Tribune.

"It must not be the same sword. This one is pretty common, definitely not worth a lot of money."

Then Thomas shows him the previous article, which lists the weapons that were stolen, including the sword, an M1 rifle, and a Japanese bolt action sniper rifle. The list matches those brought into his store last week. The article implies these weapons are of interest in a possible criminal investigation.

"I thought that guy seemed suspicious," says Rocky.

"I'll call the Briggs County Iowa Sheriff's Department to see if they're interested," says his brother.

#

"Hello, Mister Frydenberg. Whenever I hear a knock on the door, I know it must be you."

"Old habits die hard, Margaret. And again, please call me Fry."

"Come in. I just made some fresh coffee. The number of volunteer searchers is way down, so I've gone back to using my own percolator."

"That would be wonderful. The coffee at the diner tasted like it was three days old."

Frydenberg sits down at the kitchen table and stirs milk and sugar into his coffee. He takes a sip and sighs, remarking how very good it is.

After a quiet moment, he says, "I really just stopped by to see how you're doing. I'm running myself ragged, getting ready to cover the search on Saturday. I'm really sorry I couldn't stop by sooner."

"That's very nice of you to think of me. My friend told me I should be careful of what I say to reporters. I hope you understand."

"Of course, Margaret. I totally agree with your friend, because that's the same advice I would have given to you if I had been thinking properly. It's just because the story has gotten so big. When I was younger, trying to get ahead, I'm afraid I didn't always remember my ethical standards."

Frydenberg, while wondering if his nose is growing, assures Margaret that he has no interest in finding information for his reporting today. Then he goes on to probe deeply into her feelings, worries, and thoughts as if he were there to help counsel her in a difficult situation.

"I know you're a very devout woman, Margaret. That's something we all deeply admire. I have been praying that you are not being shaken in your faith." *Perhaps now he should check the sky for impending lightning*, he thinks to himself.

After a pause, Margaret admits that her faith is shaken.

"That's perfectly understandable, Margaret. How could a loving God do something like this to you?"

Frydenberg watches closely as Margaret's face grows cold. With watery eyes, she whispers, "I've thought about that a lot lately. Honestly, I just don't know."

#

Dr. Steven Ziegfeld is the assistant director of the FBI's Behavioral Psychology Department. At the request of Special Agent Donovan, he has spent the last four hours going over Agent Joad's daily case summaries that had found their way to FBI headquarters via the Western Union Telefax Network. He is preparing a preliminary analysis of Army First Lieutenant Eugene Walker, retired. He has paused his Dictaphone to better formulate a thought when the phone in his office rings.

"Did you have a chance to get through the case summary notes, Ziggy?"

"I'm halfway through writing my preliminary summary report."

"Here's the thing, Ziggy. I've gotten to know this guy since I've been here. He's as smart as anyone I've ever met, but he seems like a really decent guy, a war hero practically. He had a rough reentry from combat for a few years. But, for the last five years or so, he's been a model citizen; he got married, had a kid, he's respected in the community."

"So, what's the problem?"

"You've read the summaries. His kid's gone without a trace. I mean, they've combed the country for miles and nothing. We've rounded up every bad guy in a five-state area. The kicker is he's broke. He had opportunity and motive to the tune of a ten-thousand-dollar life insurance policy on the boy. But Ziggy, I can't for the life of me see this guy killing his son."

"Here's the thing, Donovan, I'm a psychologist; I've only done a very preliminary behavioral analysis. It all comes down to how badly he was traumatized in combat. I've reviewed the campaigns of the 77th Infantry Battalion in the Western Pacific, including Guam and Leyte. The Veteran's Administration has seen men who have endured that amount of shelling have flashbacks, troubled sleep, uncontrolled violent outbursts, and memory lapses. Many of these men have trouble leading a normal life, while others, who endured similar or even worse conditions, learn to suppress malevolent memories and tendencies."

"How can I tell which of these I'm dealing with?"

"First of all, for the purposes of this case, your best course is to assume the worst. If he's done nothing, it will all play out in time. Diagnostically, the best thing to do is have a candid talk with the wife. Keep in mind that it may take a bit of coaxing to get past her natural tendency to protect her husband. But, if he's been having outbursts, she will know. From the newspaper accounts, she's quite religious. You should be able to use that. If you ask her an unambiguous question, she will have a hard time hiding that she is lying."

"How do I deal with him?"

"With him, I suggest you subtly ratchet up the pressure. If he's been simmering, psychologically speaking, pressure might get him to boil over. And another thing, it may be difficult to get the truth out of someone like him. If I'm right, his subconscious will fight to protect him by burying all his painful memories, even new ones. His conscious mind might become lost and confused, not knowing what to believe. He may not even consciously remember doing it."

"I have to hand it to you, Ziggy. You picked up a lot in four hours."

"I've been reading the newspaper accounts all along. A whole lot of us here have been following the story. I was actually excited when you asked for my help."

"Before I forget," says Donovan, "I want to ask you about something I'm trying to get a read on. With so much time having passed, they must know that this big search is just looking for a body. Shouldn't they have realized by now that their son is almost certainly dead?"

"You would think that, but without actually seeing a body, the emotional mind just can't move that quickly. People, especially close family members, will go through a range of emotional states before they can reach a point of acceptance. Some of the wives of soldiers missing in action in the war still don't completely believe their husbands are dead."

"So, finding the boy, even if it's just his dead body, is a big deal."

"For the family, yes; it's a huge deal from a psychological standpoint. It may be their only chance to really move on."

After a pause, Donovan asks, "What if they don't find the body on Saturday?"

"That's the worst thing that could happen for the family unless..."

"Unless what?"

"Unless they already know they are not going to find him."

Donovan, silent for a few seconds, finally says, "I'm going to be needing more of your help Ziggy. For God's sake, don't take a vacation."

"Okay, Donovan. When you call this number, I'll try not to let it ring more than once."

#

Donovan is on another call when he looks up to see the sheriff's secretary, Mrs. Henry, excitedly trying to get his attention. He waves her into the office while he is still holding the phone to his ear. She hands him a note that says, "Come quick, there's a guy on the phone from Moline."

As Donovan is walking to the sheriff's office, he asks Gladys who Moline is. She looks at him incredulously as she explains that it is one of the Quad Cities. To make light of his ignorance, he smiles and says that he didn't know they all had names. The secretary rolls her eyes as she picks up the phone on her desk, saying, "I have Agent Donovan joining the call."

Mackintosh introduces Thomas Rakowski, whom he asks to repeat what he knows about the comings and goings of the samurai sword that had made its way to his brother's army surplus store in Moline, Illinois. The facts haltingly emerge as Thomas relays questions to his older brother Rocky who seems to be having trouble remembering important details. Donovan makes arrangements with the Rakowski brothers to meet with Agent Joad in the Moline store in a couple of hours.

After hanging up the phone, agent Joad is summoned to the sheriff's office. Donovan hands his partner his notes from the phone call telling him to ascertain if it is the same sword and the identity of the guy who sold it, then bought it back.

"This could be a big break, Skip. If the sword was actually stolen, it changes one huge aspect of the case."

#

Eugene is so on edge about meeting with Agent Donovan and Sheriff Mackintosh for the second time that he asks Margaret to drive the car. Eugene's bad dreams, lack of sleep, and anxiety about the purpose of being asked to come in again have his heart racing.

"Did they say why they wanted us to come in?" asks Eugene.

"The sheriff's secretary said they just wanted to give us an update on the investigation." She looks at him for a moment and then adds, "You asked me that before, Gene. Are you alright?"

"I did? I'm sorry, Margaret. This whole thing is making me a little crazy."

#

As they walk up to the building, Margaret can't stop thinking about Eugene forgetting the reason they were asked to meet with Donovan and Mackintosh so soon after they had talked about that very thing. Eugene's mind seeming to unravel has shaken her to the core.

Now seeing the sheriff's secretary waiting for them at the entrance, Margaret's mind feels numb. When she and her husband are ushered through the doorway into the ornate conference room, she feels like she has entered another world, a place where her life will never be the same again.

#

Donovan rises and shakes Eugene's hand and then holds Margaret's chair for her to sit.

"The sheriff will be joining us shortly. Thanks so much for coming in. Help yourself to coffee, water, and donuts. The donuts are fresh, so dig in before the sheriff gets his hands on them."

Donovan feels relieved as the sheriff walks in the door. He can see that the couple is on edge, and he is quickly running out of small talk. The sheriff thanks them for coming in and tells them that the purpose of today's meeting is to give them an update about what they have found out over the last two days.

"We have learned a few things since we last talked to you," says Donovan. "But I'm afraid we haven't made much in the way of real progress." He goes on to explain that they have been able to find and question all of the potential kidnapping suspects and that all but one of them have been ruled out.

"What can you tell us about the last one?" asks Margaret.

Donovan explains that FBI agents are required to go through an exhaustive process before ruling out a suspect. In this particular case, he explains, the suspect from Minnesota has met all of the criteria for being ruled out except one; he does not have a substantiated alibi for the time period in question.

"We can't officially rule him out, but at the same time, we're fairly certain that he's not our man."

"Oh, dear God," Margaret says under her breath. She reaches into her purse for a handkerchief to wipe her eyes. It's painfully obvious that she is gravely disappointed by that information. Eugene puts his arm around her shoulder.

The sheriff then launches into summarizing plans for Saturday's search. They've heard the general planning points before but today they learn the tactical details of the daylong search. He finishes by listing all of the equipment and organizations dedicated to the endeavor.

Margaret asks the sheriff what she and Eugene should do during the search.

"You're welcome to participate in any way you choose, of course. But I think it would be best if you were to stay out of sight. There will be hundreds of people in the area and dozens of reporters. We will instruct reporters to stay away from the family on the morning of the search, but we can't legally stop them if they choose to ignore us. Maybe it would be best for you to stay at a friend's house. Whatever you decide, please let me know personally, so I will be able to reach you if needed at all times during the day."

After several more minutes of questions and answers, the discussion finally winds down.

Okay, Donovan thinks to himself, *here comes the tricky part.* He is about to say, "Oh, by the way," as if what he is about to talk about is of minor importance. In fact, he is about to begin the real reason for the meeting.

"Oh, by the way, a few items came up that I hope you can help me with. First of all, Eugene, I would like to get your permission to search the hog lot. You see, the lab guys think that in the unlikely event an unfortunate accident happened in that regard that there might be a chance to find identifiable traces. As you know, it's not very likely, but you can see that if that did work, that would answer a whole lot of issues for all of us. We think of it as leaving no stone unturned, as the old saying goes."

As Donovan is finishing this dialogue that he has practiced, he feels like perhaps he had not practiced it enough.

When he is greeted with silence, he adds, "Would that be alright with you, Eugene?"

Eugene agrees but says nothing else. Donovan is hoping he may use the opportunity to ask why his hogs are still being held. There's no factual reason to hold them at this point, but Donovan, on the advice of Dr. Ziegfeld, is trying to keep pressure on the potential suspect.

"Thanks, Eugene. We really appreciate your cooperation. Now, if you could just go with the sheriff to sign the form, that will be all we need today." As Eugene is getting up to follow the sheriff, Donovan adds, "Margaret can stay here while Eugene signs the form. It'll just take a few moments."

As the door shuts, Donovan smiles at Margaret, saying, "You look very lovely today, Mrs. Walker. Your husband is a very lucky man."

After Margaret thanks him, he tells her that he has a couple of questions.

"I know you've both been under a lot of pressure, and everybody deals with pressure in their own way. I wanted to ask you if your husband has been more irritable over the last weeks?"

Margaret's face looks confused as she quietly says, "No."

"What about sleeping? Has he had trouble sleeping? That would be completely understandable, of course."

Margaret brings her hand up to touch her cross. "I...I... would say no more than anyone would expect under the circumstances."

"Has he had nightmares or flashbacks to his time in the war?"

Margaret is thinking about his screaming in his sleep as her right hand unconsciously holds the cross in her fist, "Not that I know of."

"What about memory lapses? Has he had any of those?"

Margaret has tears welling up in her eyes. "Not that he's told me about."

Donovan knows that it's time to back off. It would be just too cruel to push her anymore right now.

"Thank you, Margaret. I'm sorry if I made you feel uncomfortable. One of the hardest things about my job is that sometimes I have to upset really wonderful people like you."

Gladys Henry is stationed as a lookout while Donovan is interviewing Margaret. The sheriff is clumsily stalling the signature process to give his coconspirator more time. She was instructed to pop her head in the door, asking if they needed anything if Eugene were to leave the sheriff's office. That would be Donovan's signal to quickly wrap things up. Fortunately, Donovan was able to finish.

#

Driving home, both Margaret and Eugene feel like they have been put through a ringer once more. Margaret is upset that the kidnapping leads, like everything else, have floated away. Looking out the car window, she sees that the once brilliantly white snowdrifts have become much smaller and are infested with grime.

"My! The snow's getting dirty," she says.

She realizes that as the days pass, the bright hopes that she has continuously prayed for are becoming smaller and darker like the snow drifts, the drifts that others believe might be hiding a dark and painful truth.

"Where are you, Dicky?" Margaret says under her breath. As she is thinking about the questions Donovan asked her about her husband; she hears the question that she had just whispered reflect back into her mind. Is Donovan thinking that Eugene may have done something to Dicky? Her heart races, she feels her face flush, and she starts to feel sick to her stomach.

"Dear God," gutturally ushers from between her teeth.

#

Gladys Henry, with the help of her friend at the AAA office on First Street, has Agent Joad convinced that he will be able to make his way to the address of Rocky's shop on Rivers Drive in Moline, Illinois.

After a bit of circling in the Quad Cities, he pulls into a parking space right in front of the shop he feared he might never see.

After another half-hour, Joad, with the help of Rocky's encyclopedic knowledge of military weapons, is convinced that the M1 rifle and the Japanese sniper rifle match those in the photographs taken by the Des Moines Tribune photographer.

"Does that sword in the photo look like the one you had in your window?"

"It's the same one," says Rocky with confidence. "I remember that deep scratch," he says while pointing to the handle of the sword.

"That's great, Rocky. And the guy that sold them to you is the same guy who bought them back this morning?"

"Absolutely."

"Do you have documentation for the sale?"

"Just the ticket on the spindle," he says while pointing at the spindle peg on the cluttered sales desk.

After several minutes, Rocky is able to produce the transaction slip for both the initial sale on March 14 and today's purchase on March 16. On the first ticket, the name box is empty; on the second ticket, the name appears as Joe Anderson.

Agent Joad writes down the description of Joe Anderson in his case notebook: the man is of average height, stocky, short hair, about thirty-five. When Joad asks if he can remember anything else, Rocky says he wore a round wristwatch with a black leather band. When he can't get any more details from the shop owner, the agent worries that his boss won't be very happy with him bringing back the description matching about half of the men in the state.

"Did you get a look at his car?"

"It's black."

"Can you tell me anything else about the car?"

"Not really, just a car."

"Did you notice the license plate?"

"I think I wrote it down."

Joad, at first excited about this revelation, loses his enthusiasm as Rocky spends an hour, with the help of his brother, looking for a scrap of paper that he thought bore the car's plate number.

When pressed, Rocky remembers that the plate was yellow. Then he thinks he remembers the number ten vertically along the left side.

"That must be an Iowa plate from county number ten," says Rocky's brother. "Iowa prints each county's number on the left side of the plate"

"Do you know how the county numbers are determined?" asks Joad.

"I'm not sure, but I think they're alphabetical. I'm from Scott County; its number is 84."

Joad seems to remember seeing yellow Iowa license plates around Temperance with the number ten on them.

"I think we may have just caught a break. Think hard, Rocky. Can you remember any of the other numbers on the plate, even if it's just one or two of them?"

Rocky closes his eyes, then he says, "I think it has a four and a five on it."

#

Eugene tends to the late afternoon milking session in utter silence. He couldn't bring himself to turn on the radio, and he found he had nothing to say to the cows. As his full milk pale clangs on the cement floor, he is reminded of how that sound would often summon Holly, the cheerful cat that Dicky used to love to follow around the yard.

Thinking about Holly brings back the image of her carcass being picked apart by a crow. It isn't long before other dark memories are penetrating his thoughts, memories of other dismembered bodies. These assault his mind unmercifully as he hears himself screaming as if he is someone else attempting to stop the attack. The screaming causes the cows to jerk violently against the stanchion restraining their necks. The commotion loosens the grip of the mental fist that seems to be straining against his sanity, trying to pull it away forever.

"Dear God, help me!" he cries out. "Make it stop."

Eunice turns her head to look at him with sad eyes before turning back to her feed. The cow, seeming a sympathetic friend, somehow breaks the spell on him, at least temporarily. As he is returning to the house, he realizes that there's no way he will be able to eat.

Inside, Margaret places a half-empty pan of reheated casserole on the table for them. It's crusty and dry.

"I warmed up leftovers. I'm sorry it doesn't look very good."

Margaret looks beyond tired. Just a few hours ago, she looked so beautiful.

Now she looks bewildered and lost.

"I'm glad you didn't fuss. I really don't think I can eat anything tonight."

"I don't think I can eat anything either."

#

Agent Joad cut a half-hour off of his driving time from Moline. It wasn't until he was almost back that he realized his big mistake; he should have asked for Rocky's permission to bring back the other stolen weapons. He briefly thinks about going back to Moline but decides that he needs to give his boss the incomplete information that he did get and just admit his bigger mistake.

He begins his briefing with his confession, deciding to face the music as soon as possible. Instead of browbeating him, both Donovan and Mackintosh share stories of embarrassing rookie mistakes they had made in the past. Then Joad briefs his boss and sheriff Mackintosh about the information he did manage to obtain while referring to his notes.

"So, he lost a scrap of paper with the license plate number."

"His brother and I searched with him for an hour; no luck. The brother said he was going to keep looking and phone in if he finds it," says Joad.

"But we have a general description of a guy whose plate indicates he is from this county," says the sheriff.

"Yes, a stocky guy," adds Joad.

"Hold on," says the sheriff as he picks up his phone. "I've got a hunch."

He tells Gladys Henry to get the state police in Des Moines on the line.

"What are you thinking, Mack?"

"Hold on a second," answers the sheriff.

When he gets the state police headquarters on the phone, he identifies himself and asks them to look up the license plate number of David Davis in Briggs County. He hangs up the phone after asking them to call him back with the information. Fifteen minutes later, his phone rings. They read him the number, which he writes down on a phone message pad, which he then hands to Donovan.

"Skip, it says his plate number is ten, 45311."

"What kind of car does he drive, Sheriff?" asks Joad.

"He's at the farm almost every day. I believe it's a black Chevrolet," says Mackintosh.

"Normally, I'm not much of a hunch guy, Sheriff. But I think you may be turning me around," says Donovan.

"You know this ID is thin, right?" says Mackintosh. "A partial plate, a general description, and a car that will match a whole lot of others."

"You're right, Mack; it's probably just a coincidence. The problem is that I don't believe much in those either."

Friday—Falling Apart

Gladys is overseeing the final stages of the press conference preparations in front of the building when she sees an immaculate, black Lincoln Continental round the corner. A few seconds later, the car, led by a black and white highway patrol cruiser, pulls into the parking lot to the side of the building. She opens the door to wave at the county attorney's secretary, who has been waiting to be alerted to the governor's arrival. O'Dell is standing at the side entrance as the governor walks up to the building.

"Kenneth O'Dell," the county attorney says while holding out his hand.

"Nice to finally meet you in person, Kenny," the governor responds with a smile. "It's been a long drive to work this morning. I could really use some coffee, and if you have a doughnut around somewhere, that would be even better."

"Right this way."

The bald and rotund governor is on his second cup of coffee and third donut while seeming to not be listening to O'Dell layout a summary of the actual search plans.

"I think I've got the picture, Kenny," he says after a sip of coffee. "Let's run through the news conference."

Don Slater hands his boss the outline of the news conference. The outline is in the same format that the governor has seen on dozens of previous occasions.

"Why not let me go last, Don."

"I would have like to have done it that way, Governor, but this show has more moving parts than a standard presser. I don't want to take a chance on letting the TV guys run out of patience or film before getting to your remarks. Plus, the general going last, describing the incredible power he is bringing to bear by your authority, will place a strong exclamation point on your willingness to do whatever is necessary for the people of the state."

Mallinckrodt looks at Slater thoughtfully for a moment before smiling and nodding.

"Can I just say that I'm a little worried about volunteers," O'Dell interjects. "I understand that the number of volunteers has greatly diminished over the last week. When we started planning this thing, we were all optimistic about getting enough citizen volunteers, but now I'm starting to worry we may not get enough to meet our searching goals."

"I asked the general just yesterday if it would be possible to increase the National Guard numbers. The answer was no."

"I know that, Don. I'm just thinking we need to make as strong of an appeal as possible to get people out to search." O'Dell turns to the governor and says, "I'm just asking that at the very end of the general's remarks, either he or I make a final, strong appeal for volunteers."

"I think Kenny's got a point, Don. But I think I should do it," says the governor.

A big smile comes across Slater's face, "Brilliant, that's even better."

"I'm just glad you finally agree with me, Don," chided the governor. "Is there any Danish?"

#

While the news conference is going on, Sheriff Mackintosh is waiting on a lonely stretch of gravel road along Rural Route 2, Apex, Iowa. As David Davis's black sedan comes over the top of the hill, the sheriff briefly turns on his flashing red light. When Dub's car stops, the sheriff waves him over to his vehicle.

"Sorry, Sheriff, I run a little fast when I'm on the lonely sections of the route."

"Were you speeding?" asks the sheriff.

After a bit of hesitation, Dub says, "I'm not sure, actually."

Mackintosh laughs. He tells Dub that he didn't pull him over for his driving.

"Hop in. I'd like to ask you about these," the sheriff says as he hands Dub the photo of the weapons hanging on the wall in Eugene's grinding room.

"I'd appreciate it if you guys can recover that stuff for us."

The sheriff notices that he doesn't appear nervous; no indication yet that he might be lying.

"Is that your sword?"

"No, everything else is mine, but the sword belongs to Eugene."

The sheriff asks Dub how Eugene obtained the sword. Dub's account matches Eugene's.

"When I asked your friend about it, he seemed to be saying that his actions were not particularly worthy of the decoration he received."

"That sounds like him, but I, and everyone else in our unit, will tell you that without Lieutenant Walker's bravery, none of us would have survived."

"Have you ever heard of an Army Surplus store in Moline?"

"In Illinois? No, should I have?"

"A guy by the name of Rakowski said a man matching your description made some transactions with weapons matching those in the picture."

"One-hundred percent it wasn't me. It must have been some other really good-looking guy."

The sheriff chuckles as he tells Dub he better get back to work.

#

Sally Brown adds a tick mark next to room 214 on the switchboard call log; it's Frydenberg's twenty-fifth call of the day. This one is person-to-person to editor Ben Bray at the Des Moines Tribune.

"Thanks for returning my call, Fry. I know you're busy, but I just wanted to check in with you to see if you have everything you need to pull this one off."

Frydenberg tells his boss that he's confident he will have the news conference story on the news desk well before the deadline.

"Great. How's it shaping up to cover the all-out search tomorrow?"

"That's a different story, Chief. I'll do the best I can, but it will be a miracle from God if it comes off without a hitch. I'm going to write most of the story tonight, before the fact. That way, I will have the patchwork ready, so I can save time trying to piece the final story together ahead of the Sunday Edition deadline. Whoever decided to have this search on a Saturday should have his brain in a jar in Iowa City."

"We can't always manufacture the news, Fry. I'm sure Don Slater did his best. Are you sure you've got everything you need from me?"

Frydenberg looks down at what was once a neat outline of his plan for covering the story. Almost every other word on the triple-spaced pages is edited with blue pencil. The result of which is that he can only momentarily decipher the written plan after some mind-numbing concentration.

The reporter is feeling good about covering the mechanics of the search. The best way to convey the magnitude of the enormous search is with pictures. The paper has released two staff photographers supplemented with two freelancers under contract. He is also starting to feel good about the groundwork he is laying for the print stories. His biggest worry is if the body is discovered late in the day. In that case, beating the deadline will become much more difficult. He knows the search teams will be instructed to fire a smoke grenade upon finding the body. The circling army helicopter will then hover over the site of the body. Law enforcement officials will then set up roadblocks to keep the public out of the area. He scratches, "Tell photographers to be on alert for helicopters hovering over smoke."

As he is looking at the disorder of the outline, he resolves to find the time to retype it once again. Shaking his head, he realizes that the only way for him to operate at this point is by the seat of his pants.

Crossing his fingers, he says, "I've got it under control, Chief; it's in the bag."

#

As Madeline sees Margaret getting out of her car in the driveway, she realizes she has never seen her looking more disheveled.

"You've miss buttoned your blouse, dear," Madeline says as she pours her best friend a cup of coffee.

As Margaret looks down at her blouse, she notices that there are food stains on it as well. As tears well up in her eyes, she says, "I'm falling apart."

Madeline sets the cup and saucer in front of her, slips her arm around her shoulder, and then kisses her on top of her head.

"No one on earth could have kept it together as well as you have. Just look there," Madeline says as she points at her wall calendar. The month of March has a cross drawn on each day, starting on the sixth.

Madeline draws a cross on today's date as she says, "That's eleven crosses. Even God needed a rest after only six." After a pause, she adds, "How much can God expect one person to endure?"

Margaret is looking down, almost as if she is not listening. After a long pause, she whispers, "It's not just losing my little boy; it's slowly losing him like a saucer of water that evaporates, water that seems to never diminish until finally, one day, you notice that it is gone; his dear soul slowly fading into oblivion."

Madeline, beside herself, wanting desperately to do something to help her, softly says, "I think we should pray."

Margaret, her face flushing scarlet, eyes squinting, jaw muscles flexing, turns to face Madeline, saying, "I think it's too late for that."

Now shaken by her friend's reaction and at a loss for what to do or say, Madeline finally utters, with tentative conviction, "I know you don't mean that, Margaret."

"I can't do this anymore!" Margaret screams and breaks down, sobbing.

Madeline draws her into her arms. Sobbing with her, she says, "Let it all out. You can't hold it in anymore. Just let it all out."

#

After both women are completely drained by the longest cry of their lives, Margaret begins to confide in her darkest thoughts and fears. She whispers into her best friend's ear that she thinks Dicky is dead, and she is worried that Eugene may have had something to do with it.

Later, when she starts her car to leave, a thought hits her. Instead of going home, she drives toward Dub's apartment in the tiny village of Apex.

Dub's shirt is unbuttoned as he answers his door.

"Margaret!" he exclaims while nervously trying to button his shirt.

Margaret pretends not to notice the monumental mess in his apartment. She moves a stack of newspapers off of a chair while telling him that she wants to ask him some questions about Eugene.

"Gene has started having nightmares again," she says. "He woke up screaming Dicky's name over and over."

"I'm not a shrink, but I think that's not too surprising when you take into account what he has been, I, I mean, what both of you have been going through."

"He's having memory lapses, too."

"Really, what kind of memory lapses?"

"He has started asking me the same question he just asked a moment ago, and I think he's having flashbacks of the war."

Dub bites his lip. "He's been..., you've both been through so much."

"Tell me about the war, Dub. Neither of you has ever told me anything about that."

Dub looks away, saying, "It's hard to talk about."

"Tell me what it did to Gene."

#

Dub's heart is breaking for Margaret and his best friend. He loves them both so much. What she is asking is very difficult. But he realizes that he will do anything she asks, even this thing that he loathes to think about, no less talk about.

"We all faced a lot of fighting; we saw men, kids really, we knew getting killed. But we all knew that going in." Then, more softly, he looks away, "It was the shelling, Margaret. In the dark, the deepest darkness you can imagine hunkered down in slit trenches and bomb craters, muddy from all the rain, the shells started exploding all around us, night after night. The flashes were as bright as the sun with concussions that numbed the ears and mind back into the blackness. We were all scared to the point that Gene, the unit commander, was afraid the men would just jump up and run away, which would have gotten them killed. So, he swallowed his own fear, going from hole to hole, risking his own life, calmly telling the men between blasts that they were perfectly safe in their trenches and that the enemy was only shelling them to keep them awake. I don't think we would have been able to get through it without him."

Margaret, waiting for a moment to see if Dub would go on, finally asks, "But what happened to him?"

"Oh, God," Dub begins softly. "One of his young men, alone in a bomb crater, took a direct hit, blowing him to bits. Gene was never the same after that."

"That's terrible, but I still don't understand," Margaret says.

"There's more, Margaret, but he made me swear to never talk about it. I think he's afraid that if he has to think about it again, he will lose his mind."

"How did, whatever it was, change him?"

"He stopped caring if he died, and he lost his faith in God."

#

Agent Joad, having driven through the rolling countryside of eastern Iowa, rolls into a parking spot in front of Rocky's store yet again. Before he's gotten out of his car, Rocky's brother Thomas pulls in beside him.

"You made good time," says Thomas. "I thought you wouldn't be here for at least another half-hour."

"You don't have to worry as much about speeding tickets if you have a badge like mine," Joad says while offering a handshake.

Inside, Joad lays out a few photographs showing different men, which match the general description given by Rocky. Among them is a photo of David Davis.

"Do any of these men look familiar?"

Rocky studies the pictures while scratching his head.

"Geez, I don't know."

"Take your time, Rocky."

Rocky breathes in and out. Another car pulls up outside, which distracts him for a second. When the driver gets out and heads in another direction, he turns his attention back to the photos.

"It's hard to say for sure, maybe this one," he says while pointing to the photograph of a Minnesota fishing guide.

"How about this photo?" Joad says, pointing to a picture of Davis standing by his car.

"That kind of looks like the car, alright. Maybe that's him."

Then Joad sets those two photos side by side.

"So, do you think one of these guys could be the man?"

Rocky is growing tired of looking at pictures. The more Joad asks him if he is sure, the more he waffles. Joad has sized Rocky up as a guy with an unreliable memory.

Joad thanks Rocky and his brother for their help. He then informs them that he will be taking the other weapons that the suspect sold to Rocky. He explains that they may be able to get some fingerprints off of those.

Saturday—Consequences of Truth

Kenny O'Dell is eating a hearty breakfast in Reggie's at the unearthly hour of five a.m. He is grateful that the weather is turning out to be perfect. The week's weather, with every day's high above freezing and yesterday's high of fifty-five degrees, has melted all of the snow on open ground. The high today, expected to be in the seventies, should make short work of the small remaining drifts.

O'Dell has found the planning ordeal to be much more tiring than his typical occupation dealing with petty crimes and minor legal disputes. His mind is swimming from the lack of sleep. The one thing he feels excited about is that after today he will be out of the search planning business for good.

Glancing at the newspaper's coverage of yesterday's press conference, he wonders for the dozenth time if he is forgetting something. The scrambled eggs in his stomach are bouncing around as he realizes that if the search goes sideways, the blame will very publicly fall on him. The governor and Don Slater, in his office just yesterday, made it unmistakably clear that no political fallout was going to land on them.

As he sets his fork down after eating only half of his eggs, he looks up to see a convoy of drab-green trucks from the west stream by on US Highway 20.

"What do you suppose that's about?" says the waitress warming up his coffee for the fifth time.

"That's elements of the 133rd infantry brigade of the Iowa National Guard heading to Summit."

"Summit? Why Summit?"

O'Dell opens the Des Moines Tribune that is sitting on the counter beside him and sets it in front of her.

"That's why."

#

Margaret quickly dresses after hearing Eugene go out the backdoor on his way to the early milking session.

She is exhausted from another night of his nightmare-induced screaming. Though he promised to stay awake, their long exhausting ordeal is too much for any man to overcome. She believes he is losing his grip on sanity.

She places a sandwich on the table next to her note which says that she is going to spend the day at Madeline's house to avoid reporters and the pressures of the day's activities. She remembers Donovan's questions about Gene's state of mind. She wonders how he knew to ask that, and she's afraid to know what it means.

Pulling over the first hill out of sight of the place that has been the home of so much tension over the last weeks feels liberating. Suddenly, she feels almost elation at the prospect of a quiet respite with her best friend, Madeline. Following her normal route to the parsonage near Summit Christian Church, she finds herself driving directly past the high school, which today is the headquarters of the massive search for her son. The usually lonely little town is unrecognizable on this morning. As she is passing countless army and police vehicles parked along the road, an army helicopter thumps the air directly over the top of her car. Before long, she has to slow down to a crawl due to a confusion of pedestrian traffic jutting onto her path. Her heart is pounding as she tries to shield her face hoping against hope that no one will recognize her.

She is a nervous wreck as she runs up to Madeline's door feeling like she is running away from a mob.

"Have you been by the school?" she blurts out as Madeline comes to the door.

"Come in, dear," Madeline says as she draws Margaret into her arms. "You're safe here."

Margaret follows her best friend into the kitchen, where she is getting ready to make a batch of oatmeal cookies.

"Put on that apron over there. I think it will do us both a lot of good to make a double batch of my grandmother's oatmeal cookies."

As Margaret puts on the apron, she feels the tension start to slip away. Focusing on measuring and mixing is a tonic for her spirit. A half-hour later, they are shuffling baking sheets into the oven every eight minutes as the aroma of fresh, hot cookies fills the kitchen.

"I feel so much better," Margaret says as they relax with a coffee and a plate of warm cookies an hour after that.

"I learned it from my grandmother. She told me that whenever something is bothering me to mix up a batch of these cookies. I don't know what it is about making cookies, but it always helps me feel better."

Madeline mentioning her grandmother's advice causes Margaret to remember the coin and advice given to her by her own grandfather. Margaret, now calmer, endeavors to seek Madeline's help with these questions in her heart.

Looking intently at Madeline, she whispers, "I think God is punishing me."

#

Madeline, as a minister's wife, has found herself drawn into the role of counselor many times. She has learned to let a troubled person spill out their feelings as much as possible without dismissing their thinking out of hand, no matter how silly or crazy it may seem. In this case, however, Madeline decides to buck her instincts.

"You have been through so much, Margaret. Anyone would feel that way in your circumstance."

Margaret noticeably bristles at this. "I'm serious, Madeline!"

Madeline has also learned that confession is good for the soul.

"I'm sorry, Margaret. Please tell me what you think you've done."

"My grandfather gave me an old coin when I was ten. Anyway, he warned me that losing the coin would be a curse. My father scolded me, saying how wicked it is to believe in a curse, that it violates the First Commandment of honoring God."

"What does the coin have to do with anything?"

"Two days ago, when I was getting ready to go to the courthouse, I noticed that it was missing from my jewelry box. I know that I shouldn't have, but I became panicked that I had carelessly lost it and that this was the curse that had taken Dicky away from me for good. God has been testing me from the start. I used to believe that my faith was strong and unflappable. But God has always known the truth about me. He just needed all of this to happen to show me just how weak my faith truly is."

"You shouldn't blame yourself for a thought planted in your head by your grandfather's traditions. You were just drawn into all that in a moment of weakness."

"You don't understand, Madeline. I just can't let go of the thought that the coin has really cursed me and my family." With tears welling up, she whispers, "God knows everything I am thinking. He knows I'm putting all of this ahead of my faith in Him." Breaking down, sobbing, she blurts out, "God tests everyone at some point. He is testing me now. I know what He sees. His justice, my justice, can't, won't be denied."

Margaret is sobbing again. Madeline knows that crying is good for her; it's her broken heart trying to release the unbearable stress. She kneels on the floor next to her dear friend, wrapping her arms around her, softly saying, "Let it all out, dear," as they now sob together. Madeline wants her to cry as long as possible while knowing that just crying will never be enough.

#

Twenty minutes after putting his fork down, O'Dell turns off of the highway onto First Street at the edge of the little town that, on this day, will be stuffed with people like never before. He sees the parking lot across from the Catholic church already filling up with the school buses that will be transporting volunteer searchers to the patchwork of search grids laid out over the fourteen-square-mile area as recommended by the Civil Air Patrol.

As he heads north towards the railroad tracks, he passes the little league baseball field, which today has been commandeered to be the landing pad for two Army MH-6 "Little Bird" helicopters. He continues past the town's meager two-block-long business district, then he turns west to make his way to Briggs High School. The school's parking lot and football stadium will today be the staging area for the massive search, while its gymnasium will be used as the command post for search operations.

Turning onto Fifth Street, his nostrils are assaulted by the diesel exhaust of the long line of idling army personnel transport trucks parked on the grass directly in front of the school. As he pulls into the half-full school parking lot, he notices an empty space near the side door labeled reserved for the principal. He pulls into the spot without hesitation.

Inside the gymnasium, he finds a dozen folding tables and chairs set up on the main floor, with seating also available on the collapsible bleachers unfolded for the occasion. Against the wall, he spots what he has been looking for, five huge coffee urns with boxes of disposable cups.

Over the next hour, volunteer searchers file into the gymnasium. As they enter, Red Cross volunteers direct them to report to the Civil Air Patrol table to receive their search group assignment and bus number. From there, they are directed to the coffee line and finally to take seats on the bleachers. O'Dell has directed that the center floor area is to remain open for the three hundred National Guard troupes who will file in at 6:25 a.m. Five minutes after that, O'Dell is scheduled to welcome the searchers and introduce those giving final instructions. The hope is to have searches underway before 7:00 a.m. in order to maximize the eleven hours of daylight available.

Frydenberg has been making the rounds with the various authorities and some of the volunteers, getting names, asking questions, and writing down quotes. Ohlman, his photographer, has been busy snapping pictures and reloading his camera. O'Dell has deflected Frydenberg's question about the apparent lack of volunteers several times. His constant answer is that they will have more than enough searchers for the job.

At 6:20 a.m., O'Dell and the Civil Air Patrol officers huddle near the microphone stand. They are all really concerned by the relatively light turnout of civilian volunteers. The group decides to start the search on schedule, with additional teams being formed and sent to search as latecomers arrive. O'Dell tells the group he will request that Sheriff Mackintosh's office implore the radio stations to make frequent on-air appeals for additional volunteers.

The army troupes marching in and then standing in ranks on the gymnasium floor makes an impressive showing that quiets down the throng. O'Dell seizes the opportunity to, in turn, welcome the officers, soldiers, and volunteers before they have a chance to return to their unruly nature. After clearly stating the objective and logistics of the day's search, he turns over the microphone to Civil Air Patrol Captain Stork to explain the search strategy and tactics.

"Each assigned bus group will be led by either a Civil Air Patrol officer or a citizen leader who will be wearing a lanyard containing their credentials.

The civilian leaders were chosen because of their firsthand knowledge of that particular area. When your assigned area is completed, you will be directed to return to your bus. You will be driven to another nearby grid to continue searching. Each group will be taken to the food tent located two blocks south of here at staggered times in the middle of the day for a half-hour lunch period. Please follow directions and work quickly. We have a lot of search grids that must be finished before sunset. If you find the lost boy, your team leader will deploy a smoke grenade. When one of the two patrolling helicopters sees the smoke, it will alert authorities on the ground and then hover over the site. You are not to touch anything, that's very important. Your leader will direct you to form a fifty-foot diameter circle around the site. You will let no one inside, with the exception of the county attorney and law enforcement officials."

Watching as the buses are quickly filled and deployed, O'Dell feels relief. When he turns to go back into the gymnasium, he finds Frydenberg standing so close behind him that he is startled. Feeling frazzled and tired, he weighs to pros and cons of punching the guy in the face.

"What are you thinking at this point, Mr. O'Dell?" asks the reporter.

"Only if we can go off the record," he replies, knowing that telling the reporter he was thinking about popping him in the nose is a bad idea, especially if he gets quoted as saying it.

"Okay, off the record?"

After a pause, he says, "I'm thinking about how proud I am of this community."

After the reporter leaves, he feels a bit silly for feeding the hungry reporter such an apple-pie quote while insisting it is off the record. On the other hand, there was no way he was going to trust the reporter with what he was really thinking, even off the record.

#

As Eugene is walking back to the house, he sees Margaret just going out of sight down the road. Inside he is relieved to see Margaret's note. He is so full of anxiety that it only makes it worse having someone else around. Perhaps now alone, he can find a tiny bit of peace, but can he? He decides that he must try to look within himself for something, that thing that he has been hiding from for far too long, the truth.

Eugene walks out into the empty farmyard. He notices the old Farmall tractor under the tree. All of the snow that had buried it has now melted away. He recalls a happy memory; his son sitting on his lap on that tractor. Not knowing why, he goes to the cantankerous contraption and goes through the machinations of starting it up. Now sitting in the throbbing saddle, he tries to conjure the memory of his son in his lap.

Missing his son, he drives down the muddy road to the big rock by the creek. Sitting there, he feels terribly alone. He closes his eyes tightly and tries for the hundredth time to remember seeing Dicky walk to the house on that afternoon, the day he saw his son for the last time. Like every other time he has tried this, he just can't remember a thing.

He concludes that he just didn't look that way; he can't remember something he didn't see. So, for the first time, he tries to remember what he did see that afternoon. He remembers that Tom Magnus was with him. He can't remember the end of his discussion with him. As his heart skips a beat, he realizes he can't even remember Magnus leaving. Then, with his heart pounding, he tries as hard as he can to remember anything he did or saw after Dicky left for the house; he is terrified when he can't.

"Dear God, what is the truth?" he shouts to the sky.

The terrible dreams race through his mind; he wants to know what those mean. The visions of his son dismembered; those can't be real. The gaps in his memory; what happened during those times?

He stands up and runs as fast as he can to burn up some of the energy that's consuming him. He must find a way to think more clearly. After running in the heavy mud until he can't take another step, he rests on his haunches, trying to catch his breath. He forces himself to use his intellect to coldly consider these thoughts. Almost at once, he realizes with certainty that he must be losing his mind. It takes him a few moments to get from there to the fact that he really can't trust his memory. His thinking eventually rolls around to a terrible thought; if a crazy person is seeing a delusion such as that he is back in combat, then he could be capable of doing almost anything and quite possibly block the terrible thing out of his mind.

These thoughts, fitting together like a jigsaw puzzle, release his mind from the torture of repetitive thoughts that have been churning in his mind for days. Suddenly, overcome with utter exhaustion and hunger, he remembers the sandwich he left on the kitchen table.

Later, after devouring it, he sits on his bed. His mind and body, at the end of endurance, compel him to curl into the fetal position, and he quickly falls into the bottomless abyss of deep, inescapable sleep.

#

After thinking about the evidence connecting Dub Davis to the missing sword, Mackintosh is beginning to have his doubts. It didn't take much convincing to get Donovan to agree with him.

"We're a country mile from reasonable doubt," says the sheriff.

"The evidence is as clear as a glass of Mississippi river water," adds Joad.

"River water? I think you've spent a little too much time in the Quad Cities, Skip," chuckles Donovan.

"Well, maybe this will help clear the waters a bit," says the sheriff as he hands Donovan a file folder.

"What's in there, Mack?"

"It's the photo of the weapons that Dub Davis held yesterday. We can see if his prints on this photo match those on the weapons Joad brought back from Moline."

"That won't prove anything," says Joad. "He already admitted they were his weapons."

Mackintosh and Donovan chuckle. "I think your partner is a little green," says the sheriff.

"Think of two options, Skip," says Donovan. "In one case, Davis took the stuff to Rocky's place. In the other, it was someone else we don't know about. Now, what prints would you expect to find in each case?"

Joad's eyes widen as he says, "In case one, just Rocky's and Dub's. In case two, there could be fresh prints that didn't match either one."

"I hope we won't find your prints on them," the sheriff says to Joad.

"You won't," says Donovan before his younger partner has a chance to answer.

#

As the day unfolds, the weather steadily warms as was predicted, and as the temperature goes up, so does the number of volunteer searchers. By noon, the logistical capacity for searchers is exceeded. O'Dell orders poster signs to be placed outside to thank and turn away additional volunteers. When Frydenberg stops by again, he is relieved to be able to give him another upbeat quote.

With the work in the gymnasium now greatly reduced, Captain Stork asks O'Dell if he would like to take a ride in one of the helicopters to observe the ongoing searches. Ten minutes later, he is waiting in the little league dugout for the helicopter to land. As he straps himself into one of the two small seats with only a thin plastic bubble between himself and the wild blue yonder, he feels his pulse race. He is seriously considering begging off when the throbbing engine just behind him surges to launch them suddenly into the air. Now off the ground, the fragile machine rotates smoothly to face northeast and then tilting forward, O'Dell, with nothing to hang on to, nearly panics, feeling for all the world like he is going to fall right through the fragile bubble to his death. He closes his eyes and tries to slowly breathe but realizes that this makes him almost instantly nauseous. As he opens his eyes, he already sees searchers in neat rows walking across fields. As his mind focuses on the huge search below him, his fear diminishes. After ten minutes, as they are flying over the farm, he is almost enjoying the experience.

The pilot swings off to the east and then turns south along the path of Buffalo Creek. Green National Guard uniforms can be seen combing the creek among its trees and shrubs. He notices that only traces of snow remain in shadowy crevices. He motions for the pilot to fly lower so he can get a better look at the remaining snow. At an altitude of about fifty feet, he can see that there is not enough remaining snow to hide a small body.

Twenty minutes more and O'Dell signals the pilot to return him to town. Back at the ballfield, Frydenberg and a photographer are waiting to document his return.

"What did you see up there?" asks the reporter.

"The search is right on schedule. Conditions are perfect. I am very gratified by the magnificent effort I am seeing from this community," O'Dell says as he realizes he is sounding just like the politicians he likes to disparage.

After the candid interview, Frydenberg thanks him and tells him that he might want to consider running for higher office in the future.

Back in the gymnasium, Captain Stork reports that the search is indeed well ahead of schedule.

As the search is winding down, a troubling thought enters O'Dell's mind for the first time since he got handed the assignment of leading the search effort. As he thinks about what will happen next, he realizes that if the body is not found in the next hour, Frydenberg is going to ask him what this means to the case of the missing boy. Then, in a flash, he knows what he's going to do with that hot potato; he's going to hand it right back to the sheriff, the same guy that handed it to him.

Five minutes later, O'Dell is on the phone with Mackintosh. He tells him that the search is winding down and that they are setting up for a news conference in the gymnasium.

"It seems we've done all this searching for nothing," says O'Dell.

"It's not nothing, Kenny; it has ruled out something monumental."

After a pause, O'Dell says, "I'm going to need you here for the press conference Mack. I will open by briefly discussing the scope of the search, and then I will list all the groups that participated, name each group's leader, and thank the community at large for their help. After that, I have a feeling that I will be asked about what it means now that we didn't find the body. I am going to refer that question to you."

"I see what you mean," Mackintosh says thoughtfully. "I'll be there as soon as I can, so we can talk about how to play it."

#

Thirty minutes later, the sheriff sees Buckman standing by the entrance of the school as he makes his way out of his cruiser. The sheriff realizes that the deputy's hiatus as O'Dell's assistant is now coming to an end. Just another loose end he will have to deal with. As he walks by the deputy, he congratulates him for his work on the massive search.

He meets with O'Dell in a quiet corner of the gymnasium. After thirty minutes of planning, the two men decide to announce that this was the final search. They also decide that only after being asked will the sheriff state that the case is still active and he will follow all remaining leads as hard as possible. If asked for further information, the sheriff will report that further information will be revealed in the days ahead.

Finally, the two men make plans to meet with Donovan first thing in the morning to decide how best to push the case forward. When O'Dell points out that it's Sunday tomorrow, they agree to meet at one. Both realize that the press stories will put renewed pressure on them to get to the bottom of this never-ending case.

"I want to show you something," the sheriff says to O'Dell. "I've been carrying this index card around with me for days."

He unfolds the index card with the question, *Where's Dicky?* at the top. He draws a double line through, "Wandered off, lost." Then he puts a second line through, "Kidnapped." Finally, he draws a circle around the final item before handing it to O'Dell. The circled item is foul play.

"I'm afraid that the hardest part of this job is still in front of us," he tells the very tired-looking county attorney.

#

The day of the search kept everyone out of Donovan's hair. He has used the opportunity to review his notes and step back to look at the big picture. Five days ago, when he first set his expensive shoe down in the mud of that shabby farm in the middle of nowhere, he wanted nothing more than to find an excuse to get out of this quagmire so he could be on his way back to civilization. But three days ago, when all of the kidnapping suspects were ruled out, he didn't hesitate to call in a favor, so he could stay on the case. It was the national tragedy of an innocent boy disappearing in a snow storm that moved the powers-that-be to bring the cavalry into the frontier regions like an old melodrama. But now, as the tide of facts is turning the besieged homesteaders into possible heinous criminals, he sees nothing but trouble ahead.

He knows that with the big search over and the case notes showing most of the facts in hand, there will be pressure from the home office to turn the criminal case over to the local authorities. Five days ago, he would have jumped at the chance to cut and run. But this thing has gotten under his skin. He can't shake the feeling that he is missing something. He has come to respect the sheriff's abilities but not enough to drop this case back into the old man's lap.

Sticking his neck way out, he feels like he is placing a phone call to the nether regions. When he gets Don Slater on the phone, he asks the governor's top operative to use his influence with Washington to try to keep him on the case. After hanging up, he says a quiet prayer that this request doesn't blow up in his face.

#

As Margaret drives down the narrow road, a path now so rutted and muddy that it takes all of her attention to prevent the car from sliding into the ditch. As she gets out of her car, she pauses to feel the warmth of the fading day. The golden twilight fading in the west seems like it belongs to another time. Not long ago, agent Mackintosh had called her at Madeline's house as he had promised. He told her that despite the effort of a thousand searchers, no trace of her lost son was found. Now numbly looking at the last remnants of this long day, she fights against her own intellect, pushing her to accept the unthinkable certainty that her little boy is never going to come home again.

Her stare is interrupted by the familiar sound of bawling cows, only on this occasion much louder and more insistent than normal. Through the fog of everything that has happened today, she looks and then realizes that the cows have not been milked. Inside the house, she finds only quiet and darkness. As she looks around in the empty house, she is reminded of her fruitless searching for her son so many days ago. Then in the dark bedroom, she sees a motionless lump there on the bed. She silently moves closer; then she softly touches her husband's back; it is moving up and down ever so slowly. She tries to shake him awake.

After he finally stirs, he struggles to arrive back in the conscious world.

"Gene, you slept right through the milking time."

"Morning or evening?"

"Evening!"

"Really? Man, I can't remember the last time I slept like that."

"No one can go without sleep forever."

"I don't remember dreaming anything."

"Thank God for that."

"That's right, Margaret, thank God for that. Wait! Today was the search. Is it done?"

"They didn't find him," Margaret says as if she said that it didn't rain today.

Eugene, now fully awake, says, "They didn't find him also means that they didn't find him dead."

Margaret looks at her husband there in the dark. Her eyes steel, her teeth clenched, he can tell she is holding something back, holding it with all of her strength.

She coolly says, "You better go milk those poor cows."

"What time is it?"

"It has been dark for a while now, Eugene. Now go!"

Sunday—How I See It

After church Madeline invites the Walkers to the parsonage for a light lunch. Over coffee and finger sandwiches, the conversation is subdued and light. Pastor John had kept the sermon vague and forgettable in deference to all the drama that they and the whole church have endured over the last weeks.

Little Mikey, who had been playing alone outside, comes into the house. Seeing Margaret at the table, he casually says, "I miss Dicky."

Margaret seems frozen. Seeing this, Eugene says, "We do, too, Mikey."

With that, the little boy runs back out the door, where they can see him again playing outside the window.

Madeline screws up her courage. She says, "We should have a nice remembrance service for Dicky at some point. Not right away, of course, but when the time seems right."

Margaret sits quietly for a moment and then says, "Poor little Mikey, he's so young to be dealing with loss." Then she seems like she is going to say something else but does not.

"You mean like a funeral?" asks Eugene.

"A remembrance service can be very simple," John says. "It can be just a few prayers and letting people say a few words to try to express their loss, their feelings. It is just a small step to help people through a difficult loss."

After a long pause, Margaret finally says, "These are nice sandwiches, Madeline. You must show me how to make them sometime."

#

Donovan and Joad are working together to outline their thoughts on a legal pad in the conference room when they hear the sound of four shoes clacking in the hallway. The sheriff has brought along a canister of coffee and a box with a dozen donuts.

"Good, man!" says Joad. "I'm starving."

"What time did you guys get here?" asks O'Dell.

"Don't ask," answers Joad.

Joad pours a cup of coffee for his boss and then takes two glazed donuts before sitting down.

"Have a seat, Counselor," Donovan says to O'Dell. "I need to catch you up on the case."

"What case?" asks O'Dell.

"The moment that you announced to the world that the final search produced nothing was the moment that the door closed on the theory that a little boy got lost in a snowstorm, Kenny," says the sheriff.

"Let's not get ahead of ourselves," says Donovan to Mackintosh. Then, turning to O'Dell, he says, "Counselor, all the while your energy was being consumed by planning the search, we were following new evidence. I want to lay out that evidence for you now, fair enough?"

O'Dell nods as he pours himself a cup of coffee.

Donovan stands and walks to look out the window. He sips his coffee, then turns back to the people in the room.

"This case has always come down to three basic questions. What are they, Mack?"

"One, he wandered off, two, he was kidnapped, or three, he met foul play."

"Right, number one is natural causes. He wandered off, got lost in the storm, and died of exposure. According to Captain Stork, the farthest a boy that age could have walked is four miles, and that's under ideal conditions. An area many times that big has been searched foot-by-foot. No one knows that better than you. Do you object to ruling out number one, Counselor?"

"No," says O'Dell.

"Sheriff?"

Mackintosh shakes his head, no.

"Next is kidnapping. This is something the FBI knows a great deal about. There are two main reasons to kidnap someone, either for money or for depravity." After pausing for effect, Donovan continues, "This family has no money. In fact, the farm is teetering on insolvency. If that's not enough, the remote location makes kidnapping highly unlikely. Anyone object to ruling out kidnapping for money?"

Both say no.

"The FBI has maintained a list of sexual deviates for years now. We rounded up eleven; that was everyone on the list within two hundred miles. All were ruled out."

"What's the chance that there's a guy that's managed to stay under the radar?" asks the sheriff.

"That's a good question, Mack. It would be easier for a deviate to hide in a depressed urban area than out here in the Bible belt. That is a potential loose end, but our behavioral psychology expert believes it is highly unlikely."

"That makes sense," says Mackintosh.

"Counselor?" asks Donovan.

"Reasonable doubt is the standard; I'll defer to your expertise for now."

"What does that leave us with, Sheriff?"

Mackintosh tosses the index card with the words foul play circled onto the table.

"Now, to clearly think this through, I suggest we start with the basics," says Donovan. "The basic issue is; where is Dicky? And the first question is, is he alive or dead? Who in this room believes that the boy can conceivably be alive?

All are silent.

"The next issue is; how did the body become dead, by an accident, or by an unfriendly act."

"How can we know that?" asks O'Dell.

"We can't," adds the sheriff.

"You're right," says Donovan. "Let's stick a pin in that and move on. The next basic issue is; where's the body? And since heaven and earth have been moved to find it, I think we would have to assume that the body was hidden, okay?"

"Okay, for now," says O'Dell.

"It may have been buried, but there is no evidence for that. I mean none, whatsoever. Now, here comes the interesting part. When I asked the FBI's chief forensic scientist about the rumor that the boy was ground up and fed to the hogs, he said that unless you cut up the hog on the first day, it would be impossible to find any physical evidence; he said it would be the perfect crime. The hogs were scanned for metal, the contents on the bottom of the feeders were examined, and nothing was found."

"So, why do you have the hogs quarantined?" asks O'Dell.

"I'll come back to that in a minute," says Donovan. "The more pressing issue is why would he kill the boy?"

"Who?" asked O'Dell, "You mean Walker?"

"Yes, the boy's father."

"I can't imagine why," answers O'Dell.

"Me either," says Donovan flatly, "At least not on purpose. But what if he didn't mean to do it. What if he lost his temper with the boy? What if he pushed him or hit him in a state of rage?"

He is greeted with silence. Then, at last, O'Dell says, "That's a lot of ifs, Donovan. Do you have any evidence to substantiate any of these assertions?"

Donovan takes a sip of his coffee. "This coffee is cold," he says as he looks through a file folder. Now holding an official FBI report, he continues, "Dr. Ziegfeld, our top behavioral psychology guy, thinks Eugene Walker might fit a profile along with a large number of combat war veterans who struggle with what in layman terms is called combat fatigue. Soldiers, who were under intense artillery fire and who saw carnage of close friends combined with a few other factors, have flashbacks, memory lapses, and violent outbursts out of proportion to even moderately stressful situations."

When Donovan looks up from the report, he sees his audience silently digesting the information.

Mackintosh is the first to speak up. "I would say his money problems are more than moderately stressful. Do you have a theory, Donovan?"

Donovan picks up a legal pad and reads, "He sends the boy to the house at two-thirty on March sixth. The livestock buyer, Tom Magnus, leaves at three-fifteen. By the way, when asked, Walker avoided admitting he was selling the livestock because he desperately needs money. Later, we don't know exactly when, he finds the boy didn't go inside like he was told, and for that reason or some totally different reason like catching him doing something he was forbidden to do, his emotional state drives him to a level of violence that he didn't consciously intend. The boy dies as a result. He panics. He gets rid of the body using the things right in front of him; a sword and a feed grinder."

Setting down his legal pad, Donovan looks at the faces of the men in the room.

"You know," says Mackintosh, "I have to admit that it fits."

"How much of this can you prove?" asks O'Dell.

"Hardly any of it."

"So, what do we do?" asks the sheriff.

"What I started doing after being briefed by Dr. Ziegfeld a few days ago, at his suggestion. I put pressure on him. That's why I've continued to impound the hogs, which stops him from getting money he so badly needs. According to Ziggy, if he is suffering from this condition, he will snap if I can keep the pressure up."

"I don't know if I have the stomach for this," says O'Dell. "He's a war hero."

"If he's not suffering from this condition, Kenny, as an officer and a hero, he will be able to take it."

"We have to do this," says the sheriff. "So, how do you plan to turn up the screws?"

"First, we bring in his wife to ask her again about his behavior over the last several weeks. I casually asked her about this already, and it was obvious that she was covering for him. I think if I handle her just right, I can get the truth out of her. But, just bringing her in will probably add more stress."

"And stressing her will no doubt add stress to him," admits O'Dell. "It would me."

"Right," says Donovan. "Next, we'll bring in his best friend. I want to push him on the evidence which ties him to the weapons sale."

"When I ask him about that," says the sheriff, "He was cool as a cucumber. If he's the guy who sold the weapons, he should get an acting job in Hollywood."

"The fingerprint evidence we're waiting for should help us with that question," says Joad.

"Right," says Donovan. "But in any case, first, I'll ask him about his buddy's past behavior. If he's been losing control, his best friend will know it."

"Deputy Buckman had a run-in or two with Walker and Davis," says the sheriff.

The sheriff relates a detailed history of the altercations between Buckman and Walker, much of which involves Davis as an advocate and peacemaker. Donovan suggests bringing in the deputy to ask him a few questions.

"Give me a crack at him," suggests O'Dell. "I think a discussion about how the state looks at law enforcement officers obstructing justice might loosen his tongue."

"Mind if I sit in on that?" asks the sheriff.

"Better for the counselor to fly solo on this one, Mack. If he sweats enough, he may try to throw his boss under the bus. I don't think he'll do that if you're in the room. I want to see how big of a rat this guy is."

Donovan summarizes the strategy. They'll interview everyone around the key suspect first. Finally, they'll bring in Eugene and try to force the truth out of him, force it to explode out of him, if necessary.

Monday—Forgive Me, Father

"Nice job on the search, Melvin," O'Dell innocently starts his conversation with Deputy Buckman.

He had asked Gladys Henry, the sheriff's secretary, to get the deputy into this office as soon as possible.

"I thought I might be in trouble when Gladys told me you wanted me here right away."

The county attorney decides that he's not in the mood to pussyfoot around. He wants the deputy's honest assessment of Eugene Walker's control issues, and he is more than ready to apply whatever pressure is necessary to get it. As it turns out, it is common knowledge that the history between the two men goes back to Fort Bragg. The attorney knows that it would be easy for the deputy to slant the history in his own favor. He also knows that it would be easy for a military M.P. and later a deputy sheriff to use his authority in an inappropriate manner. In order to get a candid response from the deputy, he decides to show him right off the bat what real power feels like.

"Have a seat, Deputy." He notices the deputy looks a little pale as he sits down. "Do you know what it means to obstruct justice, Melvin?"

"Sure, it means to interfere in an official investigation."

"Yes, or no will do." The deputy looks really nervous now. "Have you ever heard of a law enforcement official who was charged with that?"

Buckman, probably not trusting his voice, shakes his head no.

"Do you think that's a serious charge?"

"Yes."

"Do you have anything you want to tell me?"

The deputy's face flushes red. O'Dell is almost afraid the deputy might throw up in his office. After a pause, O'Dell pulls a newspaper out of his briefcase and slaps it on his desk under the deputy's nose.

"How do you suppose that Frydenberg got tipped off about the sword's value?" O'Dell asks with a combination of indignancy and loathing.

Buckman's eyes betray his racing mind. Stone-faced, he says, "I don't."

"Are you sticking with that answer?"

"Yes."

O'Dell picks up his phone, pushes a button, and says, "I'll be needing that stenographer in five minutes," then slams the phone back in the cradle so hard that the bell rings inside.

Buckman really looks sick now. "Do, do I need an attorney?"

"Why would you need one? You're telling me that you didn't do anything wrong," O'Dell says sarcastically. "Do you have anything else you want to tell me?"

"Okay, okay, I told Don Slater about the sword. I swear I didn't tell Frydenberg."

"Do you think Big Don might have told him?"

"I, I really don't know, but maybe."

"What else did you tell him?"

Buckman breathes in and out, then he tells the county attorney everything he told Slater and why. O'Dell thanks him for his candor and tells him that he won't seek charges against him on the condition that he keeps telling the truth.

Now, time to switch gears, O'Dell says to himself. He asks about his interactions with Eugene at Camp Hyder. Buckman's story sounds believable, with recruits' raising Cain in the local bars whenever they were lucky enough to get a weekend pass. It was the M.P.'s impossible job to try to keep the local business owners and the camp commandant marginally happy at the same time. Naturally, it was the recruits who drew the short straw, and of course, they blamed their lot on the M.P.s. When O'Dell learns that Buckman stayed at the lonely camp in the west Arizona desert country for the duration, he asks him if he ever volunteered to serve overseas. Buckman told him that his request to do so was repeatedly blocked by the commandant.

"Now tell me about your run-ins with Walker after the war?"

Buckman explains that Eugene, along with a lot of other GIs, including himself, hit the bars pretty hard right after the war. It was a case of celebrating and blowing off steam. A lot of the guys were struggling to figure out what they would do next.

"Eugene recognized me as the M.P. from Camp Hyder when I came into Reggie's after a Saturday night shift. He and Dub had closed whatever bar they were in that night and went to Reggie's for a late breakfast."

Buckman went on to explain that when Eugene, who was hammered, found out that he had remained stateside for the duration, he became belligerent. He explained that if it wasn't for Dub, he probably would have had to arrest him.

"Was that the end of it?" asks O'Dell.

"No. There were other run-ins like that over the next few years, but Dub always managed to smooth things over. Eugene really settled down later when he bought the farm and got married."

O'Dell, who has been taking notes, assesses the deputy as telling the truth. He tries to find out if he witnessed any recent anger control incidents with Eugene with no success. When the deputy asks what he can do to get back in the good graces of the sheriff, O'Dell tells him to keep telling him the truth and to apologize.

Buckman goes directly to the sheriff's office. Inside, with hat in hand, he falls all over himself, telling the sheriff that he will never do anything like that again. The sheriff sensing that he may be able to use his repentant deputy as a counter spy at some point, decides to pretend to let him back inside the case. After explaining the strategy to pressure Eugene, the deputy relates the suspect's surprising reaction to finding a broken rosary in the barn and that he saved the item in an evidence bag.

#

Donovan, who was alerted by Mrs. Henry that Margaret had just parked her car, manages to meet her at the building door. Using his best charm to help her feel welcome, he escorts her to the upstairs conference room. Inside, he gives her a cup of coffee and sets a tray of homemade cookies in front of her.

"I promise not to keep you long, Margaret. I really have just two issues I want to ask you about, if it's alright with you."

"That's fine," she answers quietly.

"I was surprised to learn that you have a life insurance policy on your son; and a pretty big one at that."

"That was my father's idea."

"Your father?"

"He was a minister. He told us that he had seen too many families devastated by unexpected funeral expenses. He insisted we have the policy."

"What's your father doing now?" Donovan asks while writing on his notepad.

"He retired several years ago because his memory was getting too bad. I'm afraid he doesn't even know me most of the time."

"I'm so sorry," Donovan says while looking up from his notetaking. "Does your mother take care of him?"

"She died a few years ago. He's in an old folks' home."

"You poor thing. I'm sorry to bring it up."

"You didn't know."

After a pause, he says, "I want to ask you about how your husband is handling all of this, and I need you to be honest with me, Margaret; it's important." After she stares at him a moment, he adds, "Can you do that for me, please?"

When she nods, he asks, "Is he having nightmares?"

Margaret looks down and starts fumbling with her cross.

"Please tell me the truth, Margaret," he says very softly.

She abruptly moves her hand away from the cross as she says, "Yes."

"When did they start?"

"He's had a few since we've been married, but about a week ago, they started getting much worse," Margaret says while looking at her lap.

"Has he had memory lapses? You know, he doesn't seem to know about things that he recently heard or saw?"

Margaret continues to look down. Her eyes are filling with water as she nods yes.

"Just one more question, Margaret. Has he had violent outbursts with you or your son?"

Margaret's face reddens as her right hand goes to the cross as if she wants to make sure it is still there. Then she lifts it a bit with her fingers as if she is feeling its weight. "He's never been violent with me."

"What about with Dicky?"

She is now holding the cross in her fist as she remains silent.

"I'll try to make this as easy as possible. Did he yell at Dicky?"

"Sometimes," she says as tears stream down her cheeks.

"Did he ever shake him?"

"A few times."

"When he was doing that, did he seem like he could lose control?"

Margaret lets go of the cross while crying into her hands. While struggling for control, she blurts out, "I don't know! I honestly don't know!"

#

Sheriff Mackintosh volunteered to talk to Davis. When Dub comes over the hill and sees Mackintosh waiting for him there, he hops out and quickly approaches. He seems angry.

"Margaret was really upset after talking to Donovan this morning."

Instead of talking to him there, the sheriff invites him to meet at the office in an hour.

Donovan's plan seems to be working, Mackintosh thinks to himself.

When Davis comes into the sheriff's office, he is still fuming.

"Can't you guys leave the poor woman alone?"

"I wish we could," the sheriff says while trying to sound sympathetic. Then asks him again if he sold the weapons to the shop in Moline.

"Absolutely not! Why would I do that?"

"Oh, to protect your buddy, maybe."

"I don't follow you," Dub says very convincingly.

The sheriff decides to move on.

"How bad was it on Guam?"

"The worst twenty days of my life."

"Did it change you?"

A light goes on in Dub's head. He now thinks he knows where this is going.

"Yes, but not like Gene."

"I need you to tell me what happened to him on that island."

Dub knows he will do anything for his best friend—anything. He weighs his options. It's very hard to know the right thing to do. His emotions take over his judgment. This is something he needs to get off of his chest. He just hopes that it's the right thing to do.

"You want to know what changed him. Well, you've come to the right guy."

Dub tells the sheriff what it's like to be under artillery attack, shaken nearly to death and not knowing if you would live to see the next ten seconds. Then he tells the sheriff that Lieutenant Walker left his foxhole, risking his own life, going from one crater to another to tell the men that they would be safe as long as they kept their heads down. Then he tells the story of the rosary and Tommy.

"When he saw Tommy blown to bits, it changed him. Before that, he was very religious. He said prayers every day. He went to services whenever the chaplain could manage it. After Tommy was killed with his rosary in his hand, he parted ways with God."

"That was rough," the sheriff says sincerely.

"There's more. He was filled with rage. While the shells were still falling, he went out into the darkness to high ground, out past the enemy line; that was suicide. From there, he pinpointed the cave on the mountain that was hiding the Jap howitzer. That night, after the shelling stopped, he made his way back and moved one of our guns to the northwest. Then, he went back up on that hill, only this time the enemy forces were active, and he had to pull a communication wire with him. From that hill, he directed fire on that cave. When we opened fire, they immediately started firing at our position. It quickly turned into a duel between Eugene and the enemy observer, both using their skill to take out each other's guns. Our howitzer was far more vulnerable being out in the open while the Jap gun was firing out of a deep cave. It took tremendous skill for Eugene to try to land a shell at an impossibly low trajectory into that cave. As the enemy shells were closing in on our gun, Gene kept tweaking the settings, getting closer and closer until the cave exploded."

"Even then, he was nearly killed, making his way back to camp unarmed. A Jap popped up out of a camouflaged trapdoor bunker ten feet in front of him. Luckily, I was watching his return and was able to put a .30-06 round through back of his head before he could pull the trigger."

"My God," said the sheriff. "That's incredible."

"Geno was recommended for the Army Cross but wouldn't hear of it. General Broderick had to order him to accept the Bronze Star. When the star was pinned on his shirt, he turned to the men and told them that he only accepted the decoration in honor of what they, and those that died, had done."

#

Eugene makes his way into the stateliest building in Summit, St. Patrick's Catholic Church. It's eerily dark as he enters, and it's so quiet that it seems that if you sat silently in a pew, you'd be able to hear dust particles settling to the floor. His heart feels as empty as the church; as lonely as the small light yellowed with age and dimly glowing on the ornate, mahogany confessional; a structure tucked into a back corner; a light that betrays the presence of celestial justice; a justice he had learned about in catechism classes so many years ago.

Teacher, "Why does a loving God punish?"

Student, "Because it fulfills the truth of His promises."

Eugene enters the structure through a velvet curtain, then kneels in front of the familiar, one-foot-square panel with a gauze screen built into it. The priest sitting behind the screen, like all alpha predators, has been aware of his presence since the moment he touched the front door.

The coarse sound of the little window sliding open causes his heart to pound just as it did when he was ten years old.

Involuntarily, his own voice rings forth, "Bless me, Father, for I have sinned. It has been about fifteen years since my last confession, and these are my sins."

In the second that hangs in the air, Eugene sees the shadowy face of the priest, which the gauze screen makes appear as if it resides in a cloud suspended in the great beyond, a priest who now seems to be trying to decipher the face of a creature that has avoided repentance for such an eternity.

As he inhales to recite his sins, the priest breaks protocol, asking, "What's kept you away from the church for so long?"

"I became angry with God."

"So, that's your first sin. Now, tell me what the Creator of the universe did to deserve your wrath."

"It's a long story, Father."

"You may have noticed that the line for confession is extremely short. I think God, in his patience, has given you the time to tell us your long story."

Eugene starts by telling the priest that he was a good Christian until the middle of the battle to retake the island of Guam from the Japanese.

"Yes, that terrible war; what happened to you there?"

Eugene tells the priest that he had promised to say the rosary every day as an offering for God to save his life and then about the terrible shelling and giving his rosary to a terrified soldier telling him that if he prayed the rosary, he would be saved.

"Only a few seconds after I told him that, he was blown to bits. When I looked back into his foxhole, the only thing left was his dismembered hand holding a bit of the rosary." As he tells this to the priest, he contemplates this moment that is burned into his mind, recurring in his dreams, and scarring his soul, that continues to rain down from above; he wonders, is this all from the God in heaven or from the forces of evil that God allowed to enter the earth?

"And you blame God for this," the priest says, not as a question, but rather as a statement.

"I did for a long time. Now I'm not sure. I'm lost, Father. I have been for a long time."

"That was a terrible thing that God allowed to happen to you and to the boy. There are always so many terrible things like that in war. We can never know what God is planning; no human can know that. But I know that He wasn't punishing you, and He wasn't punishing him. He may have been testing you, but no one can even know that. He may have allowed that to happen for some other purpose so that something greater could happen, maybe even something that is still going to happen..." the priest's voice trails off.

Eugene's mind recall's what he did as a direct result of that incident, taking out that gun that saved dozens of lives.

"By the way," the priest interrupts his thought, "God did answer your prayer by preserving your life."

Then, the priest sensing his confessor is crying, quietly says, "Let me give you absolution, now."

"Not yet, Father. I still haven't told you my sins." Eugene breathes in and out, then he says, "I think I murdered my little son."

#

"This just came in for you," Mrs. Henry says as she hands Agent Donovan a Telefax printout.

Donovan sees it's an FBI fingerprint analysis report. As he is scanning the document, agent Joad rushes into the conference room.

"I'm on the phone with Thomas Rakowski," Joad says excitedly.

"Who's that?"

"Rocky's brother. They found the paper with the plate number."

"Well, go run it, Skip."

Donovan is just finishing the report when Joad comes back into the room.

"I'll bet you a hundred bucks that the plate doesn't belong to Davis," Donovan says as he waves the report in the air.

"Right. It belongs to a guy named Earl Jones. He's five-six, weighs one-eighty, and lives on Temperance Rural Route One."

"Go put the screws to the guy. Remind him that stealing a gun is a federal crime, 27 CFR."

"I don't think that applies to stealing a privately owned weapon, Boss."

"I'll bet you another hundred; the guy doesn't know that."

#

A half-hour later, Agent Joad, in his black suit, is standing on the front porch of a two-story farmhouse located in a grove of trees a hundred yards from an east-west gravel road on Temperance Rural Route One. The name on the mailbox is *E. Jones.*

"What are you doing on my front porch?" asks a voice from the window beside the door.

"I'd like to ask you a few questions."

"The front door doesn't open. Come around to the back."

Joad notices mud on the side of his shoes as he walks up the cracked steps leading to the back porch.

"You ain't from a church, are you?"

"I'm Agent Oren Joad of the Federal Bureau of Investigation," he says while holding up his credentials. "Are you Earl Jones?"

"What's this about?"

"Are you aware of the punishment for transporting stolen guns across state lines?

"What in God's name are you talking about?"

"Are you aware that it is a federal crime to lie to a federal agent?"

"That's what you say. I think you're trespassing."

"Not so. I knocked on the door, and you answered. Let's stop fooling around. Take a look at these pictures, and then you better start talking fast."

Joad hands him photographs of the weapons and Rocky's shop in Moline.

"Dear God," he says under his breath while turning white.

"A guy named Rocky Rakowski wrote down your car's license plate number, and I would bet you a hundred bucks he can easily pull you out of a police lineup. So, what happens next is up to you, Mister Jones. Either tell me right now where that sword is, or pack your bags for Leavenworth!"

#

Donovan, Joad, and Mackintosh, all wearing white gloves, are examining the samurai sword under a bright light in the seldom-used Briggs County evidence room.

"Are you going to have it dusted for fingerprints?" asks the sheriff.

"It wouldn't prove anything. We have a written confession from the guy who stole it. Finding Walker's or Davis's fingerprints on it gets us nowhere. It just proves they handled it at some point," says Donovan.

"Check inside the blade cover, Skip," says Mackintosh.

After struggling to find the right angle to see inside with a magnifying glass, Joad says, "Is that dried blood in there?"

Donovan takes the magnifying glass and carefully examines the point where the handle meets the blade. "I think I see blood here in the crack.

Maybe there's enough to get a blood type. Can you get a blood type done around here, Mack?"

"If they can scrape out enough dried blood, we can," replies the sheriff.

#

Chasing the blood evidence has kept Agent Joad busy all afternoon. Lab results identified the dried blood as type A positive. Following the premise that the blood could belong to the deceased boy, Joad was able to get blood types for both parents; Eugene's blood type from army records is type O negative, and Margaret's blood type from her prenatal records is A negative. After thinking about the above information for about an hour, he got one more piece of information before finding his boss and the sheriff.

"The blood on the sword is type A positive."

"That's a common blood type, isn't it?" asks the sheriff.

"Yes, almost a third of the population has that type. Margaret is A negative, that's fairly rare, about three percent. Eugene's blood is rare, too—O negative. And here's the problem. I had to look it up in the manual; if both parents are any type with negative, then the children must be negative too."

After a pause, the sheriff says, "That just means the blood on the sword isn't the boys."

"Probably," says agent Joad.

"Probably? You said that the boy's blood *must* be negative," asserts the sheriff.

"Right, but after thinking about it, I got one more blood record. David Davis has blood type O positive."

Donovan's head tilts to the side.

"You've lost me," says Mackintosh.

"Are you saying that Davis is the boy's father, Skip?" asks Donovan.

"That would fit the blood type information," answers Joad.

"Yes, but what else could it mean, Skip?"

"That it's not the boy's blood. It could be from the time of the war, or maybe even from a long-deceased samurai."

After thinking for a moment, Donovan adds, "But let's not forget that an intelligent person like Walker would not overlook the need to thoroughly clean the sword."

#

As Margaret is driving out of the county building parking lot, she remembers that Donovan's first question was about Dicky's life insurance. Why did he ask me about that, she wonders to herself? The bulk of his questions all centered on her husband, questions that pointed to the implication that he is capable of violence and the same questions he had asked her before. These thoughts overwhelm her mind causing her to suddenly put on her brakes in the middle of the road. As she is gripped in this thought, a blaring horn from behind causes her to almost jump out of her skin. Her heart now pounding, feeling lost in a jumble of racing thoughts, she drives to Madeline's house. She really needs to talk to her most trusted friend.

#

Madeline, seeing Margaret pull up to the house, realizes that she is not surprised. How much more unending tragedy can she possibly take. She decides that she must again try to nudge her best friend to take that unthinkable first step, even if just a baby step towards loosening the impossibly tangled connection that bonds a mother's heart to her living child. She imagines having to bury her adorable little Mikey. She wipes her eyes, now full of tears, as she prepares to open her door.

Not trusting her emotions, she embraces her dear friend for an eternity at the door. Then, with her arm around Margaret's shoulder, they walk slowly, as if one person, into the kitchen, still without saying a word.

Madeline pours them both a cup of coffee. She puts cream and sugar in Margaret's cup for her; oh, how well she knows her best friend. She hopes the gesture will help Margaret feel mothered.

Finally, sitting down herself, she softly says, "Tell me about it, dear."

Margaret opens up about her second interview with FBI agent Donovan, relating the gist of the conversation.

"This is the second time he asked me these questions about Eugene. What do you think it means?"

Madeline sips her coffee and then goes out of her way to speak matter-of-factly. "They are trying to judge if Eugene is capable of losing control. If he is, then they may think he did something really terrible." Then more softly, she says, "You must have suspected that."

"Do you think they could be right?" Margaret quietly asks.

"Of course not. Eugene would never harm Dicky in a million years."

After a pause, Margaret says, "That's right," under her breath. Then she adds, "Do you have anything to eat? I haven't eaten since yesterday."

"Are we talking cake or sandwich?" Madeline says with a smile.

"Mm, let's start with cake," Margaret says, with a bit brightness returning to her face.

#

While driving home, Madeline's assertions have helped her relax and unwind a tightly tangled riddle she had been carrying for days. But, in contrast to her best friend's conclusion, she is starting to believe that it is quite possible that Eugene may have done the unthinkable.

#

When Eugene comes in from the evening milking session, he's surprised to find that Margaret has set the table and dinner is simmering on the stove. He can't remember the last time they had a real supper together.

"That really smells good," he says as he enters the kitchen.

Margaret, who is stirring flour into meat drippings, says, "Just finishing the gravy."

Both quietly eat dinner. Eugene notices that Margaret seems to be miles away.

Eugene had come home intending to be totally honest with Margaret. After confessing his sin to the priest, he dutifully said the prayers of penance. Still kneeling, he promised God that he would tell the truth to the authorities but also to Margaret, no matter how difficult it might be. He still doesn't really know the whole truth; a big part of it is locked somewhere deep in his mind. But now, sitting quietly with Margaret, feeling his heart pounding, he realizes that it is now or never.

He waits until they have finished eating to ask, "Would you like to talk?"

#

Something about how Eugene asks this question causes Margaret's stomach to churn. She has been trying to find a way to start the uncomfortable conversation that part of her wants to avoid so badly. Now, with a chance to start, she feels more nervous than ever. She breathes in deeply, holding it in for a second, then deciding as she exhales that she must force herself to dive in.

"You've never really told me about the war," she says, before realizing that this isn't really what she wants to talk about.

"What do you want to know about it?"

"Did it change you?"

"Yes."

"How?"

"Many ways. I saw so many horrible and terrifying things; I really don't want to talk about that part. I saw something that caused me to part ways with God." Then quietly, he adds, "I was wrong to do that."

"Is that thing the thing you see in your dreams?"

Eugene's eyes fill with water as he whispers, "Yes," so quietly she barely hears him. Then after a moment, he adds, "But that's only half of it."

She whispers, "Can you tell me the other half?" sensing that she is asking something monumentally difficult.

She sees panic in Eugene's eyes as he says, "I don't know if I can." Then clenching his fists in his lap, he blurts out, "Yes, I will. I have to."

Margaret, frightened now, takes his hand as she says, "Please, Eugene, tell me." Her hand shaking in his, she says very softly, "No matter how terrible."

He looks intently into her eyes, then lifts her hand and kisses it tenderly. "Okay, just remember that I love you very much."

"I love you, too," Margaret says, her heart now pounding, terrified of what she is about to hear.

"The terrible thing I saw, the most terrible that is, was seeing a young soldier I had just comforted blown to bits when an artillery shell landed in his foxhole; I was just a few feet away. The thing I saw, the thing I keep seeing, is a hand; his hand is all that was left of him."

"Oh, Gene."

"The hand, Tommy's hand was holding what was left of the rosary I had just given to him."

When he doesn't say anything else for a minute, she quietly says, "That's so awful, Gene."

Gene clears his throat. "That's the first half, Margaret."

Margaret, biting her lip, not wanting to say it, says, "Tell me the other half."

"In the dream, the dream that wakes you and me up, I see the hand, but it's not Tommy's hand. It's Dicky's hand."

Margaret's mind races and she asks, "What does that mean?"

"There's a little more, Margaret. In the dream, after seeing the hand, I see Dicky's dead body lying face down in the mud."

"Did you kill Dicky?" escapes Margaret's mouth before she can stop it.

"I don't know, Margaret. I wish to God that I did, but I just don't know."

"Don't know?" screams Margaret. "What does that mean?!"

"I've thought about the afternoon when Dicky disappeared a thousand times. I've come to realize that I can't remember anything between the time I sent Dicky to the house and when I came in to eat dinner."

"Not anything?"

"I can't even remember when Magnus left. I just don't remember what happened during that time."

"Dear God!"

Tuesday—Crucify Him

When Dub pulls over the loneliest hill on his mail route, he sees a black and white cruiser for the third time.

"Here we go again," he says out loud.

As he pulls closer, he is surprised to see Buckman, not Sheriff Mackintosh, sitting in the car. As the two men make eye contact, it's the deputy who gets out of his car to stand by Dub's open window.

"I've got mail to deliver," Dub says with irritation.

"I'm not here in an official capacity. In fact, you might as well be the first person besides my wife to know that I'm getting out of the business."

"Aren't you afraid that people might think you're becoming a human being?" Dub says with surprise.

After a pause, Buckman says, "Well, it's about time."

"What are you going to do?"

"I don't know. Any mail routes available?"

"Why does everybody think this is such a great job?"

Buckman looks around at the plowed fields. He breathes in and out, then looks Dub in the eye. "I'm sure there are worse jobs around." Then after a pause, he adds, "Like mine."

"Why did you stop me?"

"Because I owe you an apology."

Dub sizes up the man in front of him. He's surprised to see that he really looks sincere.

"Why now?"

"I got myself jammed up in this thing that is happening to the Walker's. It's nothing that hurt them; it was just me trying to help myself. I got rung out on the carpet for it, and I had it coming. The whole thing made me realize what a heal I've been to you and to all the soldiers, including your best friend."

Dub seeing the sorrow in his eyes, says, "In a way, you were just doing your job."

"I wish I would have never taken the M.P. job. I wish to heaven that I would have taken my chances with you guys."

"Water under the dam," says Dub.

"Please tell Eugene that I'm sorry. I'd like to be able to tell him myself, but I can't."

"Why not?"

"That's the real reason I stopped you. I've been out of the loop for a while from the big boys. But I think they're coming after Eugene."

Buckman hands Dub a slip of paper with a name and a phone number on it.

"What's this?"

"It's the name of a lawyer in Willow Bend. Tell Eugene to call this guy. I think he's going to need him."

#

Margaret is pouring coffee when the sudden clamor of the phone on the wall behind her head gives her a start, causing her to spill coffee on her kitchen counter. Both listen for the ring pattern; one short ring is followed by two longs. The party line call is for them.

"I'll get it," says Eugene.

Margaret wipes the spilled coffee. She listens to the one-sided conversation with a sinking feeling in her gut.

"Yes, this is he... Oh, what's it about... Well, okay, I'll be there at six."

He looks nervous as he hangs up the phone. "That was the sheriff. They want me to come in for some questions."

"Should you call the lawyer?"

"Yes, but I'm not going to. I'm going to face this thing on my own. For better or for worse, I'm just going to tell the truth. What happens after that is up to God."

#

The sun, hanging low in the west, is burning into his eyes as he drives on the highway approaching Temperance. He remembers the words of the priest as he left the confessional; he had said that the truth would set him free. Now, though fully committed to the truth, he can't help but wonder if this truth will have the opposite effect. Still fearful of what the future holds for him, he calmly hardens his will to do everything in his power to accept it.

Mrs. Henry escorts him into the conference room. The side of the table in front of him has one empty chair facing the row of windows to the west. Donovan is standing behind the chair directly opposite from him. To Donovan's right is Sheriff Mackintosh, then Agent Joad, and to Donovan's left is County Attorney O'Dell. Sitting at the end of the table to the south is a woman he doesn't know sitting in front of a stenography machine.

Donovan states the date and time of day as the stenographer is recording his words. He recites for the record the matter at hand, the names of all present, and that of the person being interviewed. He states that Eugene Walker is here without an attorney and then asks him if he is willing to proceed without one. Eugene agrees.

Donovan begins by telling Eugene they are going to go through the timeline beginning at the time Margaret sent Dicky out of the house at 1:00 p.m., through 5:15 p.m., when Margaret and Eugene realized that the boy was gone.

Donovan asks what Eugene was doing when Dicky came outside.

"I was rushing to finish extra chores because a storm was coming."

Donovan asks him to continue but to be more specific.

After thinking for a moment, Eugene states that Dicky asked to drive the tractor, and since he needed to move alfalfa bales anyway, and even though he was hurrying, he agreed. Donovan has him explain how a four-year-old can drive a tractor. So, he explains how the boy enjoys sitting on his lap.

"Take me through what actually happened," says Donovan, "Step by step, please. Remember everything you can."

Eugene recites what happened as completely as possible as he is remembering it. He recalls taking the boy into the barn where it was warm, telling him to wait there and not move while he stacked bales on the tractor's payload bucket.

"Then I went back inside to get him..." Eugene's voice trails off as his expression changes as he remembers what happened next.

"What happened next?"

Eugene is remembering how Dicky didn't stay where he was told, including how he harshly scolded him. He knows that disclosing his behavior will look bad. He hesitates but knows that he must force himself to tell the unvarnished truth.

"When I came back, I found he had climbed on top of the bales, high into the air. I told him to come down at once. I picked him up. I brought his face right in front of mine. I told him to never climb on bales because it's dangerous."

"Did you shout at him?"

"Yes."

"Did you hit him?"

"No."

"Did you shake him?"

After a pause, he says, "I don't think so. If I did, it wasn't that hard."

"Are you sure?"

"Yes."

"How did he react?" asks Donovan.

"He cried," Eugene answers quietly.

Donovan moves on, questioning him about the Tom Magnus interaction and how and why Dicky left to go to the house.

"Did you watch him going to the house?"

"I don't remember seeing him doing that. I've tried and tried, and I just can't remember it."

Donovan asks him about the discussions with the livestock buyer and why he was selling his hogs. Eugene admits that he badly needs the money for overdue bills. Donovan asks him what he remembers about the buyer leaving.

"I remember telling him that he should leave to stay ahead of the storm. I was anxious for him to leave because I felt like I needed to be finishing as much of the chores as I could."

Donovan asks him what time the buyer left. After a bit of back and forth, they agree that it most likely was about three p.m.

"Now, I want you to take me through what you did between three o'clock when Magnus left and five-fifteen when you came into the house."

Eugene is looking down. The sun is setting in the window. The bright light streaming through the window over Donovan's left shoulder is blinding.

#

Donovan notices with apprehension that the sun is now blinding Eugene, precisely how he planned.

Donovan clears his throat. He is thinking that now is the time to turn up the heat to full.

"What's wrong? Look at me!"

Eugene looks up, squinting up at the silhouette talking to him.

"Tell me what you did next!"

"I-I don't remember."

"That's your story? The most important two hours of your son's life and you don't remember? Well, try harder. It's important!"

"I have tried. I've tried for days. I honestly can't remember." Then he says more quietly, "I'm telling you the truth. I wish to God that I *could* tell you."

Sensing the moment is right, Donovan shifts gears.

"Have you had other memory lapses?"

After a bit of hesitation, he admits that he has.

"How many, how often?"

Eugene haltingly admits that it's happening more and more lately.

"Bad dreams?"

"Yes."

"What about?"

"Terrible things I saw in the war."

"I want to tell you something interesting I recently learned," says Donovan. "I learned it from Doctor Ziegfeld, the FBI director of behavioral psychology. He taught me that men who have been shellshocked often suffer from lack of sleep, flashbacks, and memory lapses." He pauses for a beat to let that sink in before playing the trump card. "And in some cases, this condition results in violent, irrational, and uncontrollable outbursts."

The light is still blinding Eugene. He blinks his eyes, trying to shield them with his right hand.

Now, in a soothing voice, trying to sound motherly, Donovan says, "Does any of that sound familiar?"

Eugene nods.

"Now, let's see if any of this sounds familiar, too." Donovan picks up his legal notepad and starts reading, "The livestock buyer leaves at about three p.m. The conversation with the buyer solidifies the reality that you are going to lose the farm, bringing the tension of the last few months to a head. A bit later, we don't know exactly when, you find the boy didn't go inside like he was told. For this reason, or perhaps for some totally different reason, like catching him doing something else he was forbidden to do, you react uncontrollably. It's like you were back in the war; and it goes way too far. You are surprised to see the boy is not moving, shocked to find out he is dead. It's too much to bear; you panic. You get rid of the body using the first things you find nearby; a sword and a feed grinder."

Eugene, with a look of shock on his face, quietly says, "I don't remember any of that."

"It's a memory lapse, then, right?"

Blinking, he blurts out, "Maybe!" Looking down, with his head in his hands, he continues, "I don't know. I just don't know." Then he whispers, "I hope to God that it's not."

Donovan notices that the sun behind him has dropped below the horizon, so his subject can see more clearly now. It's now time to shift into the highest gear. Doctor Ziegfeld's words are guiding him. Ziggy told him there probably was a triggering event that started all of this, an event from the war that his mind has put in a box, that his psyche has locked shut to protect him from its unbearable pain. If Donovan can get him to relive it, then all of his memories might come flooding back. If he can lead him to it and then, at just the right moment, hit him with what he hopes will be the key, the box might pop open.

"What happened to you back in the war?"

"What? The war? Well, many things, it was terrible."

"Yes, but what was that one thing, that terrible thing, that thing that changed you? You know what I'm talking about."

#

Oh, God, Eugene says to himself. "Do we have to talk about that?"

"Yes, Eugene. It's important. It's why we're here, isn't it?"

"Dear God, please let me out of this," Eugene says so quietly that to the others, it's just a mumble. Then he remembers the priest. He remembers his promise to tell the truth. In order to be forgiven, he must tell the truth no matter how difficult. The priest also told him that if you get to the point where you don't think you can do it, then just ask God to help you try and that will be enough.

"Eugene?"

"With God's help, I'll try."

"Good, go on then."

Eugene sullenly describes the shelling. He tells them about Tommy, cowering in fear. He tells them about the explosion that blew the private, a boy too young to be there, to bits.

"What happened next, Eugene?"

"I don't remember."

"Close your eyes and try to remember."

Eugene closes his eyes. He says nothing.

"Open your eyes!" Donovan shouts.

Eugene's eyes shoot open as Donovan slams the broken rosary, the one that Deputy Buckman had noticed upset him when it was found among all the other stuff uncovered when the barn was emptied, down on the table in front of him.

"What's this, Eugene!"

Eugene screams. His mind flashes to the terrible dream in front of him, the dream that has been haunting him over and over. It flashes the image of Tommy's hand. There's that acrid smell again. Then it's the image of Dicky, dead in the mud. This time it's more real than ever. He is no longer in a room with these people; he is somewhere else, a place he can't bear to be.

"Oh, dear God! Oh, Dicky! What have I done?"

Donovan pauses as Eugene is crying, wailing, really.

With a soft but steadfast voice, Donovan asks, "Where's Dicky, Eugene?" Then, turning up the dial, his voice firm, "We need to know." After a beat, he pounces, "Tell us!"

Eugene stops crying. He looks up at the faces in the room, some looking sympathetic, and the woman typing is crying. Donovan looks defiant.

As if he has been called out of a deep sleep, he says, "I don't know. I honestly don't know." Then with Donovan still glaring at him, he adds, "I wish to God that I did."

#

After Eugene has walked out of the room, Donovan's mind is thinking about the manner of Eugene's crying. He tries in vain to read the cry. Is it a cry for mercy, mourning, or bewilderment? He realizes that it's something well beyond his experience.

After formally concluding the interrogation and sending the stenographer away, Donovan asks Joad, Mackintosh, and O'Dell to stay in the room.

As the door shuts, Donovan starts, "I want to talk about what just happened."

"What did just happen?" asks the sheriff.

"I'll tell you what didn't happen," says O'Dell, "He didn't tell us where the body is. And without a body—"

Donovan cuts him off, "Hold on, Counselor, you're jumping ahead of me."

"Okay, but nothing you are going to say will change that."

"Give him a minute, Kenny, I'd like a chance to talk about what we just heard," says the sheriff.

"Thanks, Mack," Donovan says. "My first question is, did he kill the boy?" Donovan looks from face to face as the men sit in silence. "Skip?"

"Yes."

"Why do you say that?" asks O'Dell.

"One, because we can't find the body. I think we've eliminated all other possible explanations for why that's true. And two, because he honestly can't deny that he did."

"That's two reasons that prove nothing," says O'Dell.

"You're getting ahead of me again, Counselor," says Donovan. "Right now, I'm just asking if, after seeing this testimony, these guys think he did it. We'll argue the points of law in a minute."

O'Dell is writing on his legal pad as he motions for Donovan to continue.

"What do you think, Mack?"

"We've been working on this case for quite a while. I've seen a lot of facts and a lot of twists and turns. This case is like a jigsaw puzzle. I think I'm with Donovan; when I try to put all of the pieces together, that's the picture I see."

"Jigsaw puzzle—" starts O'Dell when Donovan cuts him off.

"Before you launch into that again, Counselor, I want you to tell me this first, do you think Eugene Walker killed his son?" asks Donovan.

"Glad you asked! I don't know; and neither do you!"

"Didn't ask what you know, only what you think, but that's okay. I'll put you down as a solid no. I'm a yes, so it's three to one."

"Three to one is a hung jury," says O'Dell.

"There's a lot more evidence to look at before the jury votes," says Donovan.

O'Dell is glaring at Donovan as he takes the group through the question of if they believe Walker killed him on purpose, for the money. Everyone agrees that he did not. Next, the group, with the exception of O'Dell, concedes that they believe Walker killed him more or less accidentally when something happened to make him lose control.

Next, Donovan turns the group's attention to the question of what happened to the body. After a bit of discussion, the group, with O'Dell's lone abstention, agrees that they believe that Eugene hid the body but doesn't remember doing so.

"So, what's the point of all this, Donovan?" asks O'Dell. "I hate to burden you with reality, but without a body, it's going to be almost impossible to prove that any crime was committed."

"We do have a circumstantial case, Counselor," says Donovan. "And we have a top behavioral psychologist who will testify that Walker fits the profile of a combat soldier predisposed to and with a history of irrational, violent acts. And in addition, he suffers from significant memory lapses with one monumentally important and perhaps unbelievably convenient lapse."

"We also have a decorated war hero who can probably produce a number of comrades in arms who can testify that he selflessly saved their lives. If you think you can sway a jury around here with a head shrinker when you don't even have a body, I can tell you that you are sorely mistaken."

Donovan, in frustration, says, "I was hoping I could get him to remember if I pushed him hard enough." After a pause, he adds flatly, "It didn't work."

"So, what do we do now?" asks Mackintosh.

"It's up to you now, Mack, but I have to pack it in. There is no longer any justification for the FBI to stay on the case, and I've run out of favors I can call in to stay."

"Sorry to see you go," O'Dell says with a crooked smile. "So, what are we going to do now, Sheriff?"

The sheriff stands; he looks out the window as the fading sunset shines red in the west. He turns to face O'Dell with a thoughtful expression.

"I'm going to charge him with murder, or maybe manslaughter," the sheriff says with conviction.

O'Dell looks at the sheriff with disbelief. "Why would you do that?"

"A lot of reasons. First, he's the one and only suspect. Second, he probably did it, and I think he knows it. And even if he doesn't, I think he will go along with it because, even if he doesn't know it, I think he believes it. Lack of a body is a challenge, but this is rural Iowa; everyone knows that if the pigs got him, you'd never find the body. You're worried about a jury, Kenny? You shouldn't be; the people I talk to around here already have him sent up the river."

#

"I'm surprised you said yes," Mackintosh tells Donovan as they are driving to the sheriff's house for pot roast.

"You bailed me out from having to go to Reggie's by myself. Joad told me he wanted to ask Sally out to dinner for his last night in town."

"Sally Brown, from the Maquoketa? She'll probably talk his ears off."

"He knows, but the poor guy's been out of circulation for a couple of weeks, so I think he'll just stuff cotton in his ears and keep smiling."

Mackintosh chuckles as he says, "With Sally, that might work."

"You surprised me when you decided to push ahead with charging Walker."

"You made a good case."

"Don't give me that. I made a lousy case, and you know it. I'm between a rock and a manure pile with this one. It's the most visible assignment I'll ever have. My career would be over if I went back to Washington with nothing. That would be telling everyone in the bureau that I have no idea what happened here. Whether I believe it or not, I have to nail this guy to the cross."

"Do you believe he did it?"

"No. But I believe he could have done it. My career demands a head in a noose, and his is the only one I have to offer."

"That's pretty cold, Donovan."

"A black suit comes with a black heart."

"So, you think I'm doing the right thing?" asks Mackintosh.

"It's the correct thing. Figuring out if it's the right thing is the purview of the twelve jurors."

After a pause, Donovan asks, "Do you think you'll be able to get O'Dell on board? You won't be able to get very far without him."

"It won't take him long to realize that doing nothing isn't an option, and arresting Walker is the only play we have left."

"I hate having to cut and run, Mack. I've never had to walk away from a case so close to the end."

"I'll miss working with you, Donovan. I've been thinking about having a black suit made."

"What?"

"Sure, and can you send me a pair of those shiny black shoes, size eleven D."

"Shut up," he says, chuckling. "Seriously, Mack, I'll miss working with you, too. All kidding aside, I really will. This country living is starting to grow on me."

Wednesday—One Phone Call

Deputy Buckman is once again waiting on Dub's mail route to tell him something important. After the mail carrier rolls over the top of the hill, he waves him over.

"Hop in if you have a minute," Buckman says to Dub through his open cruiser window.

"What's up, Melvin?" Dub says after hopping inside.

"I'm afraid I have bad news again. The sheriff's secretary called me at home to tell me that Mackintosh is planning to arrest Eugene for manslaughter."

"Geez! What evidence does he have?"

"Sorry, Dub, I've been out of the loop for days. Just make sure he gets hooked up with a lawyer right away."

"Okay, I will."

"And another thing, Dub, avoid Frydenberg like the plague. He's a wolf in sheep's clothing. He's been bugging me to tell him if they are coming after Eugene. I told him that law enforcement has declined to pursue him. I figured that if I'm going down in flames, I might as well point that weasel in the wrong direction while I'm at it."

The two men discuss the situation, and then Dub asks Buckman if he's decided what he is going to do next.

"I've been talking to Captain Stork about getting into the Civil Air Patrol. I like the idea of trying to help people. I just don't have the stomach for hurting good people anymore."

#

Sheriff Sheldon Mackintosh pulls into the Walkers' farmyard alone. He has arranged things so that the press won't be tipped off until later. A younger man would probably have relished the publicity, but he has recently decided that after thirty-one years in office, he has had enough of the limelight. He is feeling every one of his sixty-six years as he knocks on the door. When Margaret Walker, who looks like she has aged ten years since the investigation started, answers the door, he feels older still.

Her eyes are full of water as she asks him to come inside. *It's as if she knows what is coming*, he thinks to himself.

"I'll get—" she starts.

"I'm right here," her husband says as he comes around the corner. "I'm ready to go, Sheriff."

#

The sheriff advises him to remain silent as the car starts the drive to the county jail. He sullenly takes the advice as he looks over his farm, perhaps for the last time. He remembers how lonely and rundown it was when he first started living here. This place gave him so much. First, it gave him something to pour his energy into, something that wasn't self-destructive. It gave him the solitude he needed to start healing his wounds. In the gentle quiet of this oasis, he regained the ability to sleep almost peacefully. The rhythms of nature—the sun, the wind, the rain, all these things that foster growth are tonic to his soul. He recalls his spirits soaring as the seeds he planted sprang forth that first year, hope of things to come. And after a few years, he was finally ready for what came next; Margaret was the medication that he thought had healed him for good.

A mile away now, going by the Brennan place, he sees a cat by the road. He remembers Holly, his milking companion and Dicky's playmate. He remembers finding Holly being picked over by a crow; he quietly cries, trying his best to muffle the sound. He turns and realizes his farm is now out of sight. Is everything gone now, he wonders; his farm, his son, his wife. *I might as well be in jail*, he thinks to himself. *Where else on earth should I be?*

He is photographed, fingerprinted, and processed. He is told that he has one phone call. Looking at the lawyer's phone number written on his hand, he thinks instead about calling Margaret to tell her how sorry he is, but what good is that?

Finally, he says, "I want to call the priest at Saint Patrick's in Summit."

When the priest finds out it's Eugene and that he's calling from jail, he tells him that he will be there in twenty minutes.

#

"So, this is what not going to confession for fifteen years gets you," the smiling priest says as the jailer unlocks the door to admit the cleric into his purgatory.

"I thought you were older," Eugene says.

"They made us work on the confessional voice in seminary. People don't like kids telling them how to live."

The priest is aware of Eugene's situation from the lengthy discussion they had during his confession.

"It appears you are being true to your conviction, to tell the truth, and face the consequences."

Eugene nods.

"Is it as hard as you thought it would be?"

"I didn't realize until the ride over here that I'm going to lose everything."

"You very well might."

"Might? I don't know if anything can stop it now, Father?"

"One thing can."

"God? That would take a miracle! Do you honestly think that God will do a miracle for someone like me? Why would He?"

The priest looks down at the Bible he is holding. He thinks about all the miracles in the book, but he also knows the importance of truth. The priest had made a promise to himself, too, during the drive from his church to this cell. He had promised that he would be truthful with Eugene, no matter how hard it might be; he owed him that much.

"No," the priest answers quietly. "I'm sorry to say that I don't." Then, as he looks Eugene in the eyes, he says, "It's not up to me, though. This book is full of miracles, and most of them start with someone facing an impossible situation, like yours."

"There's a lot of people who got cut down by the sword, too."

"That's the ones that fought for the other side, Eugene."

"But Father, does God even do miracles anymore?"

"The easy answer is yes. But the whole answer is that miracles are very rare. Every year the Vatican reviews dozens of miracle claims, but very few are verified."

"That's how saints are named, right?"

"Yes, a saint needs to have at least two verified miracles to be canonized. And the pope only names about two new saints each year."

"So, the miracles for this year are probably used up already, right?"

"There isn't a limit to the number of miracles God can do. And don't forget that the verification standard is extremely high. If a person with cancer is given only a ten percent chance of living, that person's survival can't be verified because they were given a chance. A verified miracle has to be a situation where there is no chance."

Eugene pauses for a moment, then chuckles and says, "I guess I'd settle for an unverified miracle."

"Me too," says the priest.

"Father, who is the patron saint for miracles?"

"Saint Anthony. I think he has around sixty verified miracles."

"I thought he was the patron saint of things that are lost?"

"He's both, actually."

"You mean the patron saint for things lost is also the one for miracles?"

#

The words, "You are under arrest," are still ringing in Margaret's head as she sits crying at her kitchen table. She knows she should be doing something, but for the life of her, she can't think of what it would be. Then she remembers what Eugene had told her to do earlier that morning. She cranks the phone in three short bursts. Luella Brennan, their nearest neighbor to the south, picks up her phone. Eugene had talked to her husband yesterday about the possible need for him to milk the cows and feed his steers. Luella promises to let her husband know.

Margaret thinks about calling the lawyer; Eugene had said nothing about that. She reaches for the crank but then realizes that she doesn't want to place a call like that through her party line; everyone will find out about all of this all too soon. Feeling very low, with nothing else to do, she decides to go to Madeline's house to try to clear her head.

When Madeline answers the door, both women realize that the other has been crying.

"What a sorry lot the two of us make," Madeline says while waving Margaret inside.

Margaret, confused about why Madeline is crying, asks, "What is it? Did you hear about Eugene already?"

"I haven't heard a thing; what happened?"

"Gene was arrested this morning. But why are *you* crying?"

"You poor thing," says Madeline.

"I saw it coming, but now that it has actually happened, I really don't know what to do with myself. I'm sorry to burden you with it, but I just don't know what else to do."

"I'm very glad you came, sweetheart. You're not a burden at all. In fact, I may be needing you every bit as much as you need me."

"Why, dear?"

"It's hard to say out loud."

"What is?"

"John has been going out in the evening about twice a week for a while now. It's always for some reason or another. I fought my inclination to be suspicious for a long time. Last night I gave in. I followed him. He went to Betty Meister's house. I don't know if I mentioned it to you, but John counselled her during her divorce. I thought maybe he was just continuing to help her. I felt like a fool watching from the sidewalk, but after a while, I saw them go into her bedroom and turn out the light."

Margaret, in shock, tries to search for a possible benign explanation for what she saw. She realizes that she can't. Then she thinks about the scandal this will cause and what that will mean to her dear friend's family.

"Oh, Madeline, this is terrible!" Margaret takes her friend into her arms, and they both cry together, retching in emotional pain.

After several minutes, Margaret pulls away to look at her dear friend. She affectionately wipes the tears off of her face while saying, "Aren't we the sorriest lot in the world?"

Madeline's face scrunches into something resembling a smile. A moment later, they are both laughing in each other's arms while crying at the same time. Eventually, the two women discuss Margaret's situation. Madeline, after a pause, asks Margaret directly if she believes Eugene actually killed her son.

"I just don't know what to believe anymore. Part of me can't imagine Eugene doing such a thing. He has always been very stern with Dicky. We fought about that. But it never occurred to me that he was capable of violence. But Eugene was tormented by the war, especially lately. The questions that Donovan asked me make me believe that they think that his mind, trapped in the war, could do something like this."

"What does your heart tell you, dear?"

"God help me, I think maybe he did."

Margaret feels bad about thrusting her worries on her friend, now herself facing such turmoil. She decides to lead the conversation to anything outside of their burdens, at least for a little while. She brings up a silly thing she did just before leaving the house.

"After Eugene was taken away, not knowing what to do with myself, I decided I would find that missing coin. I felt that if I could find it, I might be able to take a small bit of the weight I've been feeling away. I knew how stupid it was, but I did it anyway. I turned the house inside-out but never found it. Afterward, I felt so foolish; with everything else that is happening, I am spending my energy looking for a stupid coin. I just hope God understands."

"Don't worry about that," says Madeline. "Jesus explained that very thing; that it's a perfectly natural reaction to look everywhere for a lost coin."

"I know, but I just thought he might see this coin differently since it's connected to a superstition."

"What kind of coin is it, by the way? I never thought to ask you about that."

"It's an old German coin, a gold coin with the image of Kaiser Wilhelm on it. I think it may actually be worth something, although I would never sell it."

A surprised look comes over Madeline's face. She leaves the room for a moment. When she comes back, she hands a coin to Margaret, saying, "Does it look like this?"

Margaret, with eyes like saucers, whispers, "Where did you get this?"

"It came in with the collection money. John asked me to see what I could find out about it."

A moment later, Madeline is on the phone with the church usher. He tells Madeline that it was given to him by Berta Schmidt.

"Remember Mrs. Schmidt? She's the old woman I've told you about. She's the one living in the past. Poor thing lost her son decades ago and has not been right since."

"Is she the one who told me that her son was lost?"

"That's her. She claims all kinds of crazy things. She's really a sad case. Isn't it queer that she had the same coin as you?"

#

As Madeline drives, Margaret is looking at the coin, trying to decide if it's her family coin or just one that looks like it. Her best friend has told her that when her husband took over the church, she made an effort to visit all of the wives at home. When she met the widow Schmidt, her heart went out to her. The poor thing lives on a farm at the east edge of town. The homestead is on the far side of Buffalo Creek at the end of a lonely lane. The rundown farm seems like it is from another time and place. As they pull closer to the house, Margaret sees what she is talking about. The buildings, all once white, are now badly pealed. The front yard, with the remnants of planting beds, is overgrown with tall grass and thistles. *What a sad place to live*, Margaret thinks to herself.

"I don't know how this is going to go. I visit her about once a month; sometimes she knows me, and other times she does not."

Madeline pounds three times on the back door, and then she opens the door a bit and loudly says, "Yoo-hoo, Berta. It's Madeline, the minister's wife."

When there is no answer, she opens the door farther, and they walk through the kitchen, which has potted flowers by the windows and on the kitchen table that have not seen water in months. Part of the kitchen counter, near the sink and stove, is clear; the rest of it is covered with more desiccated flowers in bone-dry dirt. Madeline moves through the room and then extends her head to peer into the parlor.

"There you are, dear. I don't think you heard me at the door."

A scratchy voice grates the dusty air, "Oh, Madeline, so nice of you to call."

The old woman greets Margaret, asking them to sit comfortably while she prepares refreshments. When she leaves the room, Madeline whispers in Margaret's ear to just pretend to eat and drink.

When the old woman returns with a tray, she pours tea, which is cold water and sets out a plate of what she calls strudel, which is very old, burnt toast cut into squares. Madeline daintily picks up her teacup and pretends to take a sip of tea.

"Hot tea is a delight on a cold day," Madeline says while giving Margaret a knowing look.

Madeline tries to follow her host's rambling and disjointed conversation. Margaret struggles at first but gains confidence as the minutes tick by.

Finally, when she feels they have acclimated into the old woman's shadowy world, Madeline asks about the coin.

"Oh, yes, the coin. My Jurgen, that little dickens, was hiding that coin from me. I had to scold him. I'm sure you ladies know how important it is to scold the little ones. Some folks think that it's old-fashioned; don't spare the rod, it says in the Bible. Oh, well. Madeline, I almost forgot that your husband is the minister. I'm sure he's taught you that."

"Of course he has," says Madeline. "Was that coin something you have had for a long time?"

"Oh, my, no. I hadn't seen a coin like that since I was a little girl living in the old country. My father called it the fatherland. The funny thing is that when I was a little girl, I thought he was talking about his own land. You know, father's land." She chuckles, thinking of it. "Isn't it funny what we think when we're little?"

"So, where do you think that coin came from?" Margaret interjects.

The woman, not expecting the question, blinks while looking at Margaret. After a pause, she asks, "What coin?"

Madeline asks the woman about the birds outside the window. When the old woman turns her head, Madeline whispers to Margaret that she should let her do the talking.

When Berta turns back, Madeline says, "You were saying that little Jurgen had an old coin."

"Oh, yes. I asked him if that coin was his. He admitted that it wasn't. That's when I scolded him."

"Where do you think he found such an old coin?

"I think he was going through my husband's old family trunks in the attic. My husband has had to scold him for sneaking up there so many times; boys get into everything."

"You're right about that," says Madeline.

"Where is your son today?" Margaret asks.

"He's in the house, of course. Didn't you notice him walking through the room a few minutes ago?"

"No, I didn't see that," says Madeline. "Can you have him come back to say hello?"

"Oh, Jurgen! Come here, please!" Berta shouts.

When no one answers, Berta shrugs and says that he must have run outside.

After saying goodbye, they walk all around the farmyard. The farm looks like no one has set foot on it for years. Margaret's heart sinks. It's obvious that the old woman, living here alone, is living in a world all her own. As they are walking toward the car, they are startled by a screeching cat that comes running around the corner of the house. A moment later, a little boy comes running after it.

Part Three—Lost and Found

Gladys Henry is cutting out the banner headline, *"BOY 4, LOST 16 DAYS, FOUND ALIVE,"* from the Des Moines Tribune for her scrapbook. She takes note that the story's byline is not Frank Frydenberg. Frydenberg pushed the sheriff hard for access to the Walkers so he could write about their feelings after the most sensational turn of events he had encountered in his years in journalism. The sheriff, however, took great pleasure in being able to freeze the unscrupulous reporter out of the story. Mackintosh called editor Bill Bray telling him that if the Tribune wanted access to the Walkers, they would have to send someone else.

As she is pasting, line-one on her desk phone rings. It's Special Agent Donovan.

"Is Mack in, Gladys? I just heard they found him alive. I can't believe it."

"Everyone's calling it a miracle. I'm sure he'll take your call." She puts the receiver against her thigh and shouts, "Sheriff, Donovan is on line one!"

#

"Hey, Donovan, what's new, kid?"

"What's new? The paper says they found him with a senile old lady. Everyone here is hounding me for the inside story. Even Hoover called me about it."

"We're still trying to piece it together. The kid is very shy, and his language skills are poor. With Margaret's help, we got a very rough idea of what happened. Apparently, he fell asleep in the back of the livestock buyer's car. We found out from him that he stopped at the Summit grocery on the way home; he had no idea the boy was back there. The kid must have woken up and then wandered into the store to get candy, we think. That's when this old widow, Berta Schmidt, mistook him for her son, who died forty years ago, and took him home. The woman has been secluded and living in a mental fog for a dozen or more years."

The two men laugh about how the case had them chasing their tales all over the county.

"Now, here's the fun part," says Mackintosh. "The boy had taken an old German coin from his mother's jewelry box at some point. It's a long story, but the coin showing up in the church's collection basket eventually led to finding the boy there."

"I think I'm going to stick with urban crime from now on, Mack. This rural stuff is way over my head."

"You did alright, under the circumstances."

"It would be a lot easier on my shoes, too," Donovan says while laughing.

After a moment, Donovan asks about Eugene, "When I think about how I put the screws to that guy. Man, please tell him I feel very sorry about that."

Sunday, April 2—Home Twelve Days

Eugene, already dressed for church after the morning milking session, sits down at the kitchen table in front of a plate of bacon and scrambled eggs, while Margaret, wearing his favorite dress covered with a tattered apron, is flipping pancakes onto a platter.

"You look beautiful," he says so sincerely that it catches her off guard.

Almost blushing, she quietly says, "You're just saying that because of last night."

"No, sweetheart, I'm saying that because it's true."

"Well, stop it anyway," she softly says. "You're just going to get me crying again."

He goes to her and takes her into his arms, not saying a word. When she starts softly crying, he says, "Sorry, I just can't help it. I didn't think we'd be all together like this ever again."

She pushes him abruptly away, wipes her face on her apron, and then kisses him hard and fast. "Sit down and eat!"

Eugene sighs and then takes his seat as he yells, "Dicky, the pancakes are ready!"

Dicky trots into the room, "Pancakes, man-oh-man!"

Seeing the clothes his parents are wearing, he says, "Yay, it's Sunday school day!"

Both parents noted that somehow his ordeal with Berta Schmidt has improved his language skills.

Seeing the ever-growing line of mailbags leaning against the wall, he says, "We're going to have to do something with all that mail. Dub says the Apex Post Office wants their bags back."

Mail, that is all positive now, has been flowing steadily in ever since the story broke about how Dicky was found. Margaret, Dub, and Madeline have been sorting and organizing it. Some of the nicest letters, along with the many newspaper clippings are going into a scrapbook that Madeline insisted that they put together. Some of the letters contain small amounts of money. Margaret has started sending thank-you cards and longer letters to the very special ones.

"I almost forgot," Margaret says excitedly. "You have to read the latest letter from Sister Alicia." She goes to the living room, where her scrapbooking is spread out. She returns, handing Eugene the letter.

"Dear Margaret, Eugene, and Dicky,

All of the sisters were so very grateful to receive your wonderful letter. Everyone here is overjoyed that God, in His mercy, answered our humble prayers for Dicky's safe return. As I have told you before, it is our order's mission to not only serve locations far and wide as teachers and nurses but also to pray as a community, unceasingly in our Chapel of Angels. This beautiful chapel, which is housed within our church, is covered on its walls and ceiling with depictions of angels to inspire our devotion. Every hour of the day and night, three sisters pray, each with a book of petitions.

After a prayer request like yours is granted, it is our practice to pray for nine days to thank our Lord, Mary, and St. Anthony, the patron saint of lost causes.

May God continue to shine His magnificent light upon you."

Sister Mary Alicia

Eugene, eyes full of tears, reaches for the dog tag chain he has started once again wearing around his neck. He finds the cross that is now hanging there. It's the cross from the rosary fragment that was found in the barn. Also attached to the chain is the Saint Anthony medal given to him by Father Herlihy. As he is holding it in his fist, he thanks God for miraculously restoring his family.

He promises to be a kind and loving husband and father, and to follow the Lord, always, no matter how confusing or difficult that might become.

Long Winding Road—Sixty Years Later

Richard Walker, a Chicago financial executive, surprised the people in his office by taking time off, which is so rare that they all assumed he must have a terminal disease even though he swore to them that he was fine. He decided to keep the real reason for his sabbatical a secret; it was family business. His father, who had tried to patiently teach him many things, most of which made little sense to him, had told him to keep family business in the family.

After suffering the congestion of the Stevenson Freeway, he seeks out old Highway 20, so he can unwind on the curves of the forgotten two-lane road in his midlife-crisis sports car. The transition from the skyscrapers of his everyday world to the open road, small towns, and meadows occasionally littered with barns, cows, and hogs, is a welcome change.

He had thrown himself back into his work soon after his wife had died last year for several reasons. The main one, of course, was to use his work as a medicine to help him forget, a drug that, for him, is as addictive as opiates. Now, with his passenger seat so painfully empty, he realizes, once again, just how much he misses her. When he started shooting up the success ladder, his father had warned him to not take his family for granted. He had assured his father he would not, but soon, the rush of achievement became too addicting to relinquish; despite his father's warning, he knew he could never let it go.

Which brings his mind back to the one thing his father had emphasized above all else. He now hears the words of his father, "Hang onto truth, son; and above all else, be truthful to yourself." His father had told him that more times than he could possibly count.

At a small-town gas station, as he is waiting for the pump to click-off, he considers the role that truth has played in his life. He uses the idle seconds to try to heed his father's advice, to be honest with himself by truthfully looking back at the years of his life. He finds that the real truth is that if he had followed that advice, he would just be another financial analyst with a desk in a cubicle, not knowing if it's sunny or raining until he rides the elevator down to the street at five o'clock.

"Sorry, Dad," he says while hopping back into the car.

He crosses the Mississippi and makes his way through the rolling hills of eastern Iowa eventually, making his way to the village of Summit. He thinks about how different it must be to live in a rundown place like this; quaint and quiet roads without congestion, sidewalks not crowded with people, a place where everyone knows each other. He has to admit that it doesn't sound too bad. People stare at him as he emerges from his tiny, red car, now parked among dusty pickup trucks. He realizes that his clothes make him stand out like a sore thumb.

"I didn't know there was a funeral in town today," the waitress says while bringing him ice water in a chipped glass.

"I'm not here for a funeral. I came straight from Chicago. I guess I should have changed clothes."

The water tastes like scrap iron. Remembering where he is, he orders the local delicacies; a glass of milk and a cheeseburger; they taste great. He puts a twenty on the table for the meal as he thanks the waitress.

Realizing with wide eyes that he is leaving the change as a tip, she asks, "If you don't mind me asking, who are you?"

He smiles, realizing that all the other people in the café are looking at him and also realizing they probably would never forgive her if she didn't at least try to find out who he is and why he's there. He thinks about keeping it to himself in order to try to follow his dad's advice to keep family business within the family. But he feels it would be too awkward to do so.

"I'm Richard Walker. My folks used to live around here a long time ago."

"Dicky Walker?" a voice rings forth from the back booth.

Richard looks back to see a man his age in dark slacks and a wrinkled white shirt. "They used to call me Dicky."

"God Almighty! You're the last person in the world I expected to see here. I'm Michael McBride. You called me Mikey."

Richard vaguely remembers his first playmate but had not thought about him in years.

"Oh, my God, are you *that* Dicky Walker?" the waitress asks.

The revelation causes quite a ruckus in the café. Richard now wishes he had followed his father's advice. It turns out that Michael had taken over the church when his parents retired several years ago.

Suddenly, Richard remembers how his mom, when he confided to her that his marriage might fall apart, had told him about her best friend Madeline McBride, who had very difficult marital problems but had managed to work them out.

To get out of the spell of the past, he tells the group that he is just passing through and needs to get going. *What's one more lie at this point?* he tells himself.

"Sorry again, Dad," he says as he starts the car, now turning his attention to trying to decipher his dad's scrawled directions from town to the old farm.

The map says to turn right onto a dirt road just after passing the field with a huge stone at its center. He sees a boulder the size of a garage and turns onto a narrow gravel road. Hearing the stones chipping unmercifully on the fenders of his favorite car causes his stomach to churn. At the end of the road, he comes to the abandoned and overgrown farm.

As the dust is settling, he takes his mother's old scrapbook out of the trunk. The yellowed newspaper photographs show what the farm used to look like when he was a young boy.

Forcing the front door open, he finds himself inside the smallest house he has ever seen. Grossly cracked walls, floors covered in plaster rubble that used to adhere to lath slats now exposed from the sagging ceiling above. It takes a lot of concentration, even with the newspaper photos as a guide, to imagine what it was like to live here.

The barn is in much better shape. Thankfully there are a few bales of straw left, so he has a place to sit. In the muffled silence of the musty-smelling barn, he starts reading through the scrapbook for the first time. Following the articles day by day, he gains an appreciation for what his parents must have gone through. He finds the nice letters from Sister Alicia that meant so much to his mother. The photographs show huge numbers of people out looking for him. He is shocked to see that before he was found that his father had been arrested. He turns the page to see the huge headline stating that he was found alive after sixteen days. Only now that he is twice the age his parents were at that time does he have an inkling of the magnitude of their ordeal.

The last attached article from January 1962 was the Des Moines Tribune's summary of the top news stories of 1961. The Dicky Walker story was number two that year. The number one story was a campaign finance scandal sending the governor's campaign manager to jail.

The last page in the scrapbook has a plastic case securely taped to it, which holds a very old golden coin. Scratched into its plastic case are the words, *lucky coin.*

He remembers his mother telling him the story of her family's lucky coin from the old country. She had told him that she didn't want to believe it was really lucky but that she couldn't deny that it was this coin that brought me back to her. She also said that it was a miracle, for how could it have been anything else?

He stands, stretching his back, now tight from the hours spent driving. Outside he sees the stark contrast between the dilapidated and overgrown building and the grandeur of the lush crops and gently rolling countryside. Looking across the road to the west, the ground slopes down towards a creek in the distance. The view beyond is a patchwork of fields dotted with distant farmsteads. The sky above is also beautiful, the bluest sky he has ever seen, dotted with puffs of cotton. He couldn't deny that somehow, at least for today, this place feels like home.

He now turns to the reason he is here. He has come all this way to finally comply with his father's written instructions that he had received during the reading of his last will and testament ten years ago. He walks back into the barn and digs a small hole in the dirt in the southwest corner. He pulls from his pocket his father's dog tag chain, onto which is attached a small cross and a Saint Anthony medal.

He says, "This is for you, Dad." And then, not knowing why, he drops the chain into the ground and covers it with dirt. Then, following his father's last instruction, he looks at the envelope that was to be opened only after burying the chain. Inside, he sees his father's familiar scrawl, in pencil as usual, shaky from old age; a note dated just one month before his death.

"Dear Dicky,

Never underestimate how far God is willing to go to save someone. After all the prayers of so many were answered when you were returned to us after such a long ordeal involving so many hundreds of people, everyone gave thanks to God for saving you. It wasn't until I was older that I realized that God had not done all of that to save you. He had done it to save me.

Now facing death, I want to tell you something that I am now just realizing for the first time. Perhaps the incredible things that God did to save me, the things that also shook your mother's faith to its core way back then, might now, in God's long and unknowable planning, save the most important person in my life, my only son."

Love,

Dad

THE END

CPSIA information can be obtained
at www.ICGtesting.com
Printed in the USA
BVHW052032200223
658864BV00010B/138